The New Girl

Nora Valters

The New Girl
by Nora Valters

Copyright © Nora Valters 2024
Nora Valters asserts the moral right to
be identified as the author of this work.

This paperback edition (1) published by NValters Publishing
UK February 2024
Cover design © Damonza

Publisher's Note
This novel is entirely a work of fiction.
The names, characters and incidents portrayed in it are the work
of the author's imagination. Any resemblance to actual persons,
living or dead, events or localities is entirely coincidental.

All rights reserved.
No part of this publication may be reproduced, stored in a
retrieval system, or transmitted, in any form, or by any means
(electronic, mechanical, photocopying, recording, or otherwise),
without the prior permission of the copyright owner.

For more information about this and other titles by this author,
please visit www.noravalters.com

ISBN 978-1-8382301-1-1

For my grandad, Ernie

PROLOGUE

I shiver uncontrollably. Light snow flutters around me. I can only just about see it. It's almost pitch-black in this bleak, deserted forest in middle-of-nowhere Wales. I'm desperate to blow on my numb fingers, to rub my cold skin – skin so icy it feels prickly – but I don't. I don't move, I still my breathing. I have to stay silent, hidden.

I'm crouched low to the ground. My socks are soaked and muddy. Water rises up the bottom of my jeans, and the hems are caked in dirt. One sleeve of my jumper is torn from the scramble through a thorny bush. I'm thankful I'm not completely barefoot. I ran too quickly to put on shoes or a coat.

I need to focus. I'm going to have to move at some point or I'll freeze to death. But I don't know where I am or how to get out of this forest. I'll deal with that when I come to it. For now, I need to stay very, very still.

A twig cracks behind me.

Shit.

I've been found.

This can't be the end. It can't be. I will fight until I've got nothing left. I want to live. I'm not going to go easily.

The footsteps get closer. My head spins. *How the hell did I get here? How the hell did it all lead to this?*

I curse myself. I should've seen it coming. But I didn't. I was blind to it all, and now it's too late.

CHAPTER 1

Three weeks earlier

It's New Year's Eve, and I'm about to get proposed to.

My wonderful boyfriend of two years is due here at any minute to take me out and propose with a grand romantic gesture that we'll re-live and gush over for the rest of our lives.

It's 7 p.m., and I stand by the window watching the street for my fiancé-to-be's arrival. He said he'd pick me up. I don't know what that means – if he's driving over, coming in a taxi, or maybe even rocking up in a stretch limo.

It's unusual for him to plan an evening out. He's the spontaneous, ideas type, and I tend to do all the planning and booking and logistics. He'll say, 'Rach, let's go paddleboarding tomorrow!' and then I'll research where to go, how long it will take in the car, what time we should leave, and a nice place we could grab lunch. It's just one of the ways we work so well together.

So, when he said last week that he'd 'sort New Year's Eve', I just knew it was for something special. For our engagement.

I bought a sexier-than-I'd-normally-wear red dress for the occasion, dug out my fancy matching underwear, got waxed, had my nails done, blow dried my hair, and carefully applied my makeup. I want to look as good as possible in all our 'I said yes!' photos. These past few days, I've even moisturised my hands obsessively so my skin will glow in the inevitable close-up pics of my new engagement ring glistening on my finger.

At five minutes past seven, I'm getting twitchy. He's usually a few minutes late, so it's no biggie, but my nervous excitement is getting the better of me. I dash to the loo for a fast nervous wee – it'll be just my luck that he arrives at the exact moment my sexy pants are around my ankles.

He doesn't though, so I head back to the window and bounce from one foot to the other. As I watch the street, my mind wanders. We'll have a short engagement. A wonderful summer wedding. A happy marriage. Two kids minimum. A large family home with dog, cat, fish, and tortoise.

I have a thing for tortoises because of my father's old pet, Mick Jagger. He'd plod around the house when I was a child. After the accident, Mick was the only thing I liked about my court-ordered visits to see my father and sisters.

I've worked hard to put all that behind me, and my life now is perfect – a new dream job, a lovely flat, a new vibrant city to make my mark on. And with this engagement, it's about to get even better.

At eleven minutes past, my phone rings. It's Brandon, of course. Perhaps this is all part of his plan to keep me on my toes. Perhaps the limo driver got lost or the taxi was a no-show, and now he's running much later than usual.

I pick up the phone. But, like opening a shaken-up bottle of fizzy pop, my excitement bubbles up and explodes. With zero chill, I answer and squeal, "Hey, babe!"

"Hello." His voice is flat. Sombre, even.

I hear it immediately. "Everything okay, Brandon?"

"No. We need to talk."

Those are doom-laden words, aren't they? Something's gone wrong with his plans for the perfect engagement. Maybe he's lost the ring, or it was the wrong size, or something.

"Listen, I'll be happy with whatever you've got planned. Even if it's intimate, and you just come round here and get down on one knee in the kitchen after we've ordered a takeaway. I'll be happy!" I chuckle. "Soooo happy."

"Get down on one knee? What?"

He's being tight-lipped. He wants it to be a surprise, and I'm ruining everything. I bite my tongue. "Sorry, babe, talk to me."

"I'm sorry, Rach. You're such a wonderful person, but… it's over."

I laugh. "Haha, very funny! Are you trying to make me think we're splitting up right before you propose?" I laugh hysterically some more, my excitement getting the better of me.

"Rachel!" Brandon's harsh tone is like a slap.

My laughter abruptly dies in my mouth.

He continues, "I'm not joking. I don't want to be with you anymore. I'm not about to propose. Quite the opposite."

The penny drops. I don't say much else, just listen to him tell me that I've been a great girlfriend and that I'll find someone else who'll be perfect for me.

"But you moved here for me," I say miserably.

"And that's just it. I thought being in a new place would give our relationship a new lease of life. But almost immediately you started putting pressure on me to get married. I don't want that. I want to enjoy exploring and making new friends. I want to feel free, not tied down. You tie me down. I don't like it. I don't want it. We're in completely different places. I'm sorry."

He hangs up. I drop onto the sofa. It's 7.36 p.m.

I cry.

Rage – *how dare he dump me over the phone!*

Wail and flail my arms around like a wronged banshee.

Scream into a cushion.

Slump to the floor and thump my fists on the carpet, then curl into a little ball.

Gather all the belongings he's left at my flat, shove them into a bin bag and stomp on it until something cracks.

Cry some more.

Pick up my phone to call him. Change my mind and slam it back down on the table.

I enter a 'stillness' phase, sit back on my sofa and stare into space.

At 9 p.m., I look down at my gorgeous new dress and see my fancy sparkly nails and remember it's not only New Year's Eve but also a Saturday night. And I'm sitting alone in my flat with no plans.

Loneliness swims through me.

I don't know anyone in Cardiff apart from Brandon and my work colleagues. I've only been here a month and haven't made any new friends yet. The only person who I think might be becoming a friend is Pete from work, but that's very early days. We've been out a couple of times for drinks after work – once with a few others on my team and a second time with just the two of us.

My best mate still lives in Nottingham, where I used to live, and always spends New Year's Eve with her wonderful husband and wonderful four kids. I doubt she'll even pick up if I call. Her phone will be on silent or upstairs, and she'll be having too much fun to check it until morning.

I debate whether to call Mum. But she lives in Auckland now with her new family, and the time difference means she'll be fast asleep and won't answer.

But it's not a chat on the phone that I need. I *need* to get out of the flat, to be around people, to get inebriated and maybe to do some end-of-the-night crying on a stranger's shoulder in the loo.

Pete asked me last week, when we were both in work on the few days between Christmas and New Year's, if I had any plans for tonight.

"I have *big* plans with my boyfriend!" I'd replied with a Cheshire cat grin.

He'd told me he was going to a party at a friend's place and that if I was at a loose end to come along.

I'll call Pete. I can't sit around moping on New Year's Eve. It'll tip me over the edge. And I can't go the same way as I did before. I just can't. A party will be a distraction from this unbearable loneliness and devastating heartbreak for a little while. I *am* at a loose end.

I pick up my phone and dial Pete's number.

It rings and rings. *Pleeease* pick up, I will, *pleeease*.

Just when I think it's going to switch to voicemail, I hear, "Hello? Rachel?"

Pete's voice is distant and fuzzy. The line is terrible, and the sounds of a raucous party boom in my ear.

"Hey, Pete! The thing I had on tonight has... um... fallen through..." I take a breath to steady myself. "Can I come and meet you?"

"What?" he yells. "Battery about to die!"

"Can I come to the party you're at?" I yell back.

There's a crackle, but I'm certain he says, "Sure." Then I catch the word "dress" and assume he's about to give me the address. I grab a pen and paper.

He says a few words. I repeat back to him, "Cardiff Bay?"

The phone reception cuts in and out again.

I hear what sounds like ferry and water.

"Ferry Road?" I ask. "Water what?"

"Eighth floor..." he shouts above a bunch of people in the background singing Robbie Williams' 'Angel' at the top of their voices.

Another crackle. As Pete is in the middle of saying, "I'll message you—" the line goes dead. His battery's died.

I google 'Cardiff Bay ferry water' and find the Watermark building on Ferry Road in Cardiff Bay. That must be it. I search for a few more combinations of words using things like 'perry' instead of 'ferry' and so on, but can't find any address in the city that might match.

I book a taxi using the app on my phone. It'll take an hour to get here. It's a busy night, and now is the time everyone is trying to get to where they want to be for midnight. I grab the bottle of champagne that I had cooling in the fridge to celebrate my engagement. I should take it to the party, shouldn't I? Arrive with something to drink? But screw it, I pop the top and take a swig right from the bottle.

The bubbles shoot up my nose, and I snort-cough-spit the liquid up.

Nice, Rach. Real nice.

After dabbing at my face and the spill on my dress with a paper towel, I fill up my favourite mug with champagne and bring it and the bottle into the bedroom, ignoring the bin bag full of Brandon's things that sits in the doorway.

My makeup is a mess from the two rounds of crying earlier. There's no saving it. I take it off and start again. By the time the taxi arrives – pulling into my driveway and honking twice – I've had half the bottle of champers, have way-heavier-than-usual eye makeup on and have a slightly hoarse voice from singing along to my favourite playlist.

I left my phone charging in the lounge. I unplug it and check the screen. Battery low. Huh? I look at the socket – I forgot to switch it on. *Dammit.* But too late now. I grab my handbag and coat and rush out the flat. I gently shut my neighbour Ralph's front door. He's eighty-four and uses a walking frame. He often forgets to fully close his door after manoeuvring the frame in the hallway. The first time I noticed it was open, I knocked and checked if he was okay, but he said he was always doing it. So now I just close it. Easy enough to do.

I ask the taxi driver if he has a phone charger in the car. He doesn't. I'm tipsy and attempt to engage in conversation. He's not interested, offering monosyllabic replies, and then no replies at all. I take the hint and stare out the window in silence as we head from Pontcanna in Cardiff city centre to Cardiff Bay.

It's a twenty-minute drive. I don't know this part of the city at all. I haven't done all that much exploring yet. Starting the new job has been stressful, and I've just wanted to relax in the evenings. And at weekends, Brandon and I explored our local Pontcanna neighbourhood. He's living in a houseshare not too far from my flat. He wanted to have ready-made mates and didn't want to move in with me or get a place of his own. We didn't live together in Nottingham either. I thought he didn't want to live with me because he was about to propose and wanted to buy a place together as our first home. How wrong I was.

I realise nobody knows where I'm off to. I usually tell someone. I should've maybe left a note in my flat just in case something happened. But, of course, nothing is going to happen. And Pete knows I'm on my way.

Huffing on the window, I draw a smiley face in the condensation. Jittery nerves swirl in my gut. I'm not the best at meeting strangers. Brandon was brilliant at breaking the ice initially, and then I'd take over, asking questions and making a huge effort to get to know people. We made a great double act. I reach a hand over to the other side of the back seat and smooth it down. I should've been going somewhere with him tonight. He should be sitting right here.

Tears spike under my eyes. I wipe away the happy face and take a sharp breath.

"Nearly there, love," the taxi driver says.

"Great," I reply tightly, batting away the emotions.

He drops me off at an impressive apartment block close to the water. The concierge buzzes me in.

"Here for the party," I say. I realise then that Pete didn't give me the actual apartment number. "Eighth floor?"

"Go on up," the concierge says with a smile and

gestures towards the lifts.

"Thanks. Happy New Year!" I slur. The champagne has fully kicked in now.

The lobby is spacious and shiny, and so is the elevator. It spits me out on the eighth floor, the building only has nine, and I hope it's obvious where the party is at. In front of me are two doors: 8A and 8B. I can hear pumping music and chatter. I put my ear to both doors. It's definitely coming from 8A.

I take a deep breath and knock. I hope it's the right door, the right party, the right people.

The door flies open, and I almost fall through.

"Come in, come in!" a man says.

He's huge, with bulging muscles and a shaved head. He could be door security except he looks like he's channelling Elton John with large star-shaped glasses, purple sequin jacket, silver sequin trousers, no shirt, and a large gold necklace.

He pulls me into the apartment before I can say anything and closes the door behind me. This is it – I've been swallowed down into the unknown. There's no turning back now.

CHAPTER 2

"Hi, I'm Rachel. I'm a friend of Pete's. Don't suppose you know whereabouts he is, do you?"

Elton John frowns and shakes his head. "Sorry, don't know a Pete. Sure he'll be around somewhere. Lounge is through there. I'm Ivan, by the way." He trots towards the lounge, sequins glittering. But I don't immediately follow.

I take in the hallway. It's heaving with people. There are a few doors that are closed or half open. Immediately in front of me are three people. Two men and a woman in a tight three-person embrace.

The woman snogs one man, turns and snogs the other. They both run their hands all over her, then they start kissing each other.

Oh, gawd. Is this a kinky party?

She grabs a hand from each man and leads them towards one of the closed doors. She sees me watching.

"Wanna join us, gorgeous?" she asks, winking.

The men look at me. One licks his lips, and the other waggles his eyebrows suggestively.

"Umm, no. Thanks. Just looking for Pete."

She blows me a kiss, and the three of them disappear behind one of the closed doors.

I glance up and down the hallway, but no one else appears to be in the midst of sexual activity. Pete isn't here, so I take off my coat and put it on the hooks already overloaded with other people's coats and plough through to the lounge.

It's crowded, but in a good way. Immediately a cocktail is put in one hand and a napkin with three canapés is put in the other.

"Do any of these have peanuts in?" I ask the server.

"Nope, all fish."

"Excellent."

I attempt to politely manoeuvre a canapé into my mouth with one hand. An explosion of delight hits my tastebuds. Ceviche with coriander and chilli. My mouth waters. I haven't had any dinner. I was expecting to eat with Brandon. I wolf down the second and third canapés – both as incredible as the first. I give a little "mmm" out loud and determine to hunt down wherever I can get more of that food.

But someone nudges my elbow trying to get to someone else, and I remember I have a mission. And it's not eating.

I take a sip of the cocktail – it's absolutely divine. Elderflower and something. Gin, perhaps? – and take in the room.

It's an incredible apartment. One wall is entirely glass and overlooks a large terrace area, currently rammed with partygoers. There's an open-plan kitchen area, bustling with people organising the food. A bar area with a mixologist making cocktails. And a dining area, the table covered with every beverage you could imagine and buckets of ice filled with bottles.

The décor is cool, that's the only word I can use to describe it. Colourful, tasteful, with some incredible modern art on the walls and sculptures displayed on shelves and plinths. Some of the furniture looks like works of art too. There's a plush purple chair in the shape of an S on its side, or maybe it's meant to be a wave? A large fridge-freezer in the kitchen has black-and-white graffiti print all over it, and a huge clock, which looks a bit like a Jackson Pollock abstract painting, takes up one wall. The lighting is low, and there's a delightful scent wafting around. Basil, maybe?

It's stunning. I wonder who owns this place, who these friends of Pete's are.

There's a DJ set up in one corner of the room with people dancing in front of him. He's spinning laid-back house music, the kind you'd hear at an exclusive beach club in Ibiza while watching the sun go down. I can't tell if he's been paid to be here or has just brought his decks and records to play. I realise I'm smack-bang in the middle of the 'dancefloor' and people are dancing around me, giving me space as if I'm about to break out into the next viral TikTok dance routine.

And not just any people, these are cool kids – fashionable, arty, effortlessly chic. No one is really paying me any attention, but I step to the side out of the spotlight. I'm not sure these are my kind of people; I've never been a hipster. I'm more geek than glamour.

I bring my nails up to bite them, remember they've got sparkly nail polish on and drop them again. I can't see Pete anywhere. I weave my way through people to get to the door to the terrace. It's busy out there with smokers, people cooling off in the winter air and those admiring the view of the bay.

I don't spot Pete.

He must be in one of the bedrooms.

Back in the hallway, I notice how beautifully it has been decorated. The walls are cobalt-blue with huge artworks hung in a way that appears haphazard but has probably been planned meticulously. And funky-shaped lampshades on brightly patterned side tables add to the maximalist look.

I skip the room that is currently hosting a threesome and open the door at the end. It's a large bedroom with bold geometric wallpaper. A large mirror, which must've been taken down from the wall, is on the bed. Gathered around it are a group of people clutching rolled-up banknotes and snorting lines of cocaine.

"Come join," a man in a Hawaiian shirt says. He pats the bed. "Plenty for everyone!"

I hold up my hand. I've never touched illegal substances and don't plan to. That was my sisters' thing when we were younger, along with regular run-ins with the police. "No, thanks. Just looking for my mate Pete."

The man lifts his head to project his voice. "Is there a Pete here?"

Those in the group who don't have their nose to the mirror, shake their heads or mumble in the negative.

"Not here. Sorry, love," he says and sticks his head down to snort up a line.

"No worries. Have a great night." I back out, closing the door behind me.

I hesitate before trying the next door along. What will I find in there? Sex was in room one, drugs in room two, so room three might be rock 'n' roll? I chuckle to myself. I'm quite drunk. Pete, the name pops into my head. *I might find Pete in there!*

I knock back the delicious cocktail in a few gulps and open the door.

Another bedroom, but this one completely white with a large bed and mirrored furniture. Two women hunch in a corner. One appears to be reading the other's tarot cards. In the other corner, a group huddle around the huge flat-screen TV on the wall. One person sings the words off the screen to Tina Turner's 'The Best'. *Ah, I've found the karaoke room.* Pete has to be in here, he's always humming and singing to himself at the office.

A woman comes over to me brandishing a large bottle of Grey Goose vodka. "Want a shot?"

I want to down the entire bottle to blot out my heartbreak, but I'll settle for a shot. "Go on then."

She fills my cocktail glass.

"Ta," I reply and neck it back.

She tops me up again and continues around the room

topping up glasses.

A man sidles up to me. He's good-looking in a geeky way with round tortoiseshell glasses. But he's drunk and leans in a bit too close.

"Wanna sing 'Sexual Healing' with me?" he slurs and says sexual more like sessssual, which gives me the ick.

"Nope. Just trying to find Pete."

"Is Pete your boyfriend?" he asks.

"Nope." I scan the room. "He's not here."

"Have you got a boyfriend?"

"Yep," I lie. Up until a few hours ago I did, at least.

He studies my face, looks me up and down and goes to touch my hair, but I tilt back, and he thinks better of it.

"You know, you look just like that actor..." He waves his hand as if he's trying to recall the name from the deepest depths of his brain.

"Jessica Chastain?" I ask to move things along.

"No..."

"Emma Stone?"

"No..."

"Amy Adams?"

"Nah..."

"I know, Isla Fisher?"

He clicks his fingers. "That's it!"

I roll my eyes. I've lost count of the number of times I've been told, usually by drunk men, that I look like one of those actors because they have long red hair and so do I. I don't mind, it's flattering really, but not particularly original. I'm decidedly average-looking, of average height and weight, with pale freckly skin that does not do well in the sun. Brandon once told me that he loved my big smile and blue eyes. He never once compared me to a ginger movie star. He also told me that my face was nicely in proportion because my wide forehead complemented my large mouth – which was an original thing to say, and I liked the fact that he'd paid so much attention.

Urgh. Brandon. Thoughts of my now-ex turn me in on

myself. I chew the side of my mouth.

Geek Guy drifts away. I exit the room. *Where's Pete?* He must be on the terrace, and I missed him.

There's a group of women in the hallway clustered around a couple.

"It was the most romantic engagement," the woman is saying, flashing her diamond ring at her friends. "Earlier this evening, at that new restaurant in town…"

Her fiancé beams. He clutches her tightly, as if he never wants to let her go. He's smitten. She's deliriously happy.

That should've been me. I should be deliriously happy right now, a rock on my finger. The champagne, cocktail and vodka congeal in my gut and kick me from the inside. Tears threaten to spill. Needing some space, needing not to see that happy couple anymore, I dash through the one door I haven't tried yet, assuming it's the bathroom.

It is. But it's already occupied.

A woman is on her knees vomiting into the toilet. "Casey?" she asks desperately between heaves. "Will you hold back my hair?"

"Not Casey," I reply, putting my cocktail glass on the side. "But I can certainly hold back your hair."

I gather up her long box braids and hold them at the back of her head while she throws up. My grief at being dumped is temporarily cleared aside by helping her, having a purpose, being needed.

She finishes, flushes, and looks up at me. "Thanks."

"You're welcome."

"I think I need to go home."

She pushes herself off the floor, and I help her to stand. She rinses tap water around her mouth and spits it in the sink.

"You're here with Casey? Shall we go and find her?"

"Yeah." She blows her nose on some toilet roll. "Who are you here with?"

"Pete. But I can't find him. Been looking for ages. Might just give up and go home."

Her face brightens. "I know Pete! I can take you to him if you like. He was outside the last time I saw him."

"Yes, please! Thanks. But first we'd better find Casey to get you home."

"They'll be together."

We stumble out of the bathroom – the happy couple and their admirers now gone – go through the hallway, into the lounge and out onto the terrace. She holds my wrist and leads the way, stumbling through people with apologies. The uninterrupted view across Cardiff Bay and towards Bristol Channel is incredible.

"Casey," she says excitedly and hugs her mate. She taps a guy on the shoulder. "Pete, your friend's looking for you."

Sweet relief surges through me. *Finally, I've found my friend and can enjoy the party!*

The man turns around.

It's not Pete. Well, it's not *my* Pete.

He smiles at me. I smile back.

"Whoops, wrong Pete," I say with a chuckle.

"It's nearly midnight!" someone yells.

Vomit-girl grabs Casey, and Casey grabs Wrong Pete. The trio embrace, and I'm shut out.

I take a few steps back. I'm at the wrong party. I knocked on the wrong door. I probably came to completely the wrong place. My hands go clammy, and my armpits dampen. Even though it's a cold night, sweat runs down my back. I feel awkward, out-of-place. I've completely gatecrashed.

I should get out of here before whoever it is who owns this incredible apartment and has thrown this incredible party realises that they don't know me, that I'm not meant to be here.

I move towards the door back into the lounge, but I'm fighting against the traffic coming out. I hear mention of fireworks. Everyone is hustling to get a good spot, and I'm caught up and pushed towards the edge of the terrace. It's surrounded by waist-high glass panels.

Someone starts a ten-second countdown. Everyone chants. I join in, I can't help it. The fireworks go off; they're spectacular. I have the perfect view. I *ooooh* and *ahhhh*, swept up in the moment.

The DJ puts on Auld Lang Syne, and everyone links arms and sings. I sing too, even though I don't know the words. It feels magical, and just what I needed. A perfect distraction.

We all break off and hug one another.

And that's when I see them. The hosts.

I know that's who they are immediately. The sea of people part to allow them to sweep through. They almost glow. Everyone turns to look at them, nobody wants their back to them. Everyone wants to get a hug from one or both of them. I guess they're in their sixties, but have an eternal youth air about them.

They're clearly a couple. He stands slightly behind her, his hand on her waist, as if he's ridiculously proud of her and stepping back so she gets all the limelight.

She's tall, around six feet, slim and looks like a supermodel. She has naturally white, slightly wavy, super-glossy hair that reaches down to her bum and is styled in a poker-straight middle parting. Her skin is paler than pale, with not a hint of a tan. She appears almost ethereal. Heavy eye makeup enhances her mesmerising green eyes. Sharp features and high cheekbones are accentuated with contour, and her thick lips are slicked with a hot-pink lipstick. Sticky-out ears add to her quirky look. She wears a floor-length silver strapless dress nipped in around her tiny waist and long hot-pink gloves. She's achingly cool, high fashion, a 'presence'. Confidence radiates off her, and she holds herself as if a photographer is taking her picture. Essentially, she's captivating. I, along with everyone else on the terrace, can't stop admiring her.

He's an inch or so shorter. He's slender, but clearly takes care of himself, sporting a healthy tan. His greying and thinning hair is down to his chin and cut in a shaggy style, which gives him an ageing rock star vibe. He was certainly very handsome in his heyday with a square jawline, long aquiline nose, strong cheekbones, bushy black eyebrows, and brown eyes. He's dressed in dark jeans, white shirt, navy blazer, and trainers. He looks casual and low-key, but his outfit fits impeccably and is very stylish.

They're a perfect match for one another – a Hollywood casting director's dream pairing.

She leans towards a shorter man in front of her. "Joseph, darling, Happy New Year!"

She air-kisses either side of the man's face and gathers him into a hug. He looks in absolute ecstasy at her attention.

And that's when she sees me, over his shoulder. Her head tilts as she takes me in. She gives me a look with the slightest narrowing of her eyes. She knows I don't belong, that I'm not meant to be here, that she doesn't know me.

I plaster on an apologetic smile. A smile that I hope says, *I know I'm an intruder, a gatecrasher, and I'm really sorry, please don't be mean or shout or kick me out with a massive fuss or threaten to call the police or whatever.*

She gracefully finishes up her hug, the entire time keeping her eyes on mine, and strides straight for me.

CHAPTER 3

"Curious," she says, eyes boring a hole into me. "I thought I knew everyone at this party. Well, I do… because I invited them." She gives a little laugh and gestures to me. "But clearly not. And you are?"

"I'm Rachel. Look, I'm so sorry, I'm at the wrong party. I'm new in town and thought my friend was here. But he's not, so I must've taken down the wrong address. I've totally gatecrashed, and I'll be making a move now. You have a fabulous home."

I smile and go to step past her, to make my escape. But she takes me firmly by the shoulders with her pink-gloved hands.

"Nonsense," she says with a huge smile. "It's New Year's Eve! You're not going anywhere, Rachel." She turns. "Mark, darling, come here and meet Rachel. She's gatecrashed! How wonderful!"

Mark gives her a nod and finishes up his conversation.

She turns back to me and beams. I feel drawn into her orbit and have an overwhelming urge to be close to her, to bask in her attention. I get now why Joseph looked like he was in ecstasy when she hugged him. I have that exact same feeling. Her gaze warms me from the inside out.

"I'm Margie Madden." She leans in to air-kiss my cheek and hug me. "Happy New Year!"

Mark slides over. He holds out his hand. "Rachel. Mark Madden. A pleasure to meet you."

I hold out my hand, and he shakes it firmly, his other hand over the top, as if I'm the most important person he'll meet tonight.

He takes me in and says, "You look like…" He pauses to think.

"And you look like Mick Jagger," I blurt.

I'm drunk and nervous and don't want to be compared to a red-haired actor for the millionth time.

"The Rolling Stones rocker? Thanks," he says. "I'll take that."

"Oh no," I reply. "I mean my dad's old tortoise, Mick Jagger." I snort, then erupt in a belly laugh.

Mark and Margie both stare at me. I was the only one to find that funny. *Eek.*

But then Margie laughs. It turns into a howl. She doubles up laughing, clutching her middle. Mark glances at his wife and laughs too.

"I don't believe I've ever been compared to a tortoise before," he chortles.

Margie composes herself. "Well, aren't you a funny one." She links her arm through mine. "Neither of us have drinks! Come on, let's find a cocktail and get to know each other properly."

We walk back to the lounge, everyone moving out of our way. All eyes follow me, onlookers wondering, 'How did *she* get so lucky to have Margie's full attention?'

I decide to bask in it. I might as well enjoy my night. I haven't been booted out for gatecrashing, or for offending one of the hosts by comparing him to a reptile, so all good. It's highly unlikely I'll ever see any of these people again, so I'm just going to go for it, let loose, drink my heartbreak into oblivion.

Margie gets us two cocktails from the mixologist, and we sit close together on a red velvet sofa in the shape of a large pair of lips that I hadn't noticed before. We clink glasses and both take a sip. Mark comes to stand behind the sofa, his hand on Margie's shoulder. He talks to a group behind us.

"So, Rachel, tell me everything about you."

She holds eye contact. She appears absolutely fascinated by me.

"I got dumped earlier," I announce.

I'm not sure why I start my life story there, but it's as good a place as any.

"I'm sorry to hear that."

"Yep. I thought we were about to get engaged. But nope. It was over the phone too, the wanker."

"Absolute wanker," she says and appears to relish saying the word, 'wanker'.

"I know there are loads of other things to aspire to, but, for me, I just want to be married to a fantastic man and to start a family. I'd love to be a mum and a wife. Crazy, in this day and age, I know."

"That's not crazy at all."

"Don't get me wrong, I'll still work. I love my job. But I'm a hopeless romantic and have this undeniable longing for children." I take a sip of the cocktail. "But perhaps that's not going to happen for me."

"Don't be ridiculous. You're a catch. You could have any man in here. Well, apart from Mark of course, he's mine." She chuckles and kisses Mark's hand, still resting on her shoulder.

"You guys are so in love. How long have you been together?"

"We've known each other since birth. Our parents were best friends, and we grew up together. We knew from a very young age that we were meant to be. But we both went off and played the field a little at university, you know, and then got married as soon as we both graduated. I simply cannot imagine my life without him. Honestly, if he went before me... I wouldn't be able to go on." She glances up at Mark.

He feels her gaze and cuts off his conversation to gaze back. They share a tender moment.

"That's so romantic." My words hitch as emotion swells and nips at my chest. Water brims behind my eyes. "I wish…" I say through sobs, "…I had something like that."

Margie puts an arm around my shoulder and squeezes me into her. "You'll find a love like that, I'm certain."

"This is the second time this has happened – where I honestly thought I'd met *the one*, that we were about to take the next step, but instead of getting proposed to, getting dumped." I sniffle and take in a deep breath. "The time before, I got so depressed. I don't want that to happen again…" I shove away the tears with the palm of my hand. "Sorry. I'm drunk and don't want to cry. Not yet anyway. That's an end-of-the-night thing, right? And the night is still young. I want to have fun!"

Margie nods.

I'm not sure what it is – the alcohol, the attention of this glamorous woman or my absolute need to numb my pain, but I decide to throw my inhibitions out the window.

"I know what we need!" I jump up and go over to the DJ.

I pull out my phone from my handbag, tap a few things and ask him to put on a song. He takes my phone and plugs it into his equipment. I stand in the middle of the lounge in front of Margie. The music cuts out.

"This is the only dance that I'm good at," I tell her. "And it always makes me feel amazing."

Margie stands and claps her hands excitedly. "Excellent. Let's see it then!"

My music starts. A drum solo moves into a classic Egyptian folk song. It's upbeat, rhythmic, and fun.

I lift my hands, whip my hair back and forth, lift and drop my shoulders, and shake my hips. I close my eyes, smile, and feel the music. I do the entire two-minute, forty-four-second choreographed routine to the track, which I learned last year in my belly dancing class in Nottingham. Every now and then at home I chuck on this song and shimmy away. I've never done it in front of an audience before, but screw it.

Margie shakes her hips and circles her hands, and before long, there are lots of people up dancing.

My song comes to an end, and the DJ puts on some more tracks inspired by Arabic music. I keep dancing. Margie bumps her hip to mine.

"Well, who knew you were Shakira." She laughs.

"I love belly dancing. I've been going for years. I've found a class in Cardiff, but not been yet. I'm going to go next Monday when it starts again for the new year."

"Do you know, I've never done belly dancing. And I was pretty sure that over the years I'd done absolutely everything."

I hold her hands and blurt, "You'll have to come with me on Monday!"

She smiles graciously. Of course she's not going to come to a belly dancing class with me at a local community hall. She's far too classy for that. I totally got carried away.

We dance some more, and the DJ skilfully brings the music back to more generic dance stuff. Guests come up to Margie and Mark to say their goodbyes. I continue to dance and drink delicious cocktails.

When the DJ and mixologist pack away their gear, and the crowd thins out to about ten of us, Margie gathers everyone together in the lounge.

"It's time for party games," she announces.

We clap and cheer and settle ourselves on the seats around the coffee table in the lounge. Mark heads over to a chest of drawers and brings out a few boxes. He places them on the table in front of Margie. She goes through them and selects one.

"Dickhead Hoopla! I love this game!" She howls with laughter as she pulls out two giant plastic penises and explains that two people strap them to their foreheads and both get five hoops to throw onto the other person's penis.

"The winner gets the most hoops on the dick before the timer runs out," she declares and laughs some more. "Who wants to go first?"

I immediately put my hand up. "Me! Get that dick on my head!"

A few hours later, after playing numerous party games including Twister and Cards Against Humanity, I realise I'm the last person left.

"I'd better get going," I say to Margie as she's taking empty glasses to the kitchen counter and making an intoxicated effort to tidy up. Mark clears away the games.

I go to pull out my phone, but it's not in my bag. I search for it around the room, stumbling from here to there, and come across it where the DJ had his decks set up.

A stabbing sadness wrenches me in two as I pick it up. I've had an absolute blast for the past few hours, and I really don't want to return to an empty flat, to face the reality that I'm single again. All the hyped-up party energy drains away. My phone only has three per cent battery left. I open the taxi app, but there are no cars available for hours. It's 4 a.m. on New Year's Day and a busy time. I call a couple of other taxi firms, but they just ring and ring and nobody answers. How am I going to get home? I don't know anyone in this city to call for a lift.

I'll have to walk it. I open my GPS app, put my address in and search for a route from my current location. It'll take an hour. *Urgh*. I don't know this city at all. I don't know how safe this route is for a lone, inebriated female to walk, with her high heels in her hand, at 4 a.m.

My phone dies.

Double urgh.

I'll just have to follow signs to the city centre and Pontcanna and hope for the best. I don't even know Pontcanna all that well. Hopefully, I'll spot something recognisable so I can navigate to my apartment.

"Fuuuuuuck," I say out loud.

"What's up?" Mark asks.

"My phone's out of battery, there are no taxis, and I don't know the way to walk home. But I'm sure I'll be fine…" I head towards the door and try to remember where I left my coat when I came in.

"What? Nonsense. Come to bed with us," Mark says.

"Huh?" I reply, alarmed.

"What Mark means is, please stay over in one of our spare bedrooms," Margie says quickly.

"Of course, isn't that what I said?" Mark replies, swigging the last drop of whiskey in his tumbler.

"That is so kind of you, but I can't do that. I can't impose on you any longer."

Margie grabs my hand. "Shh. Let's all go to bed, right now."

She grabs Mark with her other hand, and we stumble through into the hallway. My stomach flips when I remember the threesome had been in the first door to the left, and I hope I'm not in that room, but Margie points to what was the karaoke room.

"You're in there, my dear."

She lets go of my hand and pulls Mark towards the sex bedroom. "Come on, dearest."

He grabs her around the waist and opens the door. They stagger into the bedroom, shutting the door behind them. There are a few giggles and a grunt.

I head into the spare bedroom with a smile. Good for them still having a healthy sex life after decades together. I kick off my shoes and lie on the bed fully dressed in a starfish position. When the room stops spinning, I crawl under the covers and nestle my head into the pillow. It's the comfiest bed I've ever slept in. My entire body immediately relaxes, and I let out a contented, "Ahhhh."

Honestly, I could just stay here forever.

I wake with a pounding headache and my eyes scrunched

together. I slide from the bed, use the ensuite bathroom and wobble towards the smell of coffee coming from the kitchen.

Mark potters around, grinding fresh coffee beans, putting the coffee machine on, and finding mugs.

"I feel like death," I groan as I park my bum on one of the bar stools around the kitchen breakfast bar and clutch my forehead, elbows on the counter.

"You need an espresso!" He presses a few buttons on the machine.

Margie swans in. She looks utterly fabulous. Her makeup is done, her hair swept back in a half-up half-down do, showing off some chunky gold earrings. She wears a black top with oversized puffy sleeves, a tiny white mini skirt, and some tangerine-orange over-the-knee boots. She looks as if she's off to a photoshoot with Vogue.

"You look incredible," I say.

Margie glances at me. Hesitates.

A string in my chest twangs uncomfortably. She's forgotten who I am. I've overstayed my welcome, and I need to get gone. I'm not fun, drunk, belly dancing Rachel anymore. I'm hungover, boring Rachel. The party is well and truly over – the almost silent apartment attests to that.

But she smiles broadly. "Thank you, Rachel. I've already done a 'get ready with me' video on TikTok this morning. I'm an accidental influencer." She leans against the end of the breakfast bar. "Turns out many, many people want to watch me do my makeup and put clothes on every morning." She shrugs.

Mark places an espresso in front of me and one in front of Margie. He stands next to her and picks up his phone.

"You have a lovely home," I say. I nod towards the terrace. "Such an incredible view."

"Thank you," Margie replies. "We wanted the one above, but she wouldn't sell. It's the only flat on the top floor so has 360-degree views. There are only two on this floor, one facing towards the city and this one out across the bay. So, we settled for this one." She nudges Mark. "Isn't that right, darling?"

Mark glances up from his phone. "Er, yes." And almost instantly gets engrossed in whatever is on his screen again.

She rolls her eyes.

"Must be a fantastic place to live and watch all the happenings on the bay," I say.

"Yes, it's certainly lovely being here. But we're not here all the time."

"Oh?"

"We split our time between our six properties in the UK. But probably our favourite place is our country estate in Powys. There's something so remote and bleak and yet so energising and peaceful about the Welsh countryside. And we're often on holiday, of course. We did have holiday homes abroad but found we got bored going back to the same place again and again so sold up and just rent where we fancy now. In fact, I imagine that's what this one is doing right now." She peers at Mark's phone. "What have you found?" She looks back to me. "He always likes to book his next adventure on New Year's Day."

Mark looks up. "I've found a wonderful little expedition in Peru. We'll be hunting down never-found-before archaeological sites and going into some wild, uncharted terrain. And there's a few days of white-water rafting and a visit with Mario Vargas Llosa thrown in for good measure too."

"Mario Vargas Llosa?" I ask.

"Considered one of the greatest Peruvian novelists of all time. He won the Nobel Prize for Literature in 2010."

I look at him blankly.

"*The Time of the Hero*?" he asks.

I shake my head.

"It's a great book."

I nod at him. My preferred reading is romance. The

sweet ones, the spicy ones, the trashy ones, the cliché ones. Give me all the romance, thanks. I pick up my cup of coffee, breathe in the strong fragrance and take a sip. It's delicious. The intense flavour cancels out the stale booze taste in my furry mouth. I finish the rest in one go, like the vodka shot I did last night.

Both Margie and Mark look at my left hand.

I know exactly what they're looking at. Or what they're *not* looking at.

Margie shifts position. "Sorry to be rude, but we didn't notice that last night."

"Not rude at all." I hold up my left hand, spread my three fingers and thumb and glance at the stump where my little finger should be. "I lost it in an accident when I was seven."

They both nod and look slightly concerned.

Even though they don't pry, I feel the need to explain. "I had a difficult childhood."

They both blink at me, and I get the overwhelming feeling that now is the time for me to exit. I doubt either of them had difficult childhoods. It's clear they were both born with a silver spoon in their mouths.

I stand. "Thanks for the espresso and for having me to stay. I'd better get going."

Margie takes a step towards me, blocking my way. "Oh no, Rachel. You can't leave. Not now."

CHAPTER 4

I frown, wondering what she could mean, when Mark says, "We're going for brunch at a lovely little place a few minutes' walk away. Join us! You must!"

I glance down at yesterday's red dress and high heels and think about my panda eyes from not taking off last night's makeup. "I'm not really dressed for brunch."

"Nonsense," Margie says. "You look absolutely fabulous. You can borrow a scarf and some gloves of mine. It looks a little blustery out there. But dry, thank goodness."

Before I can protest, the pair have bundled me into the hallway, found my coat and donned their own. Margie wraps a super-soft scarf around my neck and plonks some woolly gloves in my hand.

I'm surprised they don't want shot of me. But I'm not complaining. I'm not ready to go home to my empty flat just yet, not ready to spend New Year's Day on my own.

We wander around the bay to a little café that juts out into the water on stilts. We walk up the decking and are seated inside on the top floor.

It's busy. A harried server comes over to take our order, barely looking at us, barely taking a breath, stabbing at the screen of her tablet angrily.

"Chelsea," Margie says, gently touching the server's wrist. "How wonderful that we have you again."

Chelsea blushes, then beams. Her entire demeanour

changes. She becomes fully enthused with what she's doing and suddenly has all the time in the world.

"Mrs Madden. Mr Madden. A pleasure," she says sweetly. "What can I get you today?"

We give her our orders.

Chelsea smiles. "Coming right up!" She walks away with a more confident spring in her step.

"Do you come in here often?" I ask.

"No, only the once," Mark replies.

"And you remembered her name?"

"We never forget faces or names, do we, darling?" Mark says.

"Never. It's from working for years at executive level for huge firms employing thousands. It always disarms people when you remember their name," Margie says.

"What did you both do?" I ask, curiosity getting the better of me. I've been desperate to google them but my phone battery is still dead.

Mark gestures for Margie to go first.

"I worked at my family's defence manufacturing business for thirty years before retiring," she says.

"Come on, don't be modest," Mark says.

She smiles. "Fine. Daddy wanted my older brother to take it over. It had always been passed down through the male line. But my brother is a rake. A lovable rake, you must understand. Everyone adores Timothy, but he's next to useless at anything other than womanising and high-stakes poker games. So, Daddy trained me up. I took it on as CEO at twenty-five and ran it until fifty-five. It quadrupled in size under my leadership, and when dear Daddy passed away, I sold it for a hefty sum. Weapons were never my thing, and I didn't want any *Succession*-style wrangling with the kids."

"Wow," I reply, awed. "How about you, Mark?"

"I set up and sold a car technology firm."

"Now who's being modest," Margie teases.

He grins at her. "We were the first to make car

software and hardware and built-in car computer systems, that kind of thing. I'm slightly obsessed with cars. I have a large classic car collection up at our Scottish bolthole. I've recently converted my Ferrari 250 GTO to run on a fuel blend of eighty-five per cent bioethanol and fifteen per cent unleaded petrol, like King Charles' Aston Martin."

"That's cheese and wine byproduct, right?" I ask, pleased that I can join in this conversation with some trivia learnt from watching royal events on the telly.

"That's it," Mark replies, delighted.

Our food and drinks arrive, and we get stuck in.

"What do you do, Rachel?" Margie asks.

Inwardly, I cringe. I don't have an exciting job. I'm not running huge corporations. I'm not successful or powerful or distinguished in any way. "I plan out major engineering works on the railway network."

"Interesting," Margie says.

And I think she truly means it. Most people's eyes glaze over when I tell them my job.

Mark leans forward. "So, tell me..."

As we eat, he asks me numerous questions about my job. And I answer them all, happily. This is the first person in a long time – since I first started dating Brandon – that has been genuinely interested in what I do.

Chelsea comes back to clear our plates, and we order another round of drinks. I'm having a great time and don't want it to end.

"You mentioned kids earlier, how many do you have?" I ask.

They share the briefest glance with one another – an in-joke perhaps?

"Two," Margie replies. "They must both be around your age. Honestly, I lose track. One lives in Buenos Aires with his Argentinian wife and her three kids. And the other lives in Cape Town with her wife."

"Both overseas?"

"Yes. Tobias was dotty about polo as a teen and moved

to Argentina to play professionally and train polo horses. He met Bérénice and stayed. And Simone runs a vineyard and successful winery with her South African wife. They're both very happy."

"We're happy that they're happy," Mark says.

They hold each other's hands and glance at each other again in a way I can't decipher.

Margie says, "We see them every few years. But they're busy, and so are we."

"Busy being retired," Mark snorts.

"Well, *I'm* busy," Margie says. "I still do lots of charitable work, sit on a few boards as a voluntary advisor, mentor and invest in female entrepreneurs, and whatnot."

"And I sit on my arse," Mark says.

They both laugh.

From what I can tell, neither of them sits on their arse. They are not the stereotypical image of a retired couple that popular media would have people believe. They're both vibrant and clearly loving life.

Chelsea brings our drinks, and Margie asks for the bill, putting her handbag on the table. I hadn't noticed it before, but it's like a work of art.

"That handbag!" I say, admiring the light-blue shoulder bag.

"It's called a croissant bag. Perfect for a brunch outing." She chuckles.

Chelsea drops off the bill. Neither of them checks it. Margie pulls out a card and puts it on top. I pull my card out of my bag and place it on top of hers.

Mark immediately picks it up and hands it back to me. "Our treat."

"Thank you, but I'm happy to pay my share," I say.

He shakes his head. "Nobody pays for us unless they are significantly wealthier. And so far, I think that's only happened twice? Maybe three times?"

"Three times, I think," Margie replies. "There was that sheikh in Dubai that time…"

Chelsea returns and sorts the payment from Margie's card. Margie pulls out a crisp fifty-pound note and hands it to Chelsea. The server's smile goes as wide as the bay outside.

As we wander back to the Maddens' apartment, I spot a taxi and hail it.

"Best be getting home," I say.

They nod.

"I hope to see you again soon," I say eagerly.

It's true. I'd love for them to be my new friends in the city.

"Absolutely," Margie says and pulls out her phone. "Please put your number in."

I open the taxi's door, sit, put my number in her phone, and hand it back. She air-kisses my cheek. Mark closes the door for me.

"Oh!" I exclaim and knock on the window. "Your scarf and gloves." I unwind the scarf. "Could you open the window, please?" I ask the driver.

He presses a button, and the glass goes down.

Margie waves her hand. "Keep them. Give them to me next time."

"Sure?"

She nods. The driver puts up the window and pulls away. They wave. I wave back in an over-eager animated fashion, as if I'll never see them again.

When we're halfway home, my smile fades as it dawns on me that I probably won't. We have nothing in common – they're retired, wealthy, glamorous. And what exactly do I bring to the table? We operate in different spheres. But I've had a fabulous time with them, and I think they've enjoyed my company. I'd love to know more about their careers, maybe get some mentoring from Margie. And Mark seems like the type whose brain you could pick on just about any topic and find it fascinating.

The pain of my broken heart creeps back: the loneliness, the helplessness, the disappointment.

Just as we turn into my road, the sky opens. Rain lashes down. My plan to get out for some fresh air on New Year's Day goes out the window. I'll have to sit in the flat on my own. No. I have to keep busy. I'll do some cleaning or something. I can't let myself wallow in self-pity and spiral into depression like I did when Will dumped me after eight years together.

All my suppressed memories of Will come whooshing back and converge with the raw Brandon hurt to flood my senses. The driver pulls over in front of my apartment building. I pay and jump out before I can burst into tears in the taxi.

Just about holding it together, I open the communal front door, trudge up one flight of stairs to my flat on the first floor, and go to put my key in the lock.

But the door is ajar.

Did I leave it open? Unlocked? I remember leaving last night and closing Ralph's door, but did I close my own? I can't recall.

I gently push open the door. The heavy rain pounds against the windows, and the place is dark. I take a step inside. I must've left it open in my haste to get in the taxi to get to the party.

But I can feel it. A presence. The air is different, out of shape, unbalanced. It whispers in my ear, circulating when it shouldn't be. I'm not alone.

There's someone in my flat.

Silently, I nudge off my heels, pick one up and hold it out in front of me. I'm not entirely sure what protection a heeled shoe will give me, but it's better than nothing. I curse that my phone battery is empty so I can't easily call the police. If I scream loud enough one of my neighbour's should hear, shouldn't they? Not Ralph though, he's hard of hearing. Downstairs Dominic or Upstairs Seema and Hiram might though.

Creeping forward, breath sucked in, I edge towards the door to my lounge. Am I about to disturb a burglary? An opportunist thief hitting up all the empty-looking flats while the occupants are away for New Year's Eve? Will they grab what they can and make a run for it? Or fight back? Will it get ugly?

My pulse quickens, and my skin feels clammy. All the alcohol I drank last night oozes out of my pores. I push open the door.

And then I see. My chest hitches painfully.

"You," I say.

"Hello, Rachel."

CHAPTER 5

I switch on the light. The lounge illuminates. I swallow back fear.

I have to play this right. One wrong move could be deadly.

"How did you get in?" I say lightly, as if addressing a friendly neighbourhood cat that has snuck in through an open window for a quick cuddle.

My twin sisters glance at one another, look back at me and shrug in unison. They sit side by side on my sofa, one with her feet curled up next to her, the other with her feet on the table. Neither has taken their coat or shoes off. Goodness knows how long they've been in that position, in the dark.

They stare at me. Neither moves. That's a good thing. I want them both exactly where I can see them – and nowhere near me.

As if making friendly chit-chat, but knowing I won't get a straight answer, I ask, "How long have you been here?"

Two shrugs.

My heart hammers. I thought I'd escaped them. But they've found me. And so soon.

With a false smile and happy tone, I say, "How'd you get my new address?"

I certainly didn't give it to them. I didn't tell them I was moving. I found a job in a random city – I have absolutely no ties to Cardiff and have never mentioned it to them as somewhere I'd want to live. Mum knows my new address, but she wouldn't have told them.

Even though Mum is not the twins' biological mother, she was a mum to them for eight years. She tried so hard to love them. She's a nurse. It's in her nature to care and nurture and soothe and nourish. But she never forgave them for my accident and never trusted them ever again. She hasn't spoken to them or to Dad since she moved to New Zealand almost twenty years ago.

The twins glance at each other again.

With a smirk, Caroline says, "Why is your shoe in your hand?"

They both stare at my shoe.

I lower it. "Because you two gave me a fright! I thought there was an intruder in the flat."

They blink at me. Laugh. And I sigh with relief. From that small interaction, I can tell they're in an *agreeable* mood. I'm safe. For now.

I have a strained relationship with my half-sisters. Caroline and Catherine are four years older than me at thirty-nine. Caroline is a few minutes older than Catherine. They are identical twins and, unless you know them, most people can't tell them apart. We share the same father and look just like him, and just like each other. They are average height and weight and have red frizzy hair in a middle parting that falls past their shoulders, blue eyes, a face full of freckles and pale skin. They are always together. They communicate with a whole non-verbal language that I can't comprehend – the slightest blink of the left eye, or sniff, or hand gesture. It's slightly creepy. They remind me of Wednesday Addams, except there's two of them, they're ginger and they're not kooky and lovable, they're unpredictable and evil.

I want them out of my flat. But if I asked, they wouldn't go. They do what they like, when they like. I could attempt to forcibly drag them out, or call the police, but that might trigger them into doing something violent.

And that's the last thing I want. I want to keep them in this amiable mood. There's two of them and one of me. And they're ruthless. Any kind of conflict would not end well for me.

"Nice outfits," I say.

They nod and smile.

They wear the same clothes. It's usually always something to do with Disney. Today, they have on long black padded coats, *The Mandalorian* t-shirts, black leggings, thick socks, and tattered trainers. Sometimes they wear wildly inappropriate clothes – like tiny shorts with bare legs in winter or woolly jumpers in the summer. They both clutch plastic *The Mandalorian* mini backpacks in their left hands, which rest on the sofa.

"Is that Yoda?" I ask.

I'm not all that into *Star Wars*, but try to pay some attention for situations exactly like this. *Star Wars* is a favourite topic of theirs.

"Grogu," Caroline replies.

Catherine snorts contemptuously, disgusted that I got it wrong.

They talk animatedly about Grogu. They're not talking to me. It's not a conversation. They're just imparting their extensive knowledge about the subject.

My sisters have some intense obsessions – Disney being one of them. Not working and rinsing the government for every benefit they can get is another. Oh, and finding wealthy older boyfriends who'll pay for everything. They excel at that.

Caroline does most of the communicating with me. Catherine prefers to sneer unnervingly and keep her silence. But they talk respectfully and in equal amounts to one another in my presence. I've no idea how they are with other people when I'm not around. Perhaps Catherine's the life and soul of the party and annoyingly chatty? Who knows.

As they prattle to one another, not wanting to make

any sudden moves that will startle them, I slowly unwrap Margie's super-soft scarf from around my neck and pull off her gloves. I place them carefully on the radiator to dry. I'm drenched from the short sprint through the heavy rain from taxi to front door.

"I'm just going to hang this by the front door because it's wet," I say to my sisters, indicating my soaked coat.

It appears as if they're too involved in their *Star Wars* chat to hear me, but I know better. They're always watching, always listening. I come back and sit on the small armchair opposite the sofa and wait for their conversation to dry up. I know not to interrupt.

When the Grogu discussion comes to an abrupt halt, I ask "How did you get here? By train?"

If I keep asking questions then at some point they might hear one they want to answer.

They stare back at me: mute, smug. Catherine scratches the side of her nose. Caroline clears her throat. They've just said something to each other that I don't understand.

I stand. "I'm going to make a hot drink in the kitchen. Do you want a tea?"

Two nods.

I head into my separate kitchen, making sure to keep the doors open. I can't see into the lounge from the kitchen, but I can hear. I pull out three mugs, tea bags and milk. I get down a bag of sugar from the top shelf. I bought it for Brandon's tea and coffee. He liked two spoons. I don't take any. I'm thankful that I got it in for him; I wouldn't have wanted to leave the twins in my flat to nip to the shop.

I fill the kettle and turn it on. I feel gross. All I want is a shower and to brush my teeth. But the twins scare me. The flat feels different. No longer cosy, safe and comfortable, it's spiky, unpredictable, unknown, as if the ceiling will suddenly fall in without warning, or there's actually another room off the bedroom that I didn't know about. The kettle boils and switches off. I reach for it with my left hand and see the gap where my little finger should be.

They did that to me.

I was seven, they were eleven. They were obsessed with octopuses at the time, watching documentary after documentary. They were particularly fascinated by the fact that if an octopus loses one of its eight arms, it grows back. They decided to experiment on humans. On me.

At that age, I had no idea that my sisters hated me, that they were jealous of this little sibling who had stolen their dad's attention away. Even though they often broke my toys or destroyed things in the house or caused chaos if they thought I was getting special treatment, I trusted them. My love for my sisters was unconditional.

It was a Saturday afternoon. Dad was in the lounge watching telly. Mum had just got in from a long shift at the hospital and was in the shower. Caroline and Catherine lured me into the kitchen. They had a big knife in their hand. I wasn't sure where it had come from. I knew my parents hid the knives, but the twins were sneaky and saw things I didn't – like where the knives were kept and how to get hold of one.

They grabbed my left hand and placed it on the kitchen table, told me to spread my fingers, told me that it would grow back like an octopus. I didn't really know what was happening, and then – bam! – the knife came down.

I don't remember much. Apparently, I screamed, then fainted, and was rushed to hospital. They couldn't save my finger by sewing the end back on because there was no end – the twins had hidden it. To this day, no one knows what happened to it or where it went.

An accident, everyone said. An unfortunate accident.

A year after, Mum divorced Dad and moved us out. The twins weren't hers, after all. She'd met Dad when he had three-year-old twins in tow. Nothing has ever been said about who their mother was. But they were definitely Dad's. They were, and still are, the spitting image of him. Mum had tried her hardest with them – they called her

Mum, still do – but she didn't think I was safe around them.

Because, although we all called it an accident, Mum and I knew better. The twins knew what they were doing. They were eleven. They knew knives were sharp. They knew humans weren't the same as octopuses. They knew chopping off someone's finger was wrong. They had wanted to hurt me. But Dad was in denial.

"They don't have a violent streak!" he'd insist to Mum during one of their blazing rows before we moved out.

The court declared that I should visit my father and sisters every other weekend. I did, but I hated every second of it – always watchful, always on edge waiting for them to attempt to harm me again.

As soon as I turned sixteen, I stopped going. For nineteen years I've attempted to minimise contact with my sisters and father. Aiming for our relationship to only be text messages on their birthdays or at Christmas, and absolutely no in-person contact.

But they refuse to let me go.

They'd show up uninvited at my flat or work. Pull up in their car when I was walking somewhere, insist I get in and we do something together. Dad always drilled it into me that family comes first no matter what and would guilt me into spending time with them when it was the last thing I wanted.

For twenty-eight years, since I was seven, the threat that they could harm me again – at any time and when I'm least expecting it – has been a constant, sizzling undercurrent at every interaction.

And then, one month before I moved to Cardiff, it happened. They tried to hurt me again.

Around midday on a Sunday, Dad had shown up at my flat insisting we go over to my sisters' place for lunch. I said I was busy, but he wouldn't take no for an answer. At their flat, while we waited in the lounge, they had made sandwiches for us. Cheese and tomato for Dad and me.

They'd opted for something else. I went to take a bite of my sandwich and noticed a smear of peanut butter on a piece of tomato.

"That's peanut butter," I'd yelled, throwing the sandwich back on the plate and standing. "You know I'm allergic to peanuts! That could've killed me!"

Dad stood. "Calm down, Rachel. They wouldn't have done it on purpose, eh, girls?"

Caroline said, "Oops."

Catherine sniggered.

Caroline showed us her sandwich. "We're having peanut butter and jam. A bit must've got onto Rachel's sandwich."

"A silly mistake," Dad said. "No harm done."

He'd sat back down and continued eating as if his youngest daughter hadn't just come within seconds of going into anaphylactic shock.

The twins stared at me. I stared back. Catherine sniffed. Caroline rubbed her hands together. They'd done it on purpose, of course they had. And Dad had glossed over it in exactly the same way as he had when they'd cut off my finger.

Dad had growled at me to *sit the fuck down*. I did.

But I didn't eat the food. Or touch the cup of tea they'd made me. I tried not to touch anything in case they'd smeared peanut butter anywhere else in their flat.

Dad had driven me home banging on about how we should do this every Sunday and take it in turns to host and cook.

And all I was thinking was how I had to escape them once and for all. I'd immediately found another job in another city and moved without telling them. I'd felt free. *I'd got rid of them forever!*

But it's been a month.

And they're back.

I make the drinks and take them through to the lounge. Caroline and Catherine observe my every move. I watch them just as closely. I put the drinks on the coffee table, never turning my back to either of them. Catherine stands and goes to the bathroom.

"Milk and one sugar for you, and milk and two sugars for Catherine," I say cheerily.

I need to act as if the peanut butter incident didn't happen. As if they don't want to do me harm. I sit back on the armchair and take a sip of my tea. Caroline doesn't touch hers until Catherine returns. At the same time, they lift their cups, blow on the top and take a sip.

"Not the best brew," Caroline says. "Too milky."

"Why are you here?" I ask, not expecting a reply.

"New Year's resolution," Caroline says.

"Oh? What's that?" I sit up straighter.

"You," Catherine says with a wicked grin.

"*Me?*"

"This year, we have decided that our focus is you, little sister. We want to know everything there is to know about *you*," Caroline says, pointing at me.

My entire being flips. *What the hell does that mean?*

"Great," I reply, attempting not to let my panic come through in my voice.

Catherine sniggers. Caroline laughs with her.

They're winding me up. It's what they love to do. They screw with me as punishment for my being born. It'll never end.

My sisters do inexplicable things. Once, when I was at university, they came uninvited to my student house share. They were there for about half an hour. I went to the toilet, and when I returned, they were gone. And so was every piece of fruit in the five-person household. They'd stolen it from the fruit bowl on the side, from the fridge and from the cupboards. I've no idea why. I asked, of course, but never got an answer.

"When are you and Brandon getting married?" Caroline asks. "We've already picked our dresses."

"We split up. There won't be a wedding." *As if I*

would've invited them!

They glance at each other. Caroline stands and goes to the bathroom.

I know not to engage Catherine while no one else is around. It doesn't end well. Even now as adults, Catherine still likes to yell that I've insulted her or done something mean to her when I've done nothing of the sort. We look at each other until Caroline returns and sits on the sofa.

"Let's put on the telly," I say and grab the remote. "Do you still like *Keeping Up with the Kardashians*?"

They both nod.

I flick to reality shows on Netflix.

"Put season one on," Caroline says.

I put it on and watch for a few minutes. I study them surreptitiously; they're both utterly absorbed. The Kardashians are another obsession.

My body itches for a shower. The twins don't look as if they're moving anywhere. I decide to risk leaving them. What else can I do? Sit and watch them forever? This is what I've always done – attempted to get on with my life while their dark shadow hangs over me.

"I'm just going to have a shower and get changed," I say.

They don't reply or make any acknowledgement that they've heard, but I know they have.

Locking the door to my ensuite, I brush my teeth and take a quick shower. When done, with dressing gown wrapped around me, I unlock the door and check my bedroom. All clear. I put my phone on charge and stick my head around the bedroom door to look into the lounge. The twins are still absorbed in the reality show. They sprawl on my sofa as if they own it and this is their home. They still haven't taken off their shoes or coats.

I close the bedroom door. Not taking my eyes off it, I dry my hair and put on my comfies. I read and reply to a few Happy New Year messages from acquaintances in Nottingham and around the country. My bestie, Heather, has left me a voice note. I listen to it and tap out a quick reply.

There's no message from Pete. Or from Margie. I should've taken her number and messaged her to say thanks for a great night and fab brunch and organised to return her scarf and gloves. But she probably would've left me on read or messaged a few times and then ghosted me. It's better this way. I'll drop her things off with the concierge on reception at her building. I'd like to see her again, but I'm not holding my breath. I expect she has hundreds of friends and doesn't need another one.

A sneeze from the lounge draws my attention back there. I venture out of my bedroom, picking up the bin bag of Brandon's stuff and putting it by the front door. Taking a deep breath, I head back into the lounge.

Keeping Up with the Kardashians season one is coming to an end, so I switch it to season two. It's getting late, and they're showing no signs of moving from my sofa.

"Are you planning on heading off soon?" I ask.

"We're staying for dinner. Pizza takeaway," Caroline replies, not taking her eyes off the screen and not offering to pay their share.

This cannot be happening.

"Veggie pizza," Caroline adds in a tone that has a hint of menace to it.

She looks up at me and scratches the side of her head. Catherine switches her attention to me with a look that says, *I dare you to challenge us.*

"Sure," I reply tightly, quickly, not wanting to trigger anything.

I've witnessed their explosive violence first-hand. I don't remember being scared when they took my finger because I trusted them. But, less than a year later, before Mum had moved us out and put me in a different school, they'd found me crying after school because a bully in the year above had stolen my favourite pink pencil case. They asked me to point her out to them. I did, and the three of us followed her as she was walking home. I thought they were going to ask her to give it back. But down a deserted alleyway they jumped her from behind and beat her so savagely that I attempted to get between their fists and the bully's face to protect her. They threatened to kick the shit out of me. I was terrified.

While the girl bled out on the pavement, they took my pencil case out of her backpack, gave it to me and told me to never breathe a word of what had happened to anyone. The bully never came back to our school. And I never said anything. I was too frightened of my face getting smashed to a bloody pulp like the bully's. I still feel bad about that to this day.

Catherine sneers at me and flicks her eyes back to the telly.

I glance at their two tiny children's backpacks. They've not brought any overnight stuff but if they were getting a train back to Nottingham they'd need to get going soon. Otherwise, I've got no idea where they're staying tonight... *oh no*.

Caroline notices me looking at their backpacks. "We're staying here tonight."

Shit.

Inside, I draw on every ounce of strength I have in my body and send it to my internal bravery button. It presses on. A little voice in my head says: *you've managed to survive them for thirty-five years; you can cope with one night. Be strong.*

"Great," I say through a false smile, careful not to show any weakness, careful to project full confidence. "You can stay tonight, but you'll need to go tomorrow. It's bank holiday Monday but I'm busy, and the day after I'm at work. Okay?"

There's a pause. This could go either way.

"Yes," the eldest twin finally replies. She turns her attention back to KUWTK.

I let out a long, silent breath. *They'll be gone tomorrow and hopefully won't be back for a long time because it's a hassle getting from Nottingham to Cardiff to see me. Hopefully.* I order our food online and sit tensely, positioning my eyes so I'm half watching the telly, half watching them.

The pizza arrives, and Caroline demands we watch *Dumbo* – a favourite of theirs.

It's not exactly how I planned to spend New Year's Day, but at least I'm not miserable at being alone or feeling depressed, hurt, and rejected after being dumped. All that has been shoved aside to deal with the present danger of the twins in my flat.

While we're watching *Aladdin*, I make a few New Year resolutions of my own. One, to get over Brandon in a healthy way, move on quickly, put myself back out there, go on plenty of dates, find a wonderful man to marry and have kids with. Two, to find my tribe in Cardiff. Three, to learn the ropes quickly and smash it in my new job. Four, to move somewhere else in this city and do everything I can this time to make sure the twins won't find me. I must've left a loose end, and I can't do that again.

At 11 p.m., the twins stand up.

"Bedtime," Caroline says.

I stand too. "The spare bedroom is that door on the left."

They pick up their backpacks, and I follow them through the hallway. I won't ever walk in front of them in case they pulled out something sharp and stabbed me in the back. They head into the room.

"Dad wants to see you," Caroline says.

Catherine shuts the door in my face.

I gulp back fear.

I head to my bedroom, close the door, change into my pyjamas, and get into bed. But I can't sleep. I'm on high alert. I strain to hear any noises from the spare bedroom. I might get up in the morning and they're gone with all my bathroom toiletries, or need a pee in the middle of the night and find them standing at the bottom of my bed watching me, or discover they've broken or damaged something I love. I wish I had a lock on my bedroom door, but there isn't one.

I get out of bed and push and heave my bedside cabinet in front of the door. If they try to get in, that should slow them down enough for me to climb out of the window and run.

Crawling back into bed, it takes me a moment to steady my breathing.

An invasive weed has taken root and is growing fast, pushing out calm and happiness, and instead filling me with an overwhelming sense of dread and impending doom. All my muscles are tense. Restlessly, I toss and turn.

For wherever my sisters are, my father isn't far behind.

CHAPTER 6

My eyes snap open. I'm still alive. I scan my body for any anomalies, sit up and check around my bedroom. All looks well.

It's 8.07 a.m. I forgot to set my alarm last night and would've liked to have been up earlier. I had a fitful night's sleep, every tiny sound scaring me awake. I grab my dressing gown, slip my phone into the pocket, shove the cabinet out the way, and pad into the lounge.

The twins are already sitting on the sofa, dressed in the same clothes as yesterday and wearing their coats and shoes, their backpacks by their sides. Their eyes turn to watch me as I enter the room.

"Morning, would you like anything to eat?"

"We've already eaten," Caroline replies.

On and around the coffee table are empty packets of Peperami pork jerky stick (Caroline's) and steak-flavoured crisps (Catherine's). I should've known that's what their tiny backpacks were stuffed with. They don't leave home without their favourite snacks and eat them at any time of the day.

"I'm going to make a coffee and some cereal. Do you want a hot drink?"

They both shake their heads in the negative.

"Do you want to put on the telly?"

They shake their heads again.

I look around my lounge, assessing for any damage, but

all seems to be in order. I wonder what the spare bedroom will look like. Will it look like a bomb's hit it? Or perhaps I'll find a dead mouse on the pillow or a poo in the corner or something.

"Are you guys heading off now?" I ask.

They still haven't told me how they got here from Nottingham, but I suspect the train. For any normal houseguest I'd offer to drive them to the station, but I will not have the twins in my car. One would have to sit behind me, and I wouldn't be able to concentrate.

"What are you doing today?" Caroline asks, ignoring my question.

I chew the inside of my mouth. I should've been spending a fabulous day with Brandon. We were planning on going for a long walk somewhere, and then finding a cosy spot next to a fire in a pub for lunch and afternoon drinks. Buy a couple of newspapers and catch up on what was happening in the world, chat and hang out. I was going to research where we walked and find the pub, of course, that part was always left up to me.

But now, I have no plans. I don't want to tell the twins that in case they take it as an invitation to stay longer.

I don't ever lie to my sisters. They can tell.

My phone dings in my pocket and saves me from an immediate reply.

"Just going to read this," I say.

Caroline grunts and pulls out another Peperami from her backpack to eat, dropping the wrapper on my carpet. Catherine leans forward to scratch her ankle.

I sit on the armchair, keeping the twins in my periphery vision, and open the message. My heart leaps when I see it's from Margie. It reads:

Hey, Rachel. Margie here. My friend has dropped out of a spa day today and I was wondering if you'd like to join me? Starts at 10 a.m., so I can pick you up at 9.45 a.m.? Everything's already paid for so you don't need to worry about that xx

I don't even think twice about it. I reply:

Yes, please!

She sends a thumbs up emoji and asks for my address. I send it to her immediately.

I look at the twins. Relieved I don't have to lie to them, I say, "I'm going to a spa day with a friend. I need to be ready for 9.40 a.m. so need you guys to get going."

To my surprise, they nod, stand, and shoulder their backpacks.

"We're going now," Caroline says.

They walk to the front door, open it and head through. *Wow, that was easy.* But they stop and turn back to me.

"Your mobile number no longer works," Caroline says.

My pulse speeds out of control. I changed phones when I moved to Cardiff and cancelled my old number. I don't want to give my new number to them.

I use one of their tactics and don't respond. Instead, I smile sweetly. "Quick request. However you got in, please don't do that again? It gave me a terrible fright. Bye, have a good journey home."

"Until next time," Caroline says.

Catherine scowls.

They walk down the stairs without looking back. I pause, and once I hear the front door of the building open and close, I shut my front door, hurry to the lounge window, and look out at the street. I watch as they turn left out of the driveway without hesitation and walk away, side by side, in time, same leg striding out.

When I can't see them anymore, my pulse dials down a few notches, the tautness across my chest slackens, and I breathe properly again.

I head straight into the spare bedroom, preparing for the worst. But the twins have left it very tidy. As if they didn't even sleep here. I check in the cupboard, on the shelves and under the bed where I store some stuff. Nothing appears to be missing. I strip the bedsheets, drop them in the laundry basket, and pop some fresh sheets on for the next guest, whoever and whenever that might be.

As I'm making the bed, I consider how the twins found my address and got in. The only thing I can think of is that they asked my old landlord in Nottingham. I'd given him a forwarding address when I moved here so he could send on any post that looked important. The twins could've sat outside my old building for hours, days, weeks until my landlord showed up and then pounced on him. They look just like me so they'd just need to say 'we're sisters and have lost her address', and he would've immediately believed them.

But what about when they arrived in Cardiff? My elderly neighbour, Ralph, has my spare key in case of emergency, and I have a spare for his flat.

I head out of my front door and ring Ralph's buzzer. He has an internal one because he's going deaf and can't hear if you just knock.

A few moments later, I hear, "Coming!" from inside and then a few moments after that, Ralph opens the door.

"Hey, Ralph. Happy New Year! How are you?" I say loudly.

"Morning, Rachel. I'm just listening to the radio."

"I won't keep you. I just wanted to ask if you let my twin sisters into my flat yesterday?"

Ralph thinks for a moment. "Yes. I did. Lovely ladies. Look just like you. They were waiting in the street for you. Did you have a nice surprise? I wish my family were so thoughtful."

Lovely? More like manipulative and intimidating. Strangers are often charmed by their matching Disney outfits and innocent red-haired looks. The twins suck people in and then strike.

I ask, "Did you give them the key or let them in yourself?"

"I let them in. I wouldn't give anyone your key. It's safe with me."

"Great," I reply. That means they can't have made a copy so won't be able to get in again. "Please could I ask a favour?"

"Certainly."

"Please could you not let my sisters or anyone else into my flat. Although it was a lovely surprise, initially I was terrified there was an intruder."

"That's no good. Your request is noted."

"Thanks, Ralph. I'll let you get back to the radio."

He shuffles backwards and shuts his door.

Right. I've got a spa day to get ready for. All the misery of not going out with Brandon fades away. I'm ridiculously excited.

Margie appraises my flat. I can't quite believe she's here, but she rang my bell at 9.45 a.m. precisely, and I buzzed her in. It's clean and tidy, so that's something. But I know it's bland and completely lacking in any personality. Not like her and Mark's flat.

Although she hasn't said anything, heat rises to my cheeks and the urge to explain bubbles up and out of my mouth. "I was waiting to get married to buy somewhere and really put my stamp on the décor."

"You don't own this place?"

"No, I've always rented. I want to buy my first home with my husband. I think it will be more special that way. And then together we can do it up and make it our own."

"That's very sweet," she replies.

I pick up the scarf and gloves from my radiator, thankful that the twins haven't pilfered them, and hand them to her. "Here, thanks for letting me borrow them."

She pushes my hand away. "You keep them. I'd already forgotten about them."

I rub the soft cashmere between my fingers. "Thank you so much."

"My pleasure. I'm going to book a taxi."

"You didn't drive over?"

"No. I want to have a couple of drinks. Mark is at a classic car event so he can't offer lifts."

She taps on her phone. I put my coat on and wrap her scarf around my neck and put the gloves in my bag.

She continues, "Taxi is on its way."

"Brilliant. Shall we wait downstairs?"

We file out of my flat. I lock my door, and we head down the stairs and into the ground floor communal area.

Margie looks around with interest. "I do love these Victorian buildings. So distinctive. Such character."

"Yes, I'm really happy here." And my heart breaks because I'm going to need to find somewhere else. This place is now known to the wrong side of my family.

Her phone pings. "Taxi is a minute away."

"Which spa are we going to?"

"The Parkgate Hotel. Only a short drive away in the city centre. It's my favourite spa in Cardiff. It's on the top floor. You're going to love it."

"Cheers!" Margie holds out her champagne flute.

I clink it with mine. "Cheers."

She sips her champagne. "I'm pleased I went for this one. It's as delicious as I remember."

Margie picked the champagne to go with our lunch. When we'd arrived earlier – after Margie had chatted to our taxi driver the entire way – we'd been given the most delicious detox juice, I'd told them about my peanut allergy ahead of lunch, and we'd been whisked off to our treatments in separate rooms.

As the massage therapist kneaded and rubbed my body, I felt all the tension and heartache disappear to be replaced with a serene calm. I drifted off into a blissful half-sleep. After, I'd been given a sumptuous towelling robe and soft slippers and led to a private changing area to put on my swimwear.

Dressed in bikini, robe, and slippers, I headed out to the spa dining area and met Margie there. She looked just as blissed out as me.

Soothing music blends with tinkling water from a fountain on the other side of the room. I sink into the velvet tub chair and pull the cocooning robe around me.

There's a slight pause in the conversation, and a ripple of worry passes through me. This is the first moment we've not been doing something or going somewhere. Will we have much to say to one another? Do we actually have anything in common? Is she going to regret inviting me?

"That was the best full body massage I've ever had. So relaxing. Thank you for inviting me," I say.

"Thanks for coming." Margie takes a short video of her flute next to the bottle and of her taking a sip. She puts her phone down on the table. "Apologies for all this phone usage. I'll post something to my TikTok later. I didn't plan to be an influencer, but now I am, I quite enjoy it."

I dig my phone out of my robe pocket. "What's your profile?" She tells me, and I find her on TikTok. "There, I've followed you."

She doesn't really need me to, she has seventy-thousand followers.

"Thank you. I won't post anything with you in it. I keep it strictly to my face. Mark finds the whole thing abhorrent."

"He's not your Insta husband then?"

"Ha, no. Although I have floated the idea of a husband-and-wife profile called the M and M's." She laughs.

"Mark and Margie Madden – all the M's."

She laughs and looks pleased that I got her pun. "Indeed."

"But would you be chocolate or peanut?"

She laughs some more. "We're definitely both a couple of nuts."

Perhaps it's because I'm feeling so relaxed in the body,

but my apprehension about stilted conversation eases. I decide to just be myself and say what I think. "You and Mark have a lovely relationship. What's your secret after all these years?"

"We still utterly adore one another. We just *clicked* from a very young age – like two halves of the same soul slotting into place."

"That's the kind of love I want to find." I sip my champagne. "This is delicious. Are you into wine?"

"Yes. Fashion, wine, art. Anything beautiful draws my eye."

I nod.

She reaches out and touches my hand. "That's why I'm so interested in you, my dear. You are beautiful."

I blush. "Thank you, but I don't know about that…"

"It's the truth. You'll find a man who'll love you fiercely, treat you like the queen you are, and would never dream of splitting up with you over the phone." She tuts.

Our food arrives – an incredibly healthy vegan meal that makes my mouth water from just looking at it.

"*Bon appétit,*" Margie says, and we both tuck in.

"It's so good," I say after swallowing the first mouthful. "Who knew doing nothing all morning could make you so hungry."

Margie picks up her champagne flute. "And thirsty!"

"I don't know much about wine, but I do love fashion. I can't afford to buy any high-fashion stuff but I love looking at the latest trends. Who's your favourite designer? Have you ever been to any fashion shows?"

"Well…"

We chat easily and finish two bottles of champagne. I needn't have worried about the conversation. It flows like we've known each other for years. After lunch, we're shown to the hydrotherapy area. I whip off my fluffy robe, plonk it on one of the heated loungers and get into the hot tub.

Margie tucks her long white hair into a retro-looking

waterproof cap. She still has all her jewellery on, including large gold hoop earrings. Her fifties-style halter neck swimsuit is bright purple with little frills around the bust and a ruched skirt over her hips. I'm not sure why I'm surprised that she's managed to look incredibly stylish in a swimsuit, but I am. She beckons over a member of staff and talks to them for a moment.

I look down at my sensible black two-piece and am thankful that I got a bikini wax and had a pedicure a few days ago when I thought Brandon would propose, otherwise there'd be escaping spider legs and crusty feet.

The shape of Brandon lingers in my mind. I still haven't told Mum about us.

"You look contemplative," Margie says as she steps into the water next to me.

"I was just thinking I need to tell my mum about Brandon. Haven't done it yet."

A server comes over with two flutes and a bottle of champagne in a cooler bucket. He opens the bottle and pours.

Margie grins at me. "Thought we could sip bubbles while sitting in bubbles."

"Perfect," I reply.

The server hands us each a glass and retreats. We drink and ease down into the hot water. Margie snaps a few photos with her phone, now in a waterproof case. She puts it on the side.

"Are you close to your mother?" she asks.

"Yes. But not physically. She lives in Auckland. Has done for the past seventeen years."

"Oh?"

"My parents divorced when I was eight. She's a nurse and met a Kiwi doctor. They've got two kids and moved back there to raise them when I turned eighteen and moved out to go to uni. Mum thought I was old enough to fend for myself at that age."

"And were you?"

"I guess so. I just got on with it. But I miss her terribly."

"How often do you go and visit? I love New Zealand."

"Only the once."

"Once per year?"

"No. Once, ever."

Margie's eyes widen.

I continue, "I'm absolutely terrified of flying. I went to see her six years ago. It took a lot to get on that plane."

"Does she come back here?"

"No. Her entire life is there now. She has two younger kids, a fabulous husband, and a job she loves. We speak on the phone and message regularly."

"And you didn't want to move out there with her?"

"I finished uni. Got a promising job. Met someone." I shrug. "My life was here."

"And your father?" Margie asks.

I shake my head.

Margie immediately senses I don't want to talk about him and elegantly moves on. "I wasn't especially close to my mother, but our relationship was fine, you know? But I adored my father. Worshipped him. When Mother died, it was sad. But when Daddy died…" She trails off, overcome with emotion.

"I'm sorry," I say. "You don't need to tell me if it's difficult."

She knocks back the rest of her champagne, reaches over to get the bottle, tops up my glass and then her own. "One day he was in good health, the next he had lung cancer. It was a drawn-out death. He'd beg me to end his life. Tried to do it himself. Stopped eating, cut his wrists, attempted to get up to the roof of the hospital he was in so he could jump."

She wipes away a tear, sniffs and continues, "It was terrible watching him waste away. This big robust man dying with no dignity. I looked into taking him to Switzerland, but assisted dying is illegal in the UK, and I risked jail. I was still CEO of the company at that point so it wasn't an option. We can end our pets' lives humanely when they're suffering, why not our human loved ones?"

She wipes away more tears and takes a deep breath. "Anyway, that's why I'm a campaigner for assisted dying and am the patron for a couple of charities. I also fund think tanks on the topic in the UK. That's what I'm up to tomorrow, as a matter of fact. Heading to Birmingham for a couple of meetings."

"Yes, that is a divisive topic, isn't it? Amazing that you are so involved with charity."

She nods. Stands. "Shall we try out the pool?"

I follow her to the infinity pool. We swim up to the edge and look through the window at the busy city below and the magnificent skyline.

"What do you dream of doing when you hit my age?" she asks.

"I'd like to run a bed and breakfast in Devon."

"Really? Tell me more!"

"My grandma used to run one near Sherwood Forest. She's no longer with us, but I loved going to visit her. I'd help her make up the rooms, welcome the guests, cook breakfast, tell them Robin Hood stories and so on. I loved everything about it."

"Maternal grandmother?"

"Yes. Her name was Hope. That's my middle name."

"Rachel Hope…?"

"Rachel Hope Forrester."

Margie repeats my name. "That's a good strong name."

I go for a swim while Margie takes some underwater videos and selfies. I float over to her. "Shall we try out the rest?"

We spend the next hour in the heated volcanic zones, under the massaging water showers, in the sauna, and reclining on the heated loungers in the relaxation zone wrapped in our robes.

Both completely relaxed, we lounge comfortably in

silence. I pull my phone from my robe pocket and switch it back on, making sure it's on silent.

It lights up with notifications of missed calls. Before I can check them, it flashes.

"Urgh."

Margie languidly turns her head towards me. "Something up?"

"Brandon is calling me."

"The ex?"

I nod. My spa-induced serenity bursts.

She swings her legs over the lounger and leans closer to me. "If I were you, answer and see what he wants, but don't make any snap decisions. Just listen, and say you'll call him back. That way you can process in your own time."

"Right," I say. I answer. "Hello?"

"Rachel, babe. I'm so sorry for the other night. I miss you. I made a mistake. Let's forget it happened, yeah?"

Every cell in my body yearns to jump through the phone and into his arms, to pepper him with kisses and say all is forgiven. But Margie's advice rings in my ears.

"I'll think about it and call you back."

"Rach—"

"Bye," I cut him off and hang up before he can say anymore.

"Well?" Margie asks.

"He wants me to take him back. Says he's made a mistake."

"The cheek!"

But I'm stunned and don't reply.

She takes my hand. "And what do you think about that?"

"I'm not sure." And I'm not. An energy pitter-patters up and down my body. It makes me feel nauseous.

"Here's what I think. He's treated you deplorably. Any man who casually thinks he can drop a woman – over the phone on New Year's Eve, no less – and then pick her up again a few days later is not a man you want to be with. That's disrespectful. Of course, it's entirely up to you what you do, and I'll respect whatever you decide. But you're young. Don't settle for this guy because you don't want to be single. You are a catch, and don't you forget it."

A couple of hours later, Margie waves me off from the taxi. I head inside, dreading my door being open again, dreading the twins, or anyone else, sitting on my sofa. But my flat door is closed and locked, my flat empty, thank goodness.

I sit on the sofa and debate the pros and cons of making up with Brandon.

I long for him to be close, for his laughter and presence in my world. We had an amazing connection. It would be a shame to throw that away. I'll forgive and forget what he did to me this New Year's Eve, and never bring it up again. Maybe next New Year's Eve will be the engagement…

But that thought just doesn't sit right in my body. I know, deep in the depths, it's not going to happen. I want to get married, settle down, start a family. Brandon isn't on the same page.

I'm a people pleaser, and Brandon has always got what he wanted. I'm happy to go with the flow. But not this time. I'm going to put myself first for a change. I'm looking after me. Margie was right – what kind of person dumps someone and then picks them up again a few days later. I'd be disrespecting myself to let him do that to me.

Although my heart screams for me to take him back, I know in my gut and in my head that it's a bad idea. He'll only rip my heart to shreds again. It might be in a week or a year or whenever, but if he's done it once, he won't think twice about doing it again. He's using my kindness against me to get what he wants. And that's unacceptable. I'm not a doormat. I have boundaries. And he's crossed them.

I dial Brandon.

"Babe! You took your time. Shall I head over now? Got anything for dinner?"

"No, Brandon. I needed to think about it. And my answer is no."

"What do you mean, no? No, I can't come round tonight? No, you don't have anything in for dinner?"

"I'm not taking you back. We're not getting back together."

Brandon goes very quiet. I can hear his ragged breath. This is the first time I've ever said no to him.

"You've got to be fucking kidding me!" he yells.

The full force of his fury blasts me in the chest. I gasp. That was not the reaction I was expecting. I thought he might plead or go silent – definitely not blow up at me.

He shouts, "This is not the end of this!"

Shocked at his outburst, it takes me a moment to form a response. He's a lovely guy. At least, I always thought so. Calm and steady and reliable – it's what attracted me to him. But did I have him all wrong? Where has this anger suddenly come from? It's not the Brandon I know. It must've always been there but nothing I've ever done before has brought it to the surface. One thing is for sure: I do not need anyone else in my life with anger issues.

I sit taller. "We're over. I've thrown the things you left here in the bin."

He hangs up on me.

Stunned, I stare at my phone for a moment before placing it on the table. A vision of us being deliriously happy on our wedding day flashes across my mind. The same daydream that I've been entertaining for months when I thought he was going to propose.

I close my eyes to squeeze back the tears, and the vision moves on to our wedding night at a luxury hotel. I want to go in our private hot tub. Brandon wants to go to bed. We argue. His face twists, and he shouts at me. Rages. The rest of my life with him whizzes by in my mind – I'm terrified of my husband's temper, always walking on eggshells, never disagreeing or saying what I want in case it sparks an ugly moment.

No, I've done the right thing.

I'm putting me first.

I get up and head into the bedroom, changing into my cosy pjs and socks. I grab my journal and favourite pen and get comfy on my bed. I go for it, writing pages and pages detailing my heart ache and disappointment, analysing my actions, debating whether I should've done anything different and contemplating what I should do now.

After, I have a cup of tea.

And my soul feels happier, nourished from the spa day and not quite so burdened.

I feel more ready to take on the new year. Yes, my heartache is still simmering under the surface. And the shock of the twins' tracking me down and rocking up hasn't fully cleared. But this is going to be a brilliant year, I just know it.

CHAPTER 7

"I can't believe I thought it was a sex party!" I exclaim.

Pete and I howl with laughter, so much so that the person in the queue in front of us turns to look.

"I can't believe you thought I would've invited you to a sex party!" Pete replies, sucking in breath through his fits of giggles.

It's mid-morning on Tuesday, the first day back at work for many people, and the coffee shop is buzzing. It's in the building next to the building where our office is based, and I've been in here numerous times since I started this job three weeks ago – well, technically four, but no one counts Christmas week where we pretty much sang festive tunes for the entire time. I plan to come here numerous times again. The coffee is delicious, and it's the closest eatery to work, so very handy.

This is the final week of Pete showing me the ropes. I'm actually his boss, but he was tasked by the big boss to manage my induction and familiarise me with the workings of the Cardiff area rail network. It's a much bigger, much busier patch than I ran in Nottingham, and they do things differently to what I'm used to. It's also a big step up from my last role where I only managed one person. I now have an entire team.

I spent the morning grilling Pete: asking loads of questions, getting him to explain and re-explain a complex spreadsheet they use, going over what counts as our part of the track, and mapping out who operates the areas bordering ours. It was intense, so I told him, as his boss, we were going out for a coffee break. My treat. He readily agreed.

We get on like a house on fire. He's been nothing but helpful. I've settled in well and am primed to take over and run the team from next Monday when he steps back from holding my hand. I know it can't be easy showing someone more senior than you the most basic stuff, but he's taken it like a champ and done an excellent job.

He's of Mexican and Spanish heritage, was born in Swansea and raised in Cardiff, and has a strong Welsh accent. He has dark eyes, thick floppy brown hair, and big muscles from his CrossFit addiction. People warm to his vivacious character immediately. He's a year older than I am, but comes across as much younger, like a playful and over-excited puppy.

"Going to completely the wrong party means I now have new friends in the city," I say.

We take a step closer to the counter, but are still a few people away from ordering.

"Oh?" he asks.

"It was hosted by a couple called Mark and Margie Madden. They're in their sixties. I got on with them really well – after I thought they were about to throw me out for gatecrashing, that is."

Pete looks towards the counter. "That's great."

"They're well known, I think. There were loads of people there. They're both retired but had extremely successful careers in business and are ridiculously wealthy."

"Hmm," Pete replies unenthusiastically.

He's still looking at the queue, and I guess he's frustrated at how long we're having to wait.

"Margie is an accidental influencer. She's stunning and looks like a model. Here, let me show you her profile." I pull out my phone, tap a few things and bring up the app. I hold it in front of Pete.

He glances down. "I don't do TikTok. Instagram only."

"She posted one from yesterday." I open the short video for us to watch.

"You went to a spa day with her?" he asks.

"Yep! She paid for all of it. They're so generous. And she gave me some gloves and this."

I hold up the cashmere scarf that I have wrapped around my neck, which I don't think I'll take off until summer.

He pinches it between his fingers and gives it a rub, then drops it.

I smooth it with my hand. "Isn't it the softest thing ever?" I gush.

"I suppose. You're already at the gift-giving stage of this relationship, huh? It's moving fast," Pete says and purses his lips.

Is that a hint of jealousy? Up until now he's been my only friend in Cardiff. A role he's very much enjoyed, telling me about where to go out, what's on and the best places to visit. He told me that when I didn't show up to the party on New Year's Eve, he thought I'd decided to stay in. And not because I'd accidentally gone to an absolutely brilliant party on the other side of town at a multimillion-pound apartment overlooking Cardiff Bay with front-row seats for the midnight fireworks.

"You're still my number one friend," I say. My need to please rearing its head immediately in the face of his upset.

His pursed lips break into a faint smile. "I'm glad to hear that."

I'm so swept up in the Maddens that I open a browser on my phone and google them. I haven't done that yet, and I'm overwhelmed with nosiness.

"Whoa," I say and hold up my phone to Pete. "They're all over the internet!" I scroll through the results. "There's news about their businesses, their current charitable activities, profile pieces, pictures of them at high society events and even a home interiors piece. And Margie's full name is Margaret!"

"We're nearly there," Pete says and pushes my phone down so I look up.

We're two people away from ordering. Hurrah. I put my phone back in my bag. I'll internet-stalk the Maddens later.

"I need to go out later to check on some sites, if that's okay. Not anything you need to come to though," Pete says, changing topics back to work.

"Sure," I say.

I trust Pete knows what he's doing and can manage his time. He's been nothing but a conscientious employee since I arrived.

"You didn't live with Brandon, did you?" Pete asks.

I told him earlier that we'd split up, and that was the reason I was at a last-minute loose end on New Year's Eve.

"No, just me."

"Just you at Flat C, 17 Queens Road, Pontcanna!"

"Yep!"

I told him my full address once, because he was being nosey, and he likes to repeat it. I'm not sure why, but now it's become a funny little thing he does that makes me chuckle.

"Look," Pete whispers, leaning into me. "A new barista. And he is hot!"

I stand taller and look over the counter of pastries and cakes to see the man making drinks. Pete is right. "He's very attractive."

Pete grins.

It's our turn at the counter, and the server takes our orders. I pay, and we're asked to pick up our drinks at the next counter. We move along and wait, both watching the new guy work. He's wearing a white shirt with rolled-up sleeves, jeans, a black apron, and some battered converse trainers. He's short and stocky, well-muscled judging by the forearms on show, and with a square face, button nose and chubby cheeks. He turns to deliver the order to the customer in front of us, and I catch his eye. He gives me a half-smile. My heart does a little quiver.

He has sandy blond hair that is a bit spiky, a bit fluffy, and stubble. He's cute and wholesome. And looks nothing like tall, dark, and handsome Brandon.

He glances at Pete, and a look passes between them that I don't understand, but probably doesn't mean anything. The barista turns his back on us to make our orders.

Pete whispers, "He likes you." And nudges me in the ribs.

I bat away his elbow. "What? No way."

"Uh huh."

The barista turns back. "One macchiato and one mocha with an extra shot of coffee and peppermint syrup." He puts our drinks on the counter. "Let me guess…" He looks at me for a couple of seconds. "…This one is yours." He pushes the mocha towards me.

"Yes. How did you know?"

"Because you look like an interesting person, and that's an interesting drink. Not many people want peppermint in their coffee."

I'm about to say I had it once in a Starbucks, but decide not to. It's not the done thing to mention a huge chain in a small independent coffee shop now, is it? Instead, I ramble nervously, "I like peppermint tea so thought I'd give peppermint coffee a go…"

"I see," he replies.

The server on the counter gives him the next order, and he turns his back on us again. We weave our way through the busy coffee shop and spot a couple vacating a table. Pete swoops in before anyone else can claim it, sets his drink down, takes off his coat and drapes it over one of the chairs. I put my drink down and sit on a stainless-steel chair. It's still warm from the arse that graced it before me.

"Eww, I hate sitting in a chair warmed by someone else," I say and do an over-the-top grimace.

Pete laughs. He picks up the couple's empty coffee cups and moves them onto another table stacked with used cups.

He finally sits. I shrug off my coat and unwind Margie's scarf, but leave it around my neck. I take a sip of my mocha and glance up, catching the eye of the barista. He's delivering the next customer's drink but looking right at me.

I smile, blush, look away. Pete notices and glances behind him.

"He is soooo into you. You should ask him on a date, now that you're single."

"Way too soon."

"Nonsense. You need a rebound fling. It'll help you get over Brandon quicker. And you never know, barista boy over there could be your future husband. You won't know until you try."

I feel the barista's intense gaze on me again as he delivers the next customers' drinks.

"I don't know, he won't stop staring at me. I'm getting creepy vibes."

"Are you having a laugh, woman?"

"I can feel his eyes on me," I insist.

Pete slaps his forehead. "That's because he fancies you. How long were you with Brandon for? Have you forgotten how this works? When I see a woman I like, I look. I can't help it. And I hope she'll look back."

"Hmm," I reply and stir my peppermint mocha with extra coffee shot. I take another few sips. "He does make incredible coffee…"

"Precisely. Very handy the morning after a rampant sex sesh." He taps my arm. "Look, he's coming over."

The barista walks towards us, and I nearly drop the mug I'm holding. He glances at me as he passes us to clear up the table piled with dirty cups.

All the hairs on my body stand up with him so close.

Pete angles his head in the man's direction. "Ask him out on a date," he mouths at me.

Coffee cups clatter as the barista places them on a tray. He gets a cloth from his apron pocket to wipe down the table.

Screw it. I'm single again and need to get back on the dating scene. As if it's a shot of vodka for Dutch courage, I knock back the final dregs of my mocha, stand tall and stride over to the barista.

He stops cleaning and stands upright. We lock eyes. He's only just taller than me. I'm used to Brandon towering over me. But there's something very sexy about him. I catch a whiff of his aftershave; it makes my knees wobble.

"Hi, I'm Rachel. I was, er, wondering if I could take your number, and perhaps we could hang out some time?"

He smiles. "I'm Tyler. Sure. You got your phone?"

"Yeah, one sec." I hurry back to our table, ignoring Pete's smirk, and grab my phone from my bag. "Right, go for it."

Tyler reels off his digits, and I add him to my contacts list.

"Great, thanks." I gesture to the cloth in his hand. "I'll leave you to it."

"Sure thing," he replies.

"You make delicious coffee," I say. And then cringe.

I walk away, grab up my coat and bag, and give Pete a look. He gets the message, takes the last swig of his coffee, and stands. We shuffle out, pulling on our coats at the door.

"Nicely done," Pete says as we head back towards the office.

Later that day, as I walk down my road, my stomach twinges. I've been living here for the past month or so and have settled in quickly. But the twins' visit unsettled things, and now I have a slight rising panic that they'll be back at my flat waiting for me, with goodness-knows-what planned. I swallow back the fear.

I walk up my driveway and let myself into the communal area. It's quiet. There's some post for me on the side table. I scoop it up and head upstairs. My door is closed and locked. I open it.

"Hello? Anyone here?" I say into the darkness.

But the air is still.

I shut my door, kick off my boots, hang up my coat and walk through the flat turning on the lights. It's half six and already dark outside. I hate the winter and am definitely more of a summer person. I'll call Mum at 7 p.m. With the time difference, it's a good time for her because it's first thing in the morning before she heads to work.

Plonking myself on the sofa, I take off Margie's scarf and gloves and put them on the coffee table. I look at the post. From the envelopes, I can tell it's two bills and some vouchers from the supermarket I usually shop in.

I turn the first over. The seal along the back is bumpy and raised, as if it's been opened already and closed up. I check the other two envelopes – both the same. Odd. Has someone carefully prised these letters open to read what's inside? Why? Who would do that? It's pretty obvious it's nothing exciting. No. It's more likely that the letters have just got wet and rucked up going through the letterbox. I doubt they've been deliberately tampered with.

I open all three. Two bills and vouchers, as expected.

My phone lights up. I have it on silent when I'm on the bus. Not sure why, it's less annoying for other commuters, I suppose.

It's a message from Brandon. I swipe it off my notification screen. I don't want to read it.

A few more messages from him come through, and I swipe them all away. I open WhatsApp. I don't tap into our chat but can see I have six unread messages from him. I ache to read them.

But I remember Margie's advice and stay strong. Instead, I archive our chat so I don't need to see it and be tempted by those unread messages. It makes me feel better. I'm going to find someone who treats me better than he did.

My phone lights up. He's calling me.

I put my phone face down on the armrest of the sofa, head into the kitchen to get a glass of squash and return ready to call Mum. I get comfy on the sofa and pick up my phone. Four missed calls from Brandon.

I won't call him back.

I call Mum instead.

She picks up almost immediately.

"Hello, my love. You had a good day?"

We chat about a few things before I say, "I'm single again, Mum," and proceed to tell her all about Brandon dumping me on New Year's Eve. She's furious with him. It reminds me not to give in to his pestering calls and messages.

"I've got something I need to tell you," Mum says and pauses.

I hear the tremble in her voice and know it's bad news. Has one of my younger siblings failed to get into university, or crashed their car, or perhaps my step-dad's elderly mother has taken a turn for the worse?

"Okay," I reply.

There's a sniff, and my heart breaks. Mum's crying. Perhaps her mother-in-law has passed away?

"I've got breast cancer," she says.

I choke, can't speak, hear tiny explosions in my ears. It's as if a giant fist has punched me in the chest and then slapped me around the head.

She continues, her voice catching. "I'll text you the diagnosis so you can look it up. I've got a few more tests to do before they can decide on the best course of action…" Her words trail off as the floodgates open.

I join her. "Oh, Mum…" I manage.

"I might get through this. I might not. I may not have long left, or I could go on for years. Things are uncertain at the moment. That's why they're doing some more tests."

"I'm going to come out there, as soon as I can. I'll talk to work tomorrow. Book flights. I'll be there with you soon, okay?"

"Okay, my love. You'll have to face your fear of flying again."

Terror rises in me like a plane taking off. It roars in my head, flies around my insides, causes turbulence in the very depths of my soul. But it's not going to stop me this time.

"I don't care," I reply. "I have to see you, and that means flying."

"It would be lovely to have you here."

"I'll sort it, Mum."

My step-dad's voice sounds in the background. "Gotta go, Rach. Stu's driving us into work."

"Have a good day at work."

"Thanks. I love you."

"I love you, too. I'll let you know about the flight tomorrow."

We say goodbye and hang up.

My life rips out from under my feet. I'm tumbling, falling, out of control. I can't lose Mum. She's the only person I really consider my family. Yes, I have half-siblings. Yes, I have a father and stepfather. But she's the only one I'm close to. That's why I've always been so keen to set up my own family unit. To get married and have kids. To expand my family.

The thought that Mum might not be here when I get married or get to meet her grandchildren rips me into pieces. I've always wanted Mum to walk me down the aisle and do a speech. I can't imagine my future children's lives without their Grandma Valerie, without video calling her in Auckland every Sunday and visiting her every few years.

Devastated, I sob and sob and thump the armrest. The

flat throbs around me, expands and contracts. I feel like a tiny dot in the middle of it. So alone. Cast adrift.

She might not have long left. Anger flares at Brandon, for wasting my time for two years. I need to get back out there, need to meet someone. There's a great big ticking clock now. I'm not going to settle, I'll marry the right man, but I need to meet him first. I need to kiss a few frogs again to find my Prince Charming.

I pick up my phone and, before I know it, message Tyler asking him on a date tomorrow night. Although I fancy him, my gut sounds a warning. But it's probably nerves about going on a first date after two years in a relationship.

He replies almost immediately:

Sure thing. See you tomorrow. Looking forward to it.

CHAPTER 8

I raise my hand to knock on my boss' door, take a deep breath and steady myself. All morning I've been on autopilot. Getting up, getting ready, getting into work.

But inside is turmoil.

All I can think about is Mum – about her being in terrible pain, about her leaving me. I'm broken in pieces and am just about holding myself together with some sticky tape that's straining and stretching and about to snap. I didn't sleep last night, just tossed and turned until I put the side light on and sat up in bed staring into space. Hours passed in that zombie trance, and then my alarm went off.

This is the first time I've been to Kelvin's office. Even though he's my line manager, I haven't had all that much to do with him and haven't got the measure of him yet.

The big boss, Arun, conducted all my interviews. He met me on my first day and introduced me to everyone. Kelvin loitered in the background. And I've spent most of my time with Pete since I arrived.

As far as I can tell, Kelvin is a coaster and does the bare minimum. Perhaps I'm wrong, and he's very busy, but he rarely interacts with the team of seven and only briefly shows his face each day – I guess so we know he's actually here. Perhaps he does a lot of work for Arun that I'm not privy to.

Whatever he does, or doesn't do, I have to go to him to

book holiday and do any HR stuff. As soon as I arrived at work this morning I headed straight to his office. I knew vaguely where it was – Pete had gestured down a hallway when he was showing me around on my first day. It's nowhere near where the rest of the team sit in the open-plan area. It's nowhere near anyone, thinking about it. I walked past the toilets and the kitchen and a door which says 'Cleaning' on it and arrived at this door. There's no sign outside and no window in the door. But there's no other room down this hallway, and the only other door leads to the stairs, so it must be this one.

I knock, and the door swings open.

Kelvin stands on the other side, confused. "Er, Rachel, hi."

He doesn't move to invite me in. He's completely frozen with the surprise of me being at his office door. He's a big man, taller than Brandon, at perhaps six feet two or three. There's a lot of bulk on him, but it's not concentrated around his belly like so many larger men, it's all over. He's mid-fifties, but he obviously dyes his hair and beard the same dark brown. It doesn't make him look any younger; the solid colour actually looks a bit peculiar. He'd probably look better if he embraced his natural hue and accepted the greys. He's had his teeth whitened, but a couple of shades too bright. When he opens his mouth it's dazzling, startling, too much. He also has a dark tan with an orangey tinge – more Doritos-dipped than sun-kissed.

"Can I come in?" I ask.

"Sure."

He holds the door open and steps aside to allow me to walk through into the office.

It's cramped and gloomy. There's no window, and the ceiling light buzzes. The room has an old-trainers, musty smell, but it's overpowered by Kelvin's aftershave. The fragrance is so strong he must've doused himself in it, as if it was water and he was on fire. The place looks like a large cupboard. Maybe it is a large cupboard and, at some point in his two decades at this company, Kelvin has commandeered it and turned it into his office. Most of this floor is open-plan office space. There are few private offices, and only for the very senior people.

There's a desk in the middle with an extra-padded, ergonomic swivel chair behind it. In front, for visitors, is a white plastic garden chair with no seat cushion. His laptop and monitor face the back wall so I can't see what's on them. There are shelves up on one wall and behind Kelvin's desk. These aren't filled with work stuff. They overflow with Cardiff City Football Club memorabilia: signed shirts in frames, large photos of the team, mugs, scarves, pens and so on.

We skirt around each other. The small space puts us too close. It's unsettling.

He shuts the door behind me, and I hear a distinctive *click*.

"I don't think you need to lock us in," I say, lacing my tone with humour, even though alarm tickles at the edges.

"Yes, sorry. Force of habit." He immediately unlocks it.

Force of habit? Why is he in the habit of locking himself in his office? Or locking himself in with others? Why has he even got a lock on his door?

He gestures to the plastic chair. "Take a seat."

I squeeze in front of the chair and sit. It gives him enough room to shuffle around the corner of his desk to sit in his chair.

"Football fan?" I ask.

"Yeah. My hobby is collecting and selling Cardiff City FC memorabilia."

His eyes are drawn immediately to the missing finger on my left hand, and a sneer comes over his face. The few times I've been near him, he does this, even though I explained to him about my childhood accident at our initial meeting. After the first time they see it, most people don't notice it again, but he can't stop staring, his disgust evident.

I move my left hand onto my lap where he can't see it. He looks up at me, his gaze lingering for a couple of moments too long on my chest.

"What can I do for you?" he asks, impatiently.

A rush of emotion courses through me, and I feel as if I might burst into tears. My shoulders hunch, and my head tips down, the grief of Mum's diagnosis weighing heavily. Kelvin notices my damp, bleary eyes and leans backwards, repelled. He obviously has no idea how to cope with a person crying in front of him.

His cold response makes me rally. If he'd had a shred of emotional intelligence, shown me an ounce of sympathy or asked me if I was okay, I would've crumpled. Instead, I clear my throat.

"Kelvin, I had some terrible news about my mum's health last night and need to take some time off as soon as possible. The thing is, she lives in Auckland, and I need to fly out there for a couple of weeks. I can't just pop over for a visit anytime."

"You're asking to book holiday?" he says, relieved I'm not asking for anything more taxing.

"Yes. As soon as possible."

He links his fingers together, places his elbows on the desk and rests his chin on top of his knuckles. "As soon as possible is March."

"March?" I reply.

It's the third of January, I can't wait until March.

He smirks, as if he's got one up on me. "You've only just started and can't book holiday for three months. Them's the rules."

"I understand, but can this be an exception? My mum has breast cancer. I need to get out there sooner than March."

He shakes his head. "Nope. No exception. You're not special. It's in your contract. Don't like it? Leave."

I don't want to leave this job; I've only just started this job. "Perhaps I could ask HR for an exception?"

He snorts. "HR came up with the rules. But by all means, you go right ahead. Am sure they'll tell you exactly what I just did. And they won't appreciate you wasting their time, especially when we've just had this conversation."

The last thing I want is to be labelled as difficult or rude, asking for favours to bend the rules when I've only just started. If I'd been here for years, I would've immediately asked. But I've been here for weeks and haven't built up any goodwill with the HR department as yet.

I hold up my hand. "It's okay. March. I need to fill in a holiday request form and send it to you, correct?"

But I've held up my left hand, and Kelvin is hypnotised once again by my stump. He ogles it like I imagine he would a mangled car crash on the motorway.

"Kelvin?" I say and drop my hand out of sight.

"Huh? Yeah, email me a holiday request form." He stands abruptly. "That it?"

I stand too. "Yes, that's it."

"Good." He gestures to the door. "If you don't mind, I've got a busy morning."

"Thanks." I edge out from around the seat and open the door.

When my back is turned to him, I frown. *What a rude person!* He could've at least asked me how I was doing, if I was settling in okay, if he could help me with anything else. I don't like my new line manager, that's for sure.

I step into the hallway and bump into Pete. He's humming cheerfully.

"Hey, Rach!" Pete says happily. He goes into Kelvin's office. "Hey, boss!" he says in an equally jovial tone and closes the door.

I stride back down the corridor to my desk in the open-plan area.

March. It's such a long way off. I fill out the holiday form for two weeks' leave, the maximum amount I'm permitted to take in one go, and email it to Kelvin. I book a flight for the first of March to Auckland, and a return fourteen days later. If I need to, I'll change it, but I feel immediately better knowing that it's done.

But my fear of flying takes hold. The itch starts under my skin and crawls all over my body. I gasp for air. I pinch my wrist, tell myself to calm down.

Pete comes back to his desk, which is opposite mine, with a big smile on his face. He leans to one side to catch my eye.

"So, did you message Tyler?" he asks, giddy.

The interruption to my phobia panic is welcome. "Yes. We're going on a date tonight."

He claps his hands together. "Whoop! You're not wasting any time. I like it."

I smile, and he ducks back behind his laptop screen.

Kelvin appears. He points at Kalisha. She's the youngest member of our team at twenty, and joined straight out of college almost two years ago. He uses his finger to beckon her. She stands, eyes down, head hung and crosses her arms. She follows him reluctantly back towards his office.

I do not like the look of it. Is he about to reprimand her for something? She shouldn't look so scared. I make a mental note to get to know Kalisha better and to keep an eye on her interactions with Kelvin.

I check the time and open up my emails, working through a few until I find one I need to respond to in detail.

About fifteen minutes later, Kalisha hurries back towards her desk. I stand and intercept her before she can get there. "Hey, Kalisha, fancy grabbing a quick brew with me?"

She's wide-eyed with worry, but nods. We walk through to the kitchen. Thankfully, it's empty. I switch on the kettle and take down two mugs.

"Everything okay?" I ask.

"It's nothing," she replies quickly.

"What's nothing?"

"I mean to say that I really love this job, and I don't want to lose it, so if there's anything I can do for you, please let me know."

"Sure, I will do." I study her.

She shrinks into herself. "I don't actually drink tea, so am going to head back to my desk. If that's okay with you?"

"Absolutely fine. You crack on." I smile warmly at her, and she hurries out of the kitchen.

Later that evening, after wolfing down two slices of jam on toast for dinner, I'm rummaging through my wardrobe deciding what to wear. More than once, I picked up my phone to send a message to Tyler to cancel, but then changed my mind. I'm not really up for a date after hearing Mum's news. But I know she'd tell me to get on with my life. And what's the alternative? I sit at home and feel sad? No, it'll be a distraction. And that's what I need right now.

I like to keep my clothes hanging orderly: work outfits at one end, more casual in the middle and nicer, going-out stuff at the other end.

I pull out a cobalt-blue satin skirt and a lilac fluffy jumper. Perfect date attire. I'll wear with thick black tights and my black boots. I hang it up on the outside of the wardrobe door. But the bottom of the skirt is caked in mud and creased.

Weird.

I take it off the hanger and throw it in my laundry basket on top of the bedsheets from the spare room. I put back the jumper and pull out a dress. But it's the same: muddy and creased along the bottom. I check my other two dresses and purple skirt. All the same.

Maybe Brandon hung up something in the wardrobe that was dirty and it got onto my other stuff? I definitely didn't wear these things somewhere muddy. Did I?

I'm running behind, so I throw all four items in the laundry basket and grab my jeans and the lilac sweater. Brandon had a few things hanging up, but I pulled them all out on New Year's Eve and chucked them in the bin bag. Which is still by the front door. I could go and check if the muddy item is in there, but I'd need to rip open the bag because I knotted it so tightly and stuff everything into a new bag. I know something in there is broken because I stomped on it until I heard a crack, and I don't want to have to deal with all the bits. Plus, his smell will waft out. And I just can't handle all that right now.

I need to do something about the bag. Brandon has messaged and called a few times today, and I've ignored him. He'll get the message soon. But maybe I should tell him to come and pick his stuff up? Or drop it over to his? I told him I binned it, but now I feel bad about that and perhaps should give him his stuff back. I'll think about that later.

Maybe the twins put mud on my clothes when they were here, and I've only just noticed. That's the kind of random thing they would do.

I get a taxi into the city centre to where Tyler and I agreed to meet. I would've walked or got the bus, but I'm late. He said he had an idea of where we could go but wanted to run it past me first.

"Hey," I say as I jump out of the taxi and see Tyler already waiting.

"Hey!" he replies and comes forward.

He smells divine. And looks as cute as I remember.

He continues, "I was thinking we could go to this sensory art experience thing. It's meant to be pretty cool."

"Definitely. Sounds great. Lead the way," I say.

Tyler directs me down a dark, dead-end alleyway. It's a weird way to go, past large wheelie bins, but I see a sign over an open doorway with a crowd inside and music drifting out.

He heads towards the door. I reach out and touch his

arm lightly. He stops and looks at me.

"Tyler, before we go in, I just want to say that I'm not on top form. I found out last night that my mum is ill, and I've got quite a bit of stuff going on..."

His face fills with concern; his attention is squarely on me. "I'm sorry to hear that. We can skip this, if you like? And just go somewhere quiet for a chat? Are you okay?"

"Thank you for being so kind, but let's go in. And have a drink and a chat after?"

"Sure," he replies. "But if at any time you want to leave, just let me know."

We pay to get in and go through into a huge warehouse-like space with different areas. We go from one space into the next, and I panic.

"Oh crap, is this a maze?"

"No, I don't think so. I think we just follow the yellow light, see?" Tyler points up at a yellow arrow directing us through the space.

My panic subsides. "Phew! I hate mazes. Hate the feeling of being lost."

"I'm great with directions, so I'll guide us."

I nod and follow him.

The different areas are lit up with trailing lights or have things you can press or step on. There are different scents. One area looks like sweets and has a distinct smell of Fruit Pastilles. I can feel cold air, hot air, fast air, or gentle breezes. And there are fluffy walls or huge glass bubbles to touch. The music matches the area. Either fast and frantic or serene like a bubbling brook. The whole place fires up my senses, and the heavy veil of grief and heartbreak and stress and fear lifts as I focus on the present moment.

The final room is spectacular.

Tyler says, "Wow!"

I glance at him. He's looking up in wonder, completely awed. My heart does a little flip. He's very attractive.

After, we head to a nearby cocktail bar, order drinks and find a little booth to sit in.

I sip my dirty martini. It's delicious. "How long have you been a barista for?"

"Only a few weeks. I've gone back to university. I'm thirty-two and a student again. The coffee shop is a part-time job to help pay the bills."

"What are you studying?"

"Law."

"What made you go back to uni to study law?"

"I've been a jobbing musician for years. I started a law degree at eighteen but gave it up to be a drummer in a rock band. We did okay, even had a European tour, but after a few years it fizzled out. I was a session drummer and taught kids, that kind of thing. But last year I realised my heart wasn't in it anymore, and my head was telling me it was time to get a serious job."

"What changed?"

He runs his fingers through his hair. "I want to meet someone and settle down, start a family and all that. And I want to be able to support them." He takes a sip of his non-alcoholic beer.

"What kind of law do you want to specialise in?"

"Music law. Copyright infringement, and that kind of thing. I find all that fascinating because of my background."

"And have you always lived in Cardiff?"

"Nah, grew up in the middle-of-nowhere Welsh countryside. Parents still have the house there, but they're on an almost permanent cruise these days. I moved to the city at eighteen." He grins. "And how about you? I can tell by the accent you're definitely not Welsh!"

We chat easily. Two-hours-and-two-cocktails-for-me later, we exit the bar.

"How are you getting home?" he asks as we linger on the street.

"I'll get a taxi."

"I can give you a lift, if you like? I'm parked just round the corner."

He's been such a gentleman all evening; I decide he's safe. "Yes, if you're sure that's no bother."

"No bother at all. You're in Pontcanna, right? That's not too far from me."

We walk to his car and get in. It's a little Ford Fiesta, and our shoulders almost touch. A palpable frisson passes between us and hangs in the air. He backs out of the space.

"I'll head towards Pontcanna, and you can direct me from there."

"Okay," I say, feeling more confident about my bearings than I probably should be.

The car is old but immaculate on the inside, as if this is the first time it's been driven after a very thorough clean. It has a bad smell though. Tyler has a tree-shaped air freshener dangling from the rear-view mirror. It overpowers his lovely aftershave with a too spicy, too woody scent that bashes its way up my nose and immediately gives me a headache. I want to open the window for some fresh air, but it's cold and Tyler has the heater on to keep the windows from steaming up.

After two cocktails, I'm tipsy. Tyler doesn't drink and stuck to non-alcoholic beer. I go quiet while he navigates a busy junction in the city centre and assess my date. He's fun but a little intense. He's in the same place as me, wanting to find someone and start a family, and is pretty much dream boyfriend material.

"What's your favourite thing to do on a sunny day?" I ask, out of nowhere.

I remember now how much I like the getting-to-know-one-another part at the start of a relationship.

"I love a picnic in the park on a sunny day. Lazing on a blanket. Laughing, chatting, reading… kissing." He glances over towards me.

I suddenly feel very warm and unwind Margie's scarf from around my neck. I get a bit tangled, and he laughs.

The indicator *click-clack* noise goes, and the road turns into a gravelly track. He stops the car. I finally get the scarf off and look out the window.

It's a dark, deserted car park surrounded by tall trees. This isn't anywhere in Pontcanna that I recognise. The same feeling I had earlier, when I thought we were in a maze, hits me again. I don't know this city; I don't know this location.

"Where are we?" I say, my tone fast and panicky. "Why have you brought me here?"

"It's Pontcanna Fields. Only a few minutes from yours. I thought we could park up and chat some more. Sorry, I should've checked with you first."

"I think I want to head home," I say.

"No worries."

He immediately starts the engine again and exits the car park onto a road that I recognise.

"I'm the second road on the right. The first building."

He follows my directions and pulls up outside my flat.

"Thanks," I say. It was wrong going to that car park without my consent, but he brought me straight home when I asked. I undo my seat belt and turn to him. "I've had a really lovely—"

But he cuts me off by kissing me too heavily. With one hand he grabs the back of my head and pulls me towards him, with the other he grabs the top of my arm. He sticks in his tongue.

I shake my head and push away from him. It's way too much, too soon. It turns my stomach. But he's holding on too tight and closes the gap between my face and his and presses his lips to mine again.

"No," I try to say. I wriggle and manage to turn my head away from his. "No!"

He eases his hold on me and stares, an intense hunger in his eyes that I don't like – it's the same look from the coffee shop yesterday.

"Too much," I say and grab the door handle.

It's locked.

"Rachel..." He leans right over so he's practically on

top of me in my car seat.

I shove him forcefully away from me. "I said no. Let me out of the car, now!"

But he doesn't make a move.

I yell, "Unlock this car door right now or I'll scream my head off!"

Something switches behind his eyes, and he presses the button on his door to unlock the entire car.

I don't look back. I leap out the car, scarf in hand, and sprint for my building. I fumble in my bag for my keys, praying he's not following me, and let myself in. I slam the door behind me, dash up the stairs to my flat, let myself in and slam that door too. I switch on the light and slide down, my back against the door and knees to my chest.

Heart pounding, I hug my arms around myself.

I should've trusted my first impression of Tyler, listened to that red-flag twinge in my gut.

The last thing I needed was a terrible date. But I'm safe now. It's over. I won't be seeing him ever again, that's for sure.

CHAPTER 9

I sit in the middle of hundreds of people I don't know. It's Thursday morning, and there's an all-staff meeting in the large atrium in the centre of the building. Chairs have been brought in, one of which I was lucky to snag. The unlucky attendees stand around the edges, lean against the wall, or sit directly on the floor.

It's stuffy in here with so many bodies squashed in, and I'm overheating. A little niggling thought keeps popping up that there are no windows and the doors are shut and the air is running out, but I keep pushing it down. I know it's just my mind playing tricks on me and isn't real. There's plenty of air, plenty of oxygen. I take a deep breath right into the pit of my lungs to prove the point to myself.

The big bosses are delivering a round-up of last year and a looking-forward-to-the-new-year presentation. It started at 9.30 a.m. and it's now 12.30 a.m., and people are clearly flagging. It was meant to end now, but is overrunning.

Next to me is Kalisha. I purposely made a beeline for her and made sure I sat next to her this morning. I want to build a relationship with her. I sense that something isn't quite right with her, and I'm determined to find out what. On the other side is Pete. The rest of the team is scattered, but I can see Kelvin.

He arrived late and is propped against the wall near the door. He's been on his phone almost the entire time. I'm not sure he's looked up once or is taking any of this in.

Although I'm not much better.

I'm attempting to pay attention. This is important information I should be lapping up about my new workplace and the plans for the coming year. But I'm still shaken up from last night. I keep telling myself to listen carefully, and for a few seconds I hear the speaker and read what's on the slide, but then my mind wanders, and before I know it, many minutes – and slides – have passed.

I pick at the edges of my New Year's Eve gel nail polish, peeling it off in chunks. I have a little pile in my lap. It's a revolting habit, and I need to stop, but I can't seem to stay still. I have excess energy that needs to be expended. My feet have got a mind of their own, tapping, shaking, rolling from ball to heel. Kalisha and Pete don't seem to notice, thank goodness. Their attention does appear to be wholly on the presentation.

It's all gotten too much for me today. Mum's illness. Brandon. Tyler. The twins showing up out of the blue. New job. New city. Getting on a plane in a couple of months. The lack of friends and support network here.

Suddenly, everyone claps. I've got no idea why, having completely missed what the speaker said, but I clap too. I look at the stage. It was my big boss, Arun, who said something. He's shielding his eyes from the bright light directed at him, looking for someone in the audience.

Pete nudges me in the side. And Kalisha turns to me.

"Rachel? Rachel Forrester, are you here this morning?" Arun says from the stage.

Hundreds of people go silent waiting for me to do something.

Should I stand up? Wave? Say something?

I'm fine with public speaking if I've prepared. It's not my favourite thing to do, but I manage. But an off-the-cuff few words? Hell no. And in front of the entire company, all my new colleagues that I need to make a great first impression on? My thoughts are a jumbled mess. My mind goes completely blank.

There's a pause that seems to go on forever. Then I stand, the pile of picked-off nail polish flutters to the floor. I hope no one sees it.

Suddenly, there's a light on me. Whoever is doing the lighting today thinking it a wise move to single me out even further.

Hundreds of eyes scrutinise me.

I squint, hold up my hand for a half-hearted wave and squeak, "Hi!"

"There you are! Rachel has moved from Nottingham bringing exceptional skills, deep expertise and knowledge from running the planning department there for four years. We're expecting great things from her!"

Oh jeez, the pressure.

There's another pause.

Arun is expecting me to speak. But I can't think of one thing to say. Nothing generic, nothing that'll convince the few hundred people staring at me that I have exceptional skills and deep expertise.

After a beat too long, Arun saves me. He introduces someone else, another new recruit on a different team.

I sit. The light shines away from my face.

My pulse races. I've no doubt made a terrible first impression on the entire company.

Arun wraps up the meeting, people stand and file out. I bend down to grab my handbag. A few bits of picked-off gel polish fall off it. I debate whether to gather up all the flakes to put in the bin but Kalisha is behind me waiting for me to move.

In the hallway, Pete turns to me. "How was the date last night?"

"Absolutely awful," I reply.

"Oh no! So you won't want to accompany me to the coffee shop now, then?"

"Nope."

He raises his eyebrows at me. "Right. Shall I pick you

up your usual, mocha with extra shot of coffee and peppermint syrup?"

"No. I mean, yes, please pick me up a coffee, but definitely not my usual. Don't want Tyler to spit in it or something."

"Wow, that bad, huh?"

"Yep."

"I'll get you the same as me."

"Perfect."

Pete heads towards the exit, and I get the lift and walk towards my desk, sit, and switch on my laptop. I pull my phone from my bag and have a look.

There's a WhatsApp message from Tyler. Just seeing his name on my phone makes me shudder. His car's overpowering smell returns to scratch at the back of my nose. The memory of his hands gripping me too tight and his lips forced onto mine snakes across my skin. I look up from the screen and around the open-plan office, at colleagues returning from the all-staff meeting, sorting out their lunch and milling about chatting. I'm safe here at work.

I take a deep breath and read the message:

Rachel, I'm so sorry for last night. I misread the signs. I thought you were really into me and moved way too fast. Forgive me, please? I really like you and was too keen. I'm hoping you'll give me a second chance? Let's go out again, and I swear nothing like that will happen again. Let me know xx

I immediately tap out a response:

No, I don't want to go out with you a second time. Please don't contact me again.

I hit send. I wait until the ticks show the message has been delivered, and then I block Tyler from my WhatsApp so he can't message me again. There. That's the end of that. The anxious swirl in my gut eases, and I get to work.

Later that evening, I flop onto my sofa. Even though all day I've felt as if I've had too much energy circulating in my body, now I feel exhausted and don't have it in me to make dinner. I order a Chinese takeaway.

While I'm waiting for it to be delivered, I call Heather. I haven't told her yet about Brandon, or Mum, or what's happened these past few days, and I'm desperate for a catch up, to hear her voice and hear her wisdom. We've been besties since school. She has the life that I'd like one day. She's a successful sales director at a large pharmaceuticals firm, has a wonderful husband and four great kids. They live in a fabulous house with a golden retriever and a cat and are eternally happy.

Heather answers on the second ring.

I can tell by the way she says *hello* that something is wrong.

"Everything okay, babe?" I ask, worried.

"No, it is not okay, *babe*," she replies, adding a snidey tone to the last word.

She's clearly mad at me, but I've got no idea why. "What's happened?"

"You forgot Ella's eighth birthday yesterday! Your own goddaughter! She was distraught. She waited all day for a call from you, for a card, for a delivery, for anything, but NOPE! Nothing from her favourite auntie. She went to bed crying and saying it was the worst birthday ever."

I'm speechless. I can't believe I forgot Ella's birthday. I've never forgotten before – we're January birthday buddies. I always send a card and a gift and call.

"I'm so sorry," I say eventually. "I've had so much going on…"

"I don't want to hear it! Honestly, it was the last thing I needed – a wailing child on her birthday. Jez and I got up early, wrapped up gifts, put up balloons, got cake, the works, and all she kept going on about was how auntie Rach didn't love her anymore. All. Fucking. Day."

"Can I talk to her now? Will you put her on the phone so I can apologise?"

"She won't want to talk to you."

"Please, Heather."

Heather sighs. I hear footsteps padding through her house and up the stairs, a door opening, mumbled words. A few seconds later, I hear crying, and Heather comes back on the phone.

"She doesn't want to talk to you. And now she's crying again saying you ruined her birthday and that she hates you. I literally cannot deal with another evening of this. I've got a major presentation to the board in the morning, and I need to finish it tonight. Miles needs help with his impossibly hard maths homework. The youngest two have picked up a projectile vomiting bug. *And* Jez has just dumped it on me that his mother is coming tomorrow to stay for the weekend and the spare room is a tip but he's out tonight at a work thing so I have to deal with it on top of everything else I've got on my plate. *Aaargh.*"

"I can only apologise… Brandon… my mum…"

"Look, I don't mean to be a complete cow, but call me in a couple of weeks or so, yeh? When all this with Ella has blown over. And we'll have a proper chat. I really don't have the headspace tonight. Sorry. Bye."

She hangs up on me.

The doorbell goes and makes me jump. I go down and collect my takeaway, bring it back up to my flat and put it on my kitchen counter. But I don't eat any of it. My appetite has been shot clean away. Instead, I order a next-day delivery birthday card and gift for Ella, so it'll arrive tomorrow. Two days late, but better than nothing.

At lunchtime on Friday, I pull out a sandwich and a packet of crisps, which I got from the shop on the way in. I'm eating lunch at my desk today. I re-read the same email I wrote this morning for the umpteenth time. It's to the team about a new Monday morning progress meeting I'm instigating. I take over on Monday and need to get the entire team of seven on board. The wording has to be just right. It's not optional, it's obligatory to attend, but I need it to sound exciting. Most of all I need it to work, especially now Arun and the entire company are expecting 'great things' from me.

I take a bite of the sandwich. It's bland and dry, and I take an age to chew it and swallow it down.

Impostor syndrome has taken a firm hold today. I'm not usually this indecisive. I usually bash out an email, re-read it, and then send it with full confidence. But this one I keep tinkering with and delaying pressing send.

Self-doubt plagues me. *Do I really have exceptional skills, deep expertise and knowledge?*

I also don't know how to handle Kelvin. Technically, he's in charge of this department, but he's shown no interest in what I'm doing, and when I've forwarded him emails with suggestions of how we can update processes or streamline the way we do certain things, he hasn't replied. Arun did say to me to do what I thought would make the department run smoother, so that's what I'm doing. I add a line in the email saying something vague about Kelvin being very welcome to join, but not demanding his presence.

I can't procrastinate any more. I hit send.

I chuck the rest of the horrible sandwich in the bin and open the crisps. I didn't eat anything last night or this morning and need to get something down me.

My phone rings in my bag. I fish it out, and the name makes my stomach jolt.

Tyler.

Did he not get the message yesterday? Thank goodness I forgot to delete his number from my contacts list. Otherwise, I would've answered because I often get work calls on this phone from mobile numbers I don't have listed.

I cancel the call. I don't have voicemail set up so he

can't leave a message. A moment later, my phone pings with a text message. It's Tyler.

> I know you said not to contact you, but I really want you to know how sorry I am. I'd really like you to give me a second chance. Please, Rachel. Let me take you out again? Anywhere you like? xx

I don't reply. I was clear enough yesterday. I block his number on my phone so he can't call or text me.

At least Brandon hasn't contacted me in a couple of days. *He's* finally got the message now. I'll contact him about collecting his stuff when I'm ready. He thinks I binned it so there's no rush. At the moment, I don't want anything to do with him. I'm not entirely sure what I'd do if I saw him right now. Fall into his arms in tears? I'm too emotional to see an ex, especially seen as my best mate is upset with me and I don't have any other shoulders to cry on about Mum's diagnosis.

A message pops up from Margie asking if I'm free later. I reply in the negative. I'm meant to be going out with Pete tonight straight from work. He's out for lunch so I can't confirm, but we organised it a couple of days ago.

An email lands in my inbox from Kelvin in reply to the Monday morning meeting email I just sent. It says:

As long as Pete's there, no need for me.

And that's it. A moment later, another email from Kelvin arrives in reply to my holiday request.

Can't approve. Inconvenient. March 1 is a Wednesday. Take full weeks off. Better. Monday 6. Redo request.

I look at the calendar. He's right. But it really shouldn't matter, should it? I can change my flight to Friday night or Saturday morning, but that's three more days to wait before I can see Mum. I told him about her – surely he'd be compassionate enough to let me take holiday from mid-week? Obviously not. I swallow back the annoyance and go about changing my holiday request in the system and emailing it to him.

Kelvin materialises and leans against the tall shelving unit at the end of our row of desks. He looks at his phone and rests his elbow on the top of the unit. He does this every now and then, and I can't work out the purpose of it. Is it to be seen by the team? He rarely talks to anyone, just looks at his phone.

Pete comes in with a bag from the coffee shop Tyler works at. It also does food. He sits and opens the bag, taking a massive bite of a stuffed tortilla wrap.

I lean to one side of my large monitor so we can see each other. "We're still out for drinks later, right?"

He nods.

Kelvin coughs. We both glance at him. He eyes us and has clearly heard what I said. He's not expecting an invite, is he? Does he think we're organising team drinks? We're definitely not, it's just me and Pete. The last thing I want is for Kelvin to come out later. I can't stand him. But how could I tell him no? He's still my line manager. I have to maintain politeness and professionalism at all times.

Awkward.

There's a pause.

When neither Pete nor I say anything, Kelvin says, "Yeah, that'd be good. I'll come for drinks after work. Six-ish works great for me."

My hand jerks, and I drop the pen I'm holding. I bend to scoop it up from the floor and rise to face Kelvin, plastering on the fakest smile. Did he just hear an imaginary invite? He replied as if one of us asked him.

He looks at me and cocks his head. "Rachel, you've got something on your face." He points to his chin. "Right here."

Oh no. A bit of sandwich? I swipe at my face but can't feel anything.

Kelvin chuckles. "Not really."

What. A. Dickhead.

He walks away. I stare at Pete. He shrugs and continues eating. I've not felt it appropriate as yet to broach the Kelvin subject with Pete. Kelvin is Pete's boss too, and I'm still the new girl. Perhaps Pete doesn't mind him? They've worked together for years.

I pull out my bright-yellow, stress-relief fidget toy shaped like a banana. I aggressively squish, stretch, and pinch it. It was a leaving gift from my last boss in Nottingham. He had one in his office, and I always fiddled with it when I was in there.

The banana gets a bashing all afternoon. A night out with Kelvin? I can't think of anything worse. I have too much energy. My feet bounce under the desk. I pace the office whenever I take a call. Kalisha asks me the simplest question and I reply, rambling and talking way too fast and for way too long.

At half five, I pull the banana so taut that one of the seams rips and gel-like liquid in the middle squirts out.

Dammit!

I drop it in the bin and run to the toilets to wash my hands. As I'm leaving, I catch my reflection in the mirror: hollow eyes, deep forehead creases, pursed lips. I take a long breath. I've got this. I can get through a drink with Kelvin. I'll just have the one then make my excuses. Or maybe Kelvin will just have one, and then Pete and I can carry on.

I could cancel, but the thought of going home to an empty flat on a Friday night with absolutely no plans all weekend fills me with an even bigger sense of dread. I'm not entirely sure what I'd do with myself – fret, pace, pull at my hair, allow my overthinking to eat me whole. No, I need to be social.

Kelvin is lounging over the shelves again like he owns the place when I arrive back at my desk. He's got his coat on. It's six, and everyone is packing up and switching off laptops.

I don't sit back down; I pull up my coat from off the back of the chair. "Ready, Pete?"

Pete rubs his face. "To be honest, I'm feeling rotten. Blinding headache. Don't think I'm going to make it out. Sorry."

His brow is scrunched, and he squints against the harsh office lights. He doesn't look one hundred per cent, that's for sure.

My stomach sinks. That means I have to go for a drink with Kelvin on my own. Could I cancel without appearing rude? Not really. I look at my boss.

Kelvin smirks at me. "See you on Monday then," he says and strides off down the hallway towards the exit.

Phew. I've been let off the hook. But that means I have zero plans. And I really don't want to be on my own.

"See ya, Rach," Pete says and walks towards the lift rubbing circles in his temples.

"Hope you feel better soon," I say.

I put my coat on and dig out my phone from my handbag. I text Margie.

Are you still out tonight? My thing got cancelled. I'm now free, if you are?

Please, please, please let Margie be free to do something with me. Her reply is almost instant:

Yes! Come for dinner!

I do a happy dance. Margie sends another message with the restaurant name and a time. I head out of the office so pleased that I met her, so happy that our relationship seems to be blossoming, so excited that everything indicates that she'll be a great friend.

CHAPTER 10

I have an hour to kill before I meet Margie at 7 p.m. The restaurant is in the city centre, not too far from where I work, so there's not enough time to go home and get changed.

But I'm too skittery to go to a bar and get a drink. I can't sit still. And the January weather is cold, blustery, and drizzly so I can't go for a walk without getting soaked through. I head in the direction of the restaurant and into the first clothes shop I see, pick up a few garments and take them into the changing room to try on. I have absolutely no intention of buying anything, it's simply for something to do.

After, I follow my GPS app to the restaurant. It's super funky, super expensive and super exclusive with only a few tables. Exactly the kind of place that Margie would pick. I head through the door and am instantly greeted by a server in a yellow dress who asks my name. I tell her I'm with Margie Madden, and she smiles and walks me through an internal door.

The place is buzzing, full of chic couples and raucous groups. I immediately feel underdressed in my formal navy skirt suit, cream blouse, thick black tights, and sensible low-heeled black court shoes. Perfect for work, but not for this fashionable hotspot. It has emerald-green painted walls, lots of large palm plants and gold décor. There's a small jazz ensemble in one corner – a keyboard player, drummer with just one drum, a double bass and a singer crooning into one of those retro-looking silver microphones. The music is perfect for the space, bluesy and unintrusive.

The server indicates the table, and I see Margie.

And Mark.

I wasn't expecting him to be here too. But I tamp down my surprise and give them a wave. They look comfortable, at home, as if they belong here. I, however, feel like a fish out of water. Clumsy, breathless, twitchy. The server pulls out my chair, waits for me to sit and pushes it in for me, which makes me knock the table with my chest. The glassware tinkles, and a wine glass teeters precariously before Mark grabs it.

"Gosh, sorry!" I say.

I flap air to cool my face at exactly the same moment as the server pulls out a napkin and lays it across my lap. I accidentally slap her in the chin.

My cheeks burn. "Oh my gosh, I'm so sorry!"

She smiles at me, rubbing her face. "Absolutely no problem. Acadia will be with you shortly. Enjoy your meal."

I turn to the Maddens. "Oops. How are you both? Lovely to see you! Thanks for the invite," I rush out. I'm not sure what's wrong with me, it's like I'm on fast forward.

"Hi, my dear," Margie says.

"Fabulous to see you, Rachel. We're delighted you could join us," Mark adds.

I gesture around at the restaurant. "This place is fab."

"Certainly is, it's our favourite fish restaurant in Cardiff," Margie replies.

She's looking as fabulous as ever in a black lacy dress and dark eye makeup. Her long white hair trails down either side of her face and she has a gold tiara on top of her head. She looks like some kind of gothic queen.

I nod and pick up the menu. It shakes in my hand. I

put it down again. My leg jumps rapidly up and down under the table. I pick at the corners of my nails and chew at my lips.

A crash echoes across the restaurant from the kitchen, which can be seen through a long, narrow space at the back of the room. I jump. My hand flies to my mouth, catching the end of my fork. It flips up, somersaults and clatters against a small plate on the table.

Margie and Mark share a look. Is that their unspoken communication asking *why on earth did we invite this chaotic woman?* It ramps up my nervous energy.

Margie leans over and places her hand on top of mine.

Is she about to ask me to leave? I wouldn't blame her. I don't know what has got into me. It's like all the stresses of the week have built up and erupted on Friday night.

"Rachel, are you all right? You seem very fidgety and anxious. We're worried."

I study Margie's face. She appears so concerned, so warm and kind, like she genuinely cares. Mark has a similar look on his face too.

And that's it. I burst into tears. "So... sorry," I babble.

Margie gets out of her seat and crouches next to me, putting both arms around me and hugging me tight.

It's at that moment our server appears. "Are you ready to order?"

"Acadia, is it?" Mark asks.

The server nods.

He smiles. "Acadia, we just need a few minutes."

She retreats.

Margie rubs my back. "What's happened?"

I sniff. "My mum has got cancer. She told me a couple of days ago."

"Oh no. I'm so sorry to hear that," Margie says.

Mark doesn't say anything, but his expression is one of heartfelt sympathy.

"And on top of that, I've had a shit week." I take a breath and wipe my tears. "I'll be okay." I glance around at the nearby tables. People are looking our way. "Sorry for crying."

"Don't you give a rat's arse about anyone else in here. If you need to cry, then cry. Get it all out. When I heard about my father's cancer it was in public, and I howled the place down, didn't I, Mark?"

Mark nods. "You certainly did."

Margie takes her seat again. She shifts it closer to mine and puts a hand on my shoulder.

"Tell us all about it," Margie says. "Wait. Are you okay with fish and seafood and white wine? Just not peanuts, correct? Other nuts are okay?"

"No peanuts, thanks."

Margie squeezes her husband's bicep. "Dearest, will you order a few bits for the table and some wine. Unless you want anything specific, Rachel?"

I shake my head. "I don't think I have it in me to look through the menu and make a decision, so that sounds perfect. Thank you."

He places his napkin on the table. "Right you are. Let me find Acadia." He stands, catching our server's attention.

Acadia comes over promptly, and Mark reels off a few starters, mains, sides, and a bottle of wine.

Margie continues to rub my shoulder. When the server leaves to put our order in, she says, "Now then, let's hear what's happened."

As the wine comes out, then the starters and then the mains, I tell the Maddens all about my mum's cancer diagnosis, the dreadful date with Tyler, Heather's anger and my guilt at forgetting Ella's birthday, the pressure at work to perform, my dickhead boss, and my simmering fear of the impending flight to New Zealand.

They listen patiently, asking questions and fully invested in what I'm saying. I immediately feel better. Safe. Supported. It's a heady feeling. It sends me back to my early childhood. *This* is the feeling I should've had when growing up. Instead, I had the complete opposite. I was hypervigilant, always felt unsafe, and never fully supported. Mum did her best, especially when it was just the two of us, but I'd always dreamt of solid, dependable, loving parents.

I let the sensation wash over me, soak it in, allow it to take up space. The Maddens are my friends. But in this moment, they feel like wonderful surrogate parents.

My muscles relax, my breathing returns to normal, and the fizzing excess energy burns out.

I take another sip of the delicious wine. "I'm sorry to offload on you."

Margie pats her mouth with the corner of her napkin. "Not at all. What a lot to deal with. No wonder you're feeling out of sorts."

My final mouthful of a sea bass dish slides down, and I smile. "Thanks for ordering, Mark. Great choices. And the wine goes perfectly."

He waves my compliment away, smiling.

"Shall we share a dessert?" Margie asks.

Mark and I both nod, and Margie gets Acadia's attention. She tells us the dessert menu and we decide on the lavender crème brulée.

"What have you got planned for the weekend?" I ask.

Mark and Margie consider this a moment.

"Not entirely sure yet," Mark says. "How about you?"

My heart sinks. "Well, I should've been going to Snowdonia to go rock climbing with Brandon, but that's obviously not happening. It was a Christmas gift I got for him, and we booked this weekend because January can be a bit dreary, so we thought it would be something exciting to look forward to."

I wonder silently if he'll still be going without me and who he might take. But I brush that thought away quickly. I don't want to start crying again.

The dessert arrives, and we all tuck in.

"You're a climber?" Mark asks.

"I've been a few times to indoor climbing centres, but never done it outside."

Margie claps. "Well, that's what we've got planned for the weekend, then! A trip to the wall climbing centre."

"Absolutely. Three tomorrow?" Mark says.

"Sounds good," I say, excited.

We continue to chat about all sorts, and the bill arrives. Mark immediately pulls out his card.

I grab my handbag and get my wallet out. "Please let me pay for this one."

The Maddens look appalled.

"Absolutely not. We'd be mortified if you paid for us," Margie says.

"Please, it's my treat for you listening to me and all my woes earlier."

"Nonsense, anytime," she says.

"Okay, I'll pay half."

"Rachel, there's no need, honestly. But we appreciate you offering," Mark says, and he gives Acadia his card and a large wad of notes as a tip.

On Saturday morning, I decide to do some laundry. I grab my laundry basket and take it into the kitchen. I'll do the muddy stuff first, then the spare room bedsheets. I take the lid off the basket and tip it upside down onto the lino to sort into piles.

But the muddy items aren't there.

I shake out the bedsheets in case they've got caught up. But they haven't. I head back into my bedroom and open the wardrobe.

The muddy dresses and skirts are right there, hanging in my wardrobe. I'm sure I put them in the laundry basket when I saw that they were dirty on Wednesday night before my date with Tyler.

Didn't I?

I honestly can't remember. But I can't have done because they're right here hanging in the closet. I must've thought to do it and then didn't. I pull them off the hangers and take through to the kitchen. I put a load on in the washing machine and get ready to go climbing.

I drive the fifteen minutes to the climbing centre. I arrive a little early and wait inside. A few moments later, Mark comes in. On his own. I wave, and he heads over.

"No Margie?" I ask.

Last night I was under the impression she was coming.

"No. This isn't really her thing. She's done it plenty of times before and is actually pretty good, but just me today."

"Excellent," I say.

But I'm not sure if I feel excellent. Is it a bit strange as a mid-thirties woman to be hanging out with a married man in his mid-sixties who isn't your father? I'm not entirely sure, but I go with it.

"Shall we?" he says and indicates that we join the queue.

He stands a little behind me, and I take in the space. It's a large warehouse with climbing walls and a bouldering area. It's much bigger than the Nottingham climbing centre I've previously been too. There's a friendly atmosphere with nineties indie music playing and plenty of people enjoying the walls.

The queue moves, but because I'm looking at the walls, I don't immediately notice. Just as I go to take a step forward, my bum is smacked.

I spin around, ready to slap Mark's face. "What the hell?"

But he's a few steps behind me, giving a wide berth to a couple of boisterous kids barrelling their way through the queue.

A boy sheepishly says, "Sorry!" before his attention snaps back to his friend, and they bump into someone else.

The staff member on the counter beckons me forward.

Mark and I stand next to one another as she takes all our details, makes us watch a short safety video and sign various terms and conditions documents. Mark has all his own gear, but I hire mine, and she finds me the right size shoes, harness, and helmet. She inspects Mark's gear to ensure it's suitable.

Once signed in, we change and head to the main floor. The climbing walls are higher than I've been on before and loom over me. It gives me a pleasant thrill.

"Ladies first," Mark says as he sorts out the rope.

I clip into the first hook, make sure Mark is holding the rope, and start to climb. I glance back at Mark. He's concentrating on letting out the rope, but catches my eye and gives me an encouraging grin.

I peer up at the wall, trying to focus on where to put my hands and feet. I make a few moves and clip into the next bolt. I don't know Mark well, and I'm putting my life in his hands. If I fall now then it's down to his rope skills as to whether I crash to the ground or get safely lowered down. It's nerve-racking, but I have to trust that he's got me. I'm sure he doesn't want me to die on his watch.

I scramble up, my fingertips and toes finding purchase, my legs working hard to propel me. I get to the top of the wall and punch the air.

"Way to go," Mark shouts from underneath me. "Ready when you are to come down."

And this is it. The bit that always terrifies me, but in a good way. The letting go of the wall and falling backward. It goes against everything your brain is telling you to do. *Cling on!* It yells.

Here goes. I release my hold. There's always a moment of freefalling before the rope takes your weight. But the rope is slack. I fall for too long. I'm going to splat on the floor. *What a way to die!* I'm falling. *Where the fuck is Mark?* Has he messed up with the ropes? Lost his grip? Dropped the rope on purpose?

Just as my panic sets in the rope snaps taut, and I hang

there.

My heart pounds, and the rush envelops me. I always think I'm falling for too long. It's as if time stands still. Mark lowers me slowly and carefully to the ground. I put my feet on the mat, and he loosens off the rope.

"Thanks!" I say, the adrenaline lifting my spirits, giving me a glow.

"No problem," Mark says and coils the rope.

I unclip my harness. "Your turn."

He clips in, and I take up the rope, attaching it into my belay device to take his weight if he falls.

"Here goes," he says and scrambles up the wall so fast I could be watching Spider-Man.

He gets to the top and gives me the okay, and I lower him down. We move to another route and take it in turns to go up and lower each other down. We chat amiably about previous climbing sessions and the various places around the world where Mark has climbed.

Two hours pass in the blink of an eye, and before we know it, a staff member is reminding us we have five minutes left.

"That was great fun," I say as we're stepping out of the harnesses and changing.

"Certainly was," Mark replies.

"I feel so much more relaxed. Even though my hands and feet are killing me."

"I find exercise always helps to get you out of your head," Mark says.

I nod. If I'd been on my own today, I would've spent the entire time worrying about Mum, about everything.

We wander to the exit and see the torrential rain through the glass doors.

"How did you get here?" I ask.

"Walked," Mark says, peering out at the rainwater gathering in large puddles in the car park, gushing down the road gutter and overflowing the grate.

"I'll give you a lift home," I say.

"That'll be great. Thanks."

We run to my car and jump in. I start the engine. Mark looks at his phone.

"Margie says to bring you back with me. She's making Argentinian steak with our daughter-in-law's family chimichurri recipe, and Simone has sent us a case of the most perfect red wine from her vineyard in South Africa to go with it."

It takes me less than a second to decide. "Yes, that'll be lovely. Thank you." I don't want to spend Saturday evening on my own back at my flat. "Although I won't be able to help you out with the case of wine, unfortunately." I tap my steering wheel.

"Stay over. Margie will love that. We'll put you back in the spare room you stayed in before. That's known as your room now! And once you've tasted Margie's cooking, well, you'll never want to leave."

CHAPTER 11

Heavy rain pounds my car windscreen. The wipers are on the fastest setting but my visibility is still impaired.

It's just before 11 a.m. on Sunday, and I'm driving home from the Maddens' flat after a fabulous evening and a lovely breakfast. Although it's daytime, it's dark and gloomy. Ominous clouds hover in the distance, and I'm certain there'll be a storm later.

I switch on the radio and settle into the twenty-minute drive back to mine. I drum my fingers on the steering wheel to the music and lean forward to see better out the window. I feel more relaxed, ready to face the new day and the new week. A tap has been opened, and all the frazzled energy poured right out. I just need to concentrate on work and getting stuff done, and the eight weeks until I see Mum will fly by. And I'll be with her in no time. The alternative is to panic, overthink, fret, and work myself up into a frenzy of fear about the flight I'm about to take. The plane journey is inevitable, so I just need to suck it up and forget about it.

The hammering rain is deafening, so I turn up the radio just as the news bulletin comes on. The newscaster reads out the main story:

> 'A plane has crashed in the French Alps killing all those on board. The plane was carrying one hundred and forty-two passengers, including four British citizens, and six crew. An

investigation has been launched to determine what happened while first responders continue to search the wreckage.'

My heart shoots up through my mouth. I swerve off the road and stop across the entrance of an industrial estate, which hopefully isn't in use on a Sunday. My breathing hitches as I switch off the radio, turn off the engine and grab my phone from my bag.

Why did this have to happen now? *Why?* I was just about feeling calm about the flight to New Zealand. With shaking hands, I google the crash and obsessively read everything I can find. Speculation is that there was a catastrophic engine failure which meant the plane flew straight into the mountains. *OMG.* Will that happen on my flight? What are the odds?

The rain batters the roof of my car and falls in sheets against the windows. It's oppressive in this enclosed space. Vehicles roar past, kicking up spray that slams the side of my car. Headlights race by so fast it's dizzying. Occasional honking reverberates. I need some fresh air. I want to get out or lower the window to stick my head out. But I know that's a stupid idea in this weather. I'd get soaked to the bone.

I refresh google to see if there have been any new stories. I should stop this; I know I should. Put my phone away and get home, but it's a compulsion I can't control. I'm sucked into a plane crash rabbit hole.

Bang! A fist thumping on my front passenger window makes me jump out of my skin.

A large man stands there. He's in a hi-vis jacket with the hood up. A hulking figure, he's hard-faced, older, and has an air about him of someone you wouldn't mess with.

Red beard.

My heart lurches again.

Dad? Oh fuck!

"Love, move out the way," the man shouts, bringing his face close to the window and pointing at a lorry waiting to leave the industrial area but blocked by me in my car.

Not my father. A security guard.

The man stomps back to his little shed by the entrance to the estate, which I hadn't noticed before, and waves at the lorry driver.

I start my engine, pull out into a space between cars that isn't quite big enough and drive erratically back to my flat, not able to fully concentrate on what I'm doing.

I park up, run into my building and through the main front door. I shake off the rain from my coat, check the post and head up the stairs to my flat. There's a large brown box outside my front door. It has no branding on it and is about as high as my thigh and about half a metre wide. The label has my name and address with a delivery date of yesterday. One of my neighbours must've taken delivery of it and put it outside my door. We often do that for each other. I've done it for Ralph a couple of times.

But I haven't ordered anything online and am not expecting anything. The box is sealed up with parcel tape, and a little shake reveals nothing.

Who sent it? What is it?

I open my front door and step around the box leaving it on the outside for a moment. If I bring it into my flat, into my personal space then it's like I'm inviting in whatever is inside – like a Trojan horse. Is a little goblin going to jump out and destroy my flat in a crazed whirlwind? I laugh out loud at my wariness. How bad can it be? Perhaps a cleaning fairy is going to fly out and make my flat sparkle.

I bring the box inside. It's light. I shut the front door and take it through to the lounge. Pulling off coat and scarf and dropping my handbag on the armchair, I head into the kitchen for my scissors. I bring them through to the lounge and slice through the parcel tape.

Tentatively – as if I'm winding up a jack-in-the-box – I pull back the two sides. When nothing springs out, I peer in.

It's a huge bouquet of red roses. I reach in and pull them out. They're kept together with a rubber band and the stems are in a sealed plastic bag full of water. It's an impressive bunch. I pop them on the coffee table, and then tip the box upside down for a card. A piece of paper falls out. It's a delivery slip with my details on it but nothing about who sent the flowers.

Brandon. They have to be from my ex.

I thought he'd been quiet for the past few days because he'd realised I wasn't going to take him back. But maybe he was just planning this big gesture. But why wouldn't he send a card? Perhaps it's a mistake, and one should've been in there.

Well, it's too late.

If he's expecting me to call him immediately and fall back into his arms, then he's mistaken. He should've treated me better in the first place.

I find my favourite vase to put the flowers in and display them on the desk in the corner of my lounge. The vase used to belong to Mum. She'd had it for years, but had to get rid of loads of her belongings when she moved to Auckland. I took a lot of her stuff, including this vase. It has a purple and white swirl on it, and she used to have it in her bedroom displaying some dried flowers when we lived together in a little two-bedroom flat in Nottingham after she left my father and before she met Stuart.

I rub the velvety petals between my fingers, stand back, admire the roses for a moment, step forward and adjust one stem that's sticking out.

A thorn pricks my finger and draws blood. I inhale sharply and suck the pierced skin.

The vase makes me think about Mum. I send her a few messages, including a photo of the roses in her old vase. She'll be asleep now, but will see them when she wakes up and will reply then. I tell her about my weekend and ask if there's been any more news or if she's had any more test results back yet.

I also send a message to Heather apologising again and asking if Ella received her card and gift. I find my favourite playlist and put it on. I go about doing my chores while dancing and singing, eager to forget about the awful plane crash and shake away the shock of thinking I saw my father.

A few hours later, I plonk myself down on my sofa for a chill evening. Between lunch and dinner, I've done laundry and cleaned the entire flat. I check my phone – no replies from Mum or Heather. But I have a lot of notifications on Instagram. I open the app.

I follow lots of accounts, but mostly mummy influencers. I love getting top tips for when I have a brood of my own. I rarely post anything: the occasional night out or fun activity or nice view. My last post was a photo of the fireworks over Cardiff Bay on New Year's Eve, which I snapped quickly before I thought I was about to get kicked out for gatecrashing.

I have twenty-three notifications. That's the most I've ever had. I click into the list and see they're all from the same account and include likes and comments on my pictures going back years. They're all from the same account, @_leety, which has an obscure cartoon profile picture. This person has also followed me. I click into @_leety's profile and immediately see the name Tyler Lee and the first grid picture of Tyler's grinning face with a younger boy in front of a drum set. The caption reads, 'My student Ben just passed Grade 4! So proud!'

Tyler has found me on social media. Why won't he get the hint that I don't want to see him again? He hasn't sent me a DM though. Although something tells me it won't be long before he does. I block him so he can't follow me or see any of my posts.

A stone lands in my gut.

Tyler knows my address from when he dropped me home after our disastrous date. Did he send the flowers? I stare at the bunch of red roses. They're not going to make me go out with him again, but they are pretty.

I sit back on the sofa and reach over for my Kindle, which I keep on top of the low shelves next to my sofa. I can't wait to immerse myself in my romance novel. It's just got to the first steamy bit. But my fingers scrabble around on the shelf. I look, and my Kindle isn't there. Isn't where it always is, where I always leave it. I only ever read sitting right here on the sofa. I only move it when I take it on holiday or on a long train journey. But I've not been on holiday since last year, and my last train journey was six months ago. It should be right there.

I sigh and look down the side of the shelving unit. It must've fallen behind. But it's not there. I look under the sofa, check behind the back, move all the cushions. Frustration flares up. *Where the hell is it?* I pull apart my flat looking for it, searching in places it definitely won't be like under a rug in the spare room. But I know it must be *somewhere* in the flat because I've not taken it out of the front door.

Frustration transforms into anger when I can't find it anywhere and realise my flat is now a tip. I've just made more work for myself to tidy the place up again. So much for a chill Sunday evening reading a spicy love story and winding down for bed. Sleep is definitely not going to come easily tonight. I'm wound right up, practically vibrating.

My Kindle didn't just grow legs and walk out of here for a jaunt in Cardiff.

The twins.

They were the last ones in my flat. And they have a history of hiding or taking things. Outside, the rain picks up pace and clatters against my windows. The twins both have phones, but I only message Caroline because Catherine never replies. I haven't sent a message to her in almost a year. I have a new phone number and, if I want answers, I'm going to have to reveal it.

Gritting my teeth, I bash out a message to Caroline:

Hey, it's Rachel. This is my new number. When you were here, did you move or take my Kindle?

Lightning flashes behind my curtains. The storm that has been threatening all day has finally hit. A second later, a loud rumble of thunder cracks right over the top of my building.

And, in perfect timing, my phone dings with a notification.

It's a reply from Caroline. I didn't think she'd respond. It reads:

No.

CHAPTER 12

On Monday morning, I wait for the bus at the bus stop less than a minute's walk from my front door.

I could drive into work, but I find it easier, cheaper, and quicker to get the bus. There's a bus stop right outside my office building, and it's a direct route. There's no car parking where I work so if I drove, I'd need to pay exorbitant daily parking charges, deal with the hassle of finding a space every morning and walk to my office building anyway.

I could afford it, I get paid a good salary and have a large amount in savings, but I'd rather my money stays in my savings account, waiting for when I've met a husband and can buy our dream family home together.

The bus rolls up. There's always a queue, and I wait my turn to get on, tapping my debit card on the reader and moving down into the bus. On some mornings, I get a seat; on others, like today, I have to stand. I shuffle down the bus and stand between the seats holding onto the cold handrail above my head.

Usually, I'd listen to an audiobook or music. Or scroll through property for sale in Devon that might be suitable to turn into a bed and breakfast – and daydream about my life in the far future, when the kids have flown the nest, and my husband and I want a little business to run in our later years. But not today.

Today, I'm too distracted. I stare into space, and

absolutely not at any other commuter. That's an unspoken commuter rule that I don't plan on ever breaking.

I can't stop thinking that if the twins didn't move my Kindle, then what the hell happened to it? The twins don't lie. They'll avoid answering questions and keep their silence, but will never say something untrue. When Mum asked them where my finger was after they'd chopped it off, they stayed silent. Didn't fib and say they didn't know. Just blinked at her and gave nothing away.

So, I believe them. They didn't move it. Otherwise, Caroline wouldn't have responded. Was someone else in my flat? But why would they just take my Kindle and nothing else? No, I don't believe that. I must've put it somewhere and just can't remember. But why can't I remember?

Or maybe the twins have started lying. Which is an alarming thought.

Sleep evaded me last night as I went over and over this conundrum, and I yawn widely. A little noise escapes, earning me an amused glance from a woman sitting on the seat nearest me. Without thinking, I release my grip on the handrail and get out my phone. The bus lurches to a stop, and I get thrown into the crowd of commuters jammed in the space down the middle of the bus.

"Sorry!" I say as hands haul me back to my feet.

I grab the handrail again. The driver is heavy on the brakes, and we pitch forwards and jerk backwards all the way into the city centre. More people get on, and we all squeeze together. It's uncomfortable with all these bodies pressing into me, and today I feel overwhelmed by it. Suffocated. At every stop people jostle me from behind to get off or push me from the front when more people get on. And it's stifling hot. The driver has the heater on full blast because it's a cold day, forgetting that this many people squashed together create their own heat.

I take a deep breath and remind myself that I've done this many times before and all has been fine. Nothing slipped into my pocket or stolen out my bag. Never hurt or molested. Nothing awful has ever happened to me on the bus. It's just a bunch of people wanting to get to work or to lectures. That's it.

With one hand still clutching the handrail, I check my phone with the other. Mum has replied. She still has more tests to do and is waiting for the results of some others, so there's no further news or updates on her diagnosis or treatment plan. I wish I was there with her. I wish I lived nearer.

The bus lurches again, and I get a sharp elbow in the ribs. The man doesn't apologise. I grit my teeth. The windows are all steamed up, and I haven't kept track of where I am or which stop I'm at.

"Excuse me," I say to the person sitting nearest the window.

They pull out an earbud to hear me properly.

"Please could you wipe the window a bit and let me know where we are?"

They look at their gloved hand, clearly making a decision as to whether to wipe with glove on or glove off, when the man who elbowed me tells me gruffly what stop we're coming up to.

"Thank you. This is me then."

The person sitting by the window breathes a sigh of relief and pops their earbud back in.

I press the bell and shuffle and squeeze past bodies to get to the door at the front of the bus. Someone knocks into me, and my phone slips through my fingers. It drops to the floor of the bus with a clunk and skids through feet and under a chair.

"Shit, sorry! I dropped my phone!"

I attempt to bend down to retrieve it, but there are too many people around me. The bus eases to a stop. *My stop!* Shit. The last thing I need right now is to lose my phone.

"This is my stop!" I announce loudly in the hopes that the driver might hear me. "But I've dropped my phone!

It's under that chair!"

I point to where I think it's gone, and commuters attempt to bend to pick it up.

The bus doors open, and I know I only have seconds before they shut again. I don't actually know where the next stop is in the city. I've only ever gone this far on the route. Although I know I'm perfectly capable of putting on my GPS app and navigating my way to work from another bus stop, I really don't want the hassle, and I really don't want to be late for work this morning – on the first day I'm taking over the team. That will not give the right impression.

A man finally picks up my phone from the floor and goes to hand it to me, but people are shoving me attempting to get out, and I'm being carried along in the crush and can't reach it.

"Here," he says loudly, and two nearby commuters pass the phone along.

I grab it from them. "Thanks!"

The doors shut again.

"Wait! This is my stop!"

I barge through bodies, not caring if I'm bumping into people or stepping on feet, and the doors open again.

With a shouted thanks to the driver, I burst through the crowd, stumble down the two steps and spill onto the pavement with wobbly legs. I suck down air. The bus doors close, and it drives away.

"Alri, mush. Y'alright?" a woman waiting at the stop asks me.

Clumsy, distracted behaviour is not normal for me – it's like I'm not quite in my body. I pull myself together and stand straighter.

"Yes, thanks. Dropped my phone on the bus and nearly missed my stop."

"Ah, yeh, nightmare, mush," she replies.

I smile at her and walk the few steps into my office building.

There's a queue to swipe through the turnstiles to get to the lifts, and I join it. That little incident has thrown me off balance, but I just need to take a few breaths and reset.

Someone taps me on the shoulder. "Are you Rachel Forrester?"

I turn and look at the tall man. Although he must be someone I work with, I don't recognise him. He's well-built, has a beanie hat on and his coat collar turned up like he's trying to hide his face.

"Yes," I reply with a suspicious frown. "Why?"

He points over his shoulder. "Receptionist is calling you."

"Rachel!" the receptionist bellows. She stands behind her desk frantically waving at me.

I step out of the queue and head towards her desk.

She's out of breath and clearly annoyed.

"Did you not hear me shouting your name?"

"Um, no, sorry. Was in my own little world."

She rolls her eyes. "This was left for you a few moments ago."

She reaches behind her desk and hands me a coffee cup, steam rising through the drink hole in the lid. I take it from her and look at the branding on the cup. It's from the coffee shop that Tyler works in. I sniff it, and get the distinct smell of peppermint.

"Who left it?" I ask. But I already know.

"Didn't say his name, was in a bit of a rush. Blond guy."

"Thanks," I say, but she's already dealing with the person next to me.

The queue is now to the door. Whoever designed this building did not take into account the lift usage at rush hour. I join the back and tap my foot impatiently. I look at my watch. I have ten minutes to get to my desk before 9 a.m. I can't be late, not today.

The coffee cup is warm in my hand. I open the lid and peer at the liquid. It looks and smells like a peppermint mocha with an extra shot of coffee. I take the tiniest sip and swoosh the liquid around my mouth like I'm tasting fine wine. It tastes like my favourite coffee. I'm not sure why I think Tyler might tamper with it – drop in some poison or drugs or laxatives or something – but I seem to be very suspicious today.

Tyler just won't get the hint, will he? Blocked everywhere digitally so now he's physically coming to my work. I did tell him I worked here, and he knew the building because his coffee shop is minutes away. I put the lid back on and note the bin near the turnstiles that I could drop it in on the way past. But I'm still quite a few people away.

Screw it. I take a swig of the coffee. After the morning I've had so far, I need it. It's delicious. Tyler does know how to make nice coffee; I'll give him that. But drinking it does not mean I'm going to give him a second chance. No way. It's just a waste to bin perfectly good coffee. Tyler will go away eventually if I ignore him.

I finally arrive at my desk at 8.59 a.m. All the team, including Pete, are already there waiting for me. I dump my bag on my chair and the empty coffee cup in the bin and grab up my pen, notebook, and laptop.

"Shall we?" I say confidently to the team and gesture to the row of meeting rooms at the end of the floor.

I booked this work-in-progress meeting for 9 a.m. every Monday and am grateful I printed out what I needed on Friday afternoon, otherwise the first ever meeting would've started late. I need to ensure it goes well.

An hour later, after a very encouraging first work-in-progress meeting, I lead the team back to our desk area. I smell him before I see him. Kelvin's way-too-strong aftershave assaults my nose. He didn't make it to the team meeting, didn't even stick his head in to show face. And now he's leaning over my desk with a smug look.

"Kelvin?" I ask as I reach my desk.

He steps aside. "Receptionist just brought this up for you. None of the team were around to take it so she asked me to." He points to my desk. "Apparently, it's the second time today that someone has dropped off something for you. Got a secret admirer or something, have we?"

All the team are now back at their desks and listening to everything Kelvin is saying. Pete remains standing.

Kelvin smirks. "Whoever it is, is really bad at poetry."

I stare at my desk. There's a large plush teddy holding a card in its arms sitting on top of a box of chocolates. Kelvin must've read the card. That is not cool.

I pull out the card and read the typed text. It's a poem:

Chocolates are sweet,
And I think you're pretty neat.
Teddies are cute,
And I hope me showing you my love like this doesn't make you puke.

I frown, flip the card to look at the back. It's blank. There's no name or indication of who sent this.

Kelvin bursts out laughing. In a whiny voice, he recites the poem in front of the entire team.

"Chocolates are sweet, and I think you're pretty neat. Teddies are cute, and I hope me showing you my love like this doesn't make you puke!"

He places his fingers in his mouth and mimes vomiting with the sound effect thrown in for good measure.

I glare at him, colour rising to my cheeks.

The team aren't sure how to react. No one laughs along with Kelvin, but there are a few raised eyebrows and smiles before they all choose wisely to get on with their work. This is their boss after all, more senior to me, so they can't outright defy him by not acknowledging him altogether.

I'm furious. How dare he read my personal message and tell the entire team to embarrass me! I bite my top lip to stop myself from saying something I'll regret. I need to show the utmost professionalism in front of the team and deal with this when I've calmed down. I've only just got through the first month of my probation period and have two more months to go. I can't risk going about this all wrong and pissing off Kelvin now. I give him a tight smile, sit, turn on my monitor and plug it into my laptop, pretending Kelvin and the teddy aren't even there.

He chuckles some more to himself and points at Kalisha. Across all the team desks, instead of walking the few steps to Kalisha's desk, he shouts, "Kalisha, remember we've got our weekly one-to-one at half two today."

She shrinks into her chair and nods quickly in reply. Kelvin strides off. Pete finally sits. When everyone has their eyes on their monitors and are deep into work, I pick up the teddy. It's soft and, yes, cute. But who sent me this? I'm thirty-five years old and not three-to-five years old. The chocolates are all white chocolate – my least favourite. Was it Brandon? Tyler? Did whoever send me this also send me the roses yesterday? Why aren't they leaving their name?

I open the chocolates, stand, and go around to each team member to offer them some.

"Take as many as you like," I say.

All morning, I've been considering the best way to approach Kelvin to tell him how inappropriate I felt his earlier behaviour to be, and at lunch, I'm ready to head to his office and confront him. I finish eating a sandwich at my desk, push out my chair and am about to stand when Kalisha appears in front of me clutching her stomach and looking miserable.

"Are you okay?" I ask her.

"I really don't feel well. Terrible period pain. Are you okay if I head home? I can log on at home and carry on working, but just need a hot water bottle and to lie on my sofa, if you know what I mean."

She glances in the direction of Kelvin's office and back

to me.

I should probably check with Kelvin, he is meant to be the team leader after all, and I'm only second-in-command, but I sense she's doing this to avoid her one-to-one meeting with him this afternoon.

I could be wrong, of course, but I immediately reply, "Yes. Of course. Let the team know and don't log on later if you're not up to it. Just rest up."

"Thank you," she replies.

She quickly tells the team members who are still at their desks and hurries out.

Does Kelvin do weekly one-to-ones with any of the other team members? He certainly doesn't with me. Why just her? Something isn't right, and I'm going to get to the bottom of it. I pick up my notebook and pen and head towards Kelvin's office at the end of the quiet hallway.

As I'm approaching, Pete's distinctive laugh pierces the silence. The door to Kelvin's office is ajar.

I'm about to turn around and come back later after Pete's finished, when I hear Kelvin say, "It won't be long now until the new girl's gone."

I shouldn't eavesdrop, I know I shouldn't, but what the hell does that mean? Kelvin can only be referring to me, can't he?

Pete doesn't reply verbally.

Kelvin continues, "You should've had that position, kiddo. I told Arun that you applied and should be promoted. But everything's coming together nicely."

There's some mumbling that I can't make out, and then Kelvin laughs and claps his hands.

He adds, "Right, you'd better get back out there."

I hurry away silently and back to my desk, my mind reeling.

After work, I head home, get changed, put the teddy and card next to the roses, have a quick dinner and head out again to meet Margie at a local community hall for a belly dancing class.

All afternoon my head was spinning with that overheard conversation. Pete went out on site visits, and I had various meetings and calls, so I didn't have time to properly process and decide what to do.

I arrive before Margie. I introduce myself to the teacher and explain I've done it before and am at intermediate level. She's pleased and asks me to stand near the front because the beginners always want to be at the back. I oblige. Margie comes in, spots me and heads over. She takes in the chilly hall, the faded dusty curtains, peeling paint, and the stacks of plastic chairs along the back.

And I take her in. She's wearing harem trousers cuffed at the ankle and a crop top with her flat stomach on show.

She sweeps me up in a hug. "Hi, darling."

"Those trousers are epic!"

"I thought I'd dress the part. Not often you can get your belly out with no judgement."

The teacher introduces herself to the class and, starting at the other end to us, approaches each of the attendees individually.

"How's your day been?" I ask Margie.

"Interesting. I spent the day at a female entrepreneurs and investors networking event in Oxford. Hosted by the university. Some fascinating people and ideas."

"Wow, sounds brilliant."

"It was. And you?"

"It's been... odd," I reply.

"Do tell!" Margie says.

I tell her about Tyler and the coffee drop and how I know it was him because it was my favourite coffee.

"And what's that?"

"A peppermint mocha with extra shot of coffee."

"I see. Yes, that is a pretty unique order."

I then tell her about the teddy, chocolates, and terrible poem. She's laughing at the bad poetry when the teacher comes over to us.

Margie confirms she's a complete beginner.

Once the teacher has moved on, I say, "And I overheard something—"

But before I can continue, the teacher claps to get everyone's attention and pulls forward two boxes.

"Dancers, please take a scarf from this box and a shimmy belt from this one. The scarf is to hold and the shimmy belt goes around your waist and makes a fabulous tinkling noise when we get those hips moving!"

From the boxes I take a turquoise floaty scarf and a yellow shimmy belt. Margie grabs hers, and we both grin at each other as the class starts.

The teacher turns on the music, and my mind immediately relaxes as I focus on it. And with every movement I feel looser and stronger. I get lost in the class, all the stress of the day melting away as I shimmy and bounce and sway in a figure of eight.

At the end, we all clap one another and pop the props back in the boxes.

"You're a natural," I say to Margie as we're waiting in the queue to pay the teacher. "Did you enjoy it?"

"I thoroughly enjoyed it! I can't believe I've never done it before."

"She's an excellent teacher. I'm so pleased I found a class here."

Margie nudges me. "Go on, you overheard something…"

"Oh, yes."

I tell her about hearing Kelvin and Pete in Kelvin's office. She listens intently.

"Hmm. I wish I'd been a fly on the wall. I'm an excellent judge of character," she says.

"I don't know what to think."

We get to the front of the queue. I hand over some cash to the teacher, and Margie pays on her phone using a QR code that the teacher shares. Margie adds a tip. The teacher sees the amount and nearly falls over.

As we're walking out of the hall and back to our cars in the little car park, Margie says, "Have you considered that perhaps Pete's friendship isn't genuine? That he's bitter at being passed over for promotion and is planning something with Kelvin? It sounds to me as if Kelvin is a coaster and is put out that you've been hired. You're obviously excellent at the job and will hugely show him up and undermine him in all ways. Maybe this is Arun's strategy to get rid of dead wood. And Pete is potentially too enmeshed with Kelvin after years of working together to see him for what he really is."

"Maybe." I nibble at my nails and chew the skin around them.

Margie hugs me. "Look out for yourself, my dear. Some people in workplaces want to do as little as possible for their salaries and once they find a cushty job will do anything they can to stay in it. Believe me, I've come across quite a few in my time running Daddy's business."

"I bet. But I really thought Pete was my friend, that he was a genuine guy."

A sadness creeps over me. Up until I met the Maddens, he was my only friend in Cardiff. I thought we'd be friends for life. We just immediately clicked.

"Perhaps he is," Margie says wisely. "And this is all Kelvin. Pete has just got himself caught up and now can't extricate himself from it."

An idea pops into my head. "What are you doing on Friday?"

"No plans. Shall we go out?"

"Yes. And I'll bring Pete. You can see what you make of him. I trust you, Margie. I know you'll give me your honest opinion."

"Right you are. Friday it is."

CHAPTER 13

The high-pitched *squeak* of a brake pedal cuts through me and sets my teeth chattering. This morning the bus is near-empty, and I get a prized seat downstairs near the front. I've no idea why Tuesdays are so much quieter than Mondays, but I'm not complaining. The seat is comfy, and I attempt to ignore the fusty, wet-dog smell coming from the upholstery to enjoy the journey.

I put my earbuds in and turn on an audiobook. It's one about getting over a heartbreak that I downloaded this morning. I'm a sucker for any non-fiction audiobook about love and relationships.

The intro starts, but I'm not paying attention and don't take in a word. I stare out the window watching the world whizzing by.

I spoke to Mum briefly this morning while I was getting ready for my day and she was winding down from hers. We chatted amiably about all sorts, just like we always do, but this time there was a heaviness over the conversation – an elephant on the line, as such. Her cancer. Neither of us brought it up. She told me that there was no more news on a message so I wasn't going to chase her again. If she had news, she'd tell me immediately. I didn't tell her about Tyler or the overheard conversation or about anything that might worry her. I kept it light.

A pregnant woman gets onto the bus. I immediately jump up and offer her my seat.

"No worries. There's an empty one right behind you," she replies, cradling her bump, her engagement ring and wedding ring sparkling on her hand.

I touch my own stomach. I'd love to be pregnant. I'd love to be married.

The brakes squeal again. I rub my eyes. They feel tired even though they've only been open a couple of hours. I had another restless night. The Pete and Kelvin thing swirling.

I'll remain friends with Pete and give him the benefit of the doubt. Perhaps Margie is right, and he's been swept up in something that he wants no part of, but because Kelvin is his boss, can't get out of. When we're not in work, when we're out at a bar or restaurant, or in a neutral place, I'll ask Pete outright and see how he reacts.

With Kelvin, I need to watch my back. I plan to do a great job, have a brilliant first three months and sail through my probation period with no glitches. I pull out my phone, stop the audiobook and start a Notes list with everything inappropriate that Kelvin has done to date. And I'll add everything from now until March. It'll be evidence that shows Kelvin is a poor boss to take to Arun once my employment is one hundred per cent confirmed. I'll do it the proper way by keeping a record and bringing it up in a professional setting. I'm not sneaky. Confronting Kelvin now will cause drama, irreparably damage the team's respect for me, and more than likely get me fired. I'll bide my time, but be on constant alert.

I press the bell for my stop and put my phone back in my bag. I jump off the bus along with a handful of others and walk the few steps towards my building.

And that's when I see him. Tyler.

He comes charging towards me, as if he's about to rugby tackle me onto the hard pavement and crack my head open. I brace myself for impact, but he stops inches from me.

I back away a few steps and find myself against the

glass frontage of my work building. He stands in front of me in just his coffee shop branded t-shirt, apron, jeans, and trainers. No coat. He must be freezing. But I don't ask, I don't want to get into conversation with him.

His stocky build hems me in. My body temperature switches to scorching. I tug at Margie's scarf around my neck to loosen it. But, because of the way I've tied it, end up doing the opposite. It's too tight and feels as if it's getting tighter, like a noose strangling me.

Tyler holds up a takeaway cup. "I thought I'd hand-deliver this."

The smell of coffee rises up. My mouth salivates at the expectation of drinking the delicious brew.

"I don't want it, Tyler. You really shouldn't be here. I told you very clearly that I don't want to see you again."

Tyler chews his lip. "I know, but I was really hoping you'd give me a second chance, that you'd reconsider?"

"No! I'm not interested. Do not contact me again."

Tyler looks crestfallen. "Okay, I understand. Here, take this anyway. It's your favourite."

He thrusts the coffee cup at me, but I refuse to take it from him. "No, thank you."

"Take it," he says, his tone turning angry.

"No. Get out my way. I need to get to work."

I move to the side, but he blocks me.

His face turns into a snarl, and he lifts the cup as if he's about to throw it in my face. I flinch, expecting scalding liquid to hit, but he chucks the cup on the ground. The lid flies off, and hot coffee splashes onto my boots and up my trousers. The smell is no longer delicious, it's bitter.

I tut and shake off my trousers. Thankfully, they're navy so the stain isn't too obvious, but the smell is going to follow me around all day – and straight into my first meeting at 9 a.m. with Arun. A meeting that I'm now running late for because of Tyler.

I shove past him and hurry through the rotating doors into the reception area of my work building, grabbing my swipe card from my pocket and heading to the end of the queue for the elevators.

A hand grabs my bicep and jerks me back.

"I'm so sorry, Rachel," Tyler says.

That's it. I shake my arm out of his grip and shout, "Don't touch me! Get the hell away from me *right now*."

He recoils. All around, my colleagues stare. The last thing I need is to make a scene that everyone talks about, 'Did you see the lover's tiff the new girl had in reception this morning!' but I'm past caring. Tyler needs to fuck off. Now.

The security guard appears next to us, takes one look at me, and reads the situation. He turns to Tyler.

"Do you work here, sir? Because if not, I'd suggest you leave immediately."

The guard's deep voice is enough to push Tyler back. He puts his hands up, scurries through the rotating doors and hurries off in the direction of the coffee shop.

"Thank you," I say to the security guard.

He nods at me and goes back to his post by the door. I join the queue, and my skin crawls with all the eyes on me. I pull out my phone and tap out a message to Margie telling her about what just happened. I'd usually tell Mum or Heather or both, but Heather hasn't replied to my message from the other day, still in a mood at me for forgetting Ella's birthday, and I don't want to stress Mum out any more than she already is.

Margie replies:

What an idiot. Have got everything crossed he stays well away from you now xx

I check the time, hoping I might have a few minutes to head to the bathroom to wash the coffee out of my trousers and dry them under the hand dryer, but I don't. I'm already running late for my first monthly meeting with Arun.

Later that evening, as I get in from work, I see that my neighbour Ralph's front door is wide open. He usually leaves it ajar, never open all the way.

I stick my head in, but can't hear a thing. It's eerily quiet. No clatter from the kitchen or snoring or telly going. I expect he's sitting quietly in the lounge reading a book. He's told me before that's his favourite thing to do. He's going deaf so I don't shout for him or knock. And I'm not just going to waltz in to his flat uninvited and scare the life out of him. I lean in, try not to look around too much like I'm being nosey, and shut the door.

He's got a three-bedroom flat. He never goes in the third bedroom because it's full of his long-deceased wife's things that he can't bear to part with but doesn't want to look at either.

"Door to that room's always shut," he'd told me when I'd first moved in. And then he'd gone off on a tangent about the first time he and a mate had been arrested for syphoning petrol out of a car so they could put it in a motorbike they'd just stolen. He'd been a rebellious sixteen-year-old, apparently.

I let myself into my flat and sink into my sofa. I'm exhausted. It's been a long, stressful day. Arun completely threw me in at the deep end this morning. I was still jittery from the Tyler encounter and worried about being late and stinking of coffee so not on top form, but Arun didn't even notice. I'd barely sat down before he'd briefed me on a large project that had been stalling for more than a year and told me he wanted me to get it moving and finished in the next two months. He instructed me to go away and think about it for a few hours and to come back to him that afternoon with a workable plan. He also said to report straight to him and not to involve Kelvin.

All morning, I planned it out and went back and presented my idea to Arun after lunch. He signed it off and told me to get on with implementing it. It's an ambitious plan. I had to make some big decisions, which, if they work out, will be spectacular, but, if they don't, will cost us millions and piss off many stakeholders who we really don't want to piss off – passengers, train operating companies, other departments, my big boss Arun's big bosses.

I pinch the bridge of my nose. My brain hurts. A whopper of a headache is coming on. I slowly turn my head from one side to the other to stretch out my stiff neck. My gaze lands on the top of my shelving unit. I stop.

My Kindle. It's right there in the place where it lives, where it should've been on Sunday night.

I grab it to make sure it's real, turn it on and scroll through my library. It's working fine, and everything appears to be on there.

What is wrong with me? Was it there all along, and I just didn't see it? I ripped apart my entire flat on Sunday night looking for it. And then had to put the whole place back together again.

Five years ago, I spiralled into a deep depression when Will dumped me after eight years together, and something is happening again now. But this is different to before. Last time, I completely shut down. Went to bed, and couldn't do much of anything other than cry. This time, I'm tired but wired. It's distracting, and making me forget things and not see things when they're right in front of me.

I put the Kindle back on the shelf and look at my hands. Turn them back and front, notice the gap where my little finger should be. I need to keep functioning, to hold it together for Mum and this trip in a couple of months' time. I can't fall apart now; I need to stay strong.

The headache kicks in. The smell of the roses, before so sweet, is now nauseating. And there, next to the flowers, clasping the card printed with that terrible poem, is the teddy.

It stares at me with black beaded eyes.

A shiver ripples across my back. It's creeping me out, that teddy. As if whoever gave it to me is watching my every move. I get to my feet as fast as the throbbing pain across my forehead allows, grab a bin bag from the kitchen, stuff the roses and the teddy in it and take it downstairs to put in the large wheelie bin outside. I come back in and, to make myself feel marginally better, kick Brandon's stuff in the bin bag by the door. I still haven't dealt with that yet, but I will.

I take a deep breath, happier now the teddy and roses are out of my flat, and decide to eat a quick dinner and go straight to bed for an early night. I need to rest my mind. It's been working overtime these past few days, dealing with all the crap that this new year has thrown at me. After a good sleep, I'll feel refreshed for the next few days at work.

And I just have to hope this weird place I'm in will pass quickly.

CHAPTER 14

"*Sí, mama.* I'll sort the balloons. Uh-huh. *Siete. Cero. Sí,* am sure they'll have blue, if not silver… The largest size possible, *bueno*…"

In the front seat of the taxi, Pete chats on the phone to his mum about his dad's seventieth birthday party on Sunday.

We're stuck in Friday evening rush-hour traffic from the city centre to Cardiff Bay. We left work, hailed a taxi and are on our way to meet Margie and Mark at a bar for a few end-of-the-week drinks. I'm pleased Pete's on the phone, it's giving me a moment to decompress after a seriously busy week.

The project I'm leading for Arun has ramped right up and is now in full swing. I've been working overtime and firing on all cylinders to get it moving and completed in just two months' time. Arun has high expectations, and I'm under a massive amount of pressure to deliver. My team has been brilliant, all of them stepping up, all of them thrilled to be working on something so important and exciting. Kelvin hasn't paid any attention. Pete has been just as keen as his colleagues.

Tyler hasn't hassled me in person again. But the coffee deliveries haven't stopped. On Wednesday, Thursday, and this morning he's left me a coffee on reception so it was there when I arrived. Three times I picked it up, emptied it out in the kitchen sink on my floor and chucked the cup in the recycling box.

Should I go to the police? Surely, it's harassment or stalking now? But I don't feel frightened or threatened by the behaviour. Just irritated. And he's leaving gifts. Not exactly sinister, but still worrying. Would the police take that seriously? And besides, I've been so busy with work that I haven't had time. Perhaps I'll do it this weekend. I let out a sigh at the thought and decide against. I've got so much on my plate at the moment that I don't want to have to deal with the police too right now. If it escalates then I will. And surely the coffee deliveries will fizzle out soon enough when they don't produce any response.

I'm looking forward to a few drinks tonight to unwind. Mark and Margie are excited to meet Pete, and Pete seems excited to meet the Maddens in return. I'll wait for the right moment tonight to ask him about the Kelvin conversation I overheard. All week, Pete has been a stellar team member and given me no reason to think he's involved in some plan with Kelvin to get rid of me. But I'm not going to forget about what I heard.

We finally arrive, pay the driver and head into the bar. It's down some stairs and, on first glance, looks dingy and a bit cramped, but actually opens up into a large basement space, with DJ at one end, bar along one side and a few seats along the other. It's already heaving with Friday-after-work drinkers. I spot Mark and Margie and wave. They're sitting on high stools around a tall circular table, their backs against the wall.

I lead Pete through the crowd towards them.

They both slide off their stools to greet us. Mark and Pete shake hands. Margie hugs me and goes straight in to hug and air-kiss Pete, who happily reciprocates. Mark gives me a brief hug.

"You're looking gorgeous!" I say to Margie.

She's wearing low-rise flared jeans, a sequin butterfly top that shows off her midriff, a bunch of gold chunky chains around her neck, and a black baseball cap. Her hair is in low braided pigtails. She looks like 2000s-era Mariah Carey crossed with a gangster crossed with Pippi Longstocking. And it totally works.

"Thanks, my dear."

I catch a whiff of Margie's fragrance. "And your perfume's lovely."

"It's the new Dior one. Lemony and fresh. I love it."

The Maddens slip back onto their stools, and Pete and I take the ones opposite. There's a fifth stool which has Margie's large tote bag on it.

"This place is awesome," I say loudly over the music, the chatter, the laughter, the sounds of a busy bar. I take in the place and recognise the DJ. "Oh! It's the guy who was playing at your New Year's Eve party."

"Certainly is," Margie replies with a big smile. "That's Karl. He's brilliant."

Mark nudges the cocktail menus towards us. "We've got a tab going so order whatever you want."

Pete points to the cocktails in front of the Maddens. "What are you two drinking? Is that a jelly baby on the side?"

Mark turns his drink so we can see it better. "Yes, it's an alcoholic jelly baby made here especially for this cocktail. It's spicy, made with chilli vodka." He points out the cocktail on the menu. "It's this one. It says to drink the drink and then eat the jelly baby."

I ease out of my jacket, put it over my stool and sit on it. I grab my phone from my bag and put the torch app on to read the cocktail menu.

"That's better," Pete says, huddling closer to me to use the light too.

"I think I'm going to get the chilli one first. Start the night with a kick," I say and sway to the music.

A woman bumps into me. "Sorry!" she immediately says.

"No worries," I shout back.

"Think I'm going to go for the chilli one too," Pete

says. "I'm a massive fan of spicy things."

"So am I," Mark replies. "What's the hottest thing you've ever eaten?"

"I'll go to the bar," I say and slip off my stool.

Mark gives me the tab number, and I wade through people to the bar, spot an opening and order. A few moments later, I'm heading back to our table with two elaborate-looking and spicy-smelling cocktails. I pop them on the table and smile – the Maddens and Pete are deep in conversation about their favourite places to go out in Cardiff.

Margie takes out her phone. "Do you guys mind if I snap a photo of your cocktails before you start? I forgot with ours."

"Of course," I say and push our drinks together.

She takes the photo and drops her phone back in her bag. I give Pete his drink, and we both take a sip.

"Whoa!" I say as the chilli hits.

Pete's cheeks colour. "That's insane!" He takes another sip. "It's a bit like drinking a super-hot Thai green curry."

We all laugh, clink our glasses together and say cheers, take a drink and put the cocktails back on the table just as a man bumps into it. All the glasses rattle. We grab them to stop any from tipping over.

"So sorry!" he shouts.

"No bother," Pete replies.

Margie smiles warmly at Pete. "Pete was just telling us about a Mexican place in the city that he really rates because they took his Mexican grandfather there when he visited, and he loved it – so it must be good!"

"It does an amazing *sopa de camarones*—" Pete says.

"Shrimp soup," Mark interjects for my benefit.

"—that is described as *punishingly* hot."

"Margie, we *have* to go there," Mark says.

She laughs and takes a video of the venue, slowly moving from left to right. She seems to stop on me.

"Don't include me," I say, suddenly feeling self-conscious about the thought of being in Margie's TikTok video to her seventy thousand followers.

She blows me a kiss. "I never include anyone other than me. I think the top of your head is on show, that's it."

"It's got such great vibes in here," I reply. "We walked in, and I immediately felt relaxed and happy and ready for a great night."

Margie puts her phone away and points at the menu. "We need to decide what cocktail to have next!"

A few cocktails later – including one that came in a teapot and another that was smoking – I pick up my phone from the table and say, "Everyone get close! I'd like to take a photo for my mum, just to prove I have friends." We all huddle together, and I snap a quick selfie of us. "Perfect." I put my phone back on the table and jump off the stool. "Just going to the loo."

"Me too," Pete says. "I'll come with you."

We head towards the toilets at the end of the bar, and there's a quiet spot where no one seems to be standing. Now's my moment. I pull Pete towards me.

"Pete, can I ask you something?" I shout in his ear above the music.

"Sure!" He leans in to me to hear better.

"Is there something going on with Kelv—"

But Pete spots someone he knows.

"Juan!"

He waves and gives me a quick look as if to say, *I'll be one moment*, and dashes over to the person he's seen.

They hug and slap each other's backs as if they've not seen each other for a long time. The few times I've been out with Pete, he's always bumped into somebody he knows. He knows a lot of people in this city.

My full bladder nudges me, and I decide not to wait for Pete. I get in the slow-moving queue for the ladies' bathroom.

A few minutes later, Pete heads towards the gents – of

course with no queue – and says, "I'm going to head to the bar after. You want anything?"

"I'll have the smoking one again please. Thanks!"

He gives me a thumbs up and disappears into the gents. I glance back towards the busy dancefloor. From the queue, I can just about see in front of the DJ booth. My stomach somersaults. All the relaxed, happy feeling speeds away faster than a Japanese bullet train.

Ginger hair.

There.

Two heads of it.

Oh fuck, the twins are still in Cardiff?

I lean out from the queue, keeping my foot in my space, and squint at the spot where I just saw the two redheads. It's dark, and the flashing lights make it hard to tell. But there's no one there that I can see with red hair. I imagined it, thank goodness.

I step back into the queue with a smile at the woman behind me.

After I've had a wee, checked my hair and slicked on some more lip gloss, I head back to the table. Mark and Margie are having a moment, snogging each other's faces off. Pete must still be at the bar. I decide not to disturb them. I'll send that photo to Mum and look at my phone until they come up for air.

I go to grab my phone off the table. But it's not there. I scan the table and frantically look under it, in my bag, in my coat pockets. I check all the floor nearby.

"Everything okay, Rach?" Margie asks.

"No," I wail. "My phone's gone! I left it on the table!"

"It can't be far." Mark gets off his stool to check the floor with me.

Margie scans the table once again, moving my bag out the way to check.

"Fuck!" I say. "I can't lose my phone! It has my life on it."

My heart sinks at all the lost photos and screenshots

and notes and my entire diary and all the apps' data. I use it for absolutely everything.

"It'll all be in the cloud," Mark says reassuringly. "You'll be able to download everything back onto a new phone."

I shake my head. "I needed to sort out the storage on my iCloud ages ago because it was full. I hadn't got round to it."

"Ah," Mark says.

"Someone's taken it, haven't they? It's been nicked. Should we ask at the bar, see if they have CCTV?"

Pete arrives and slides two smoking drinks onto the table. His face is scrunched up. He does not look happy.

"Pete!" I grab his arm. "I've lost my phone. It's not on the table anymore. I think someone's taken it!"

Pete stares first at Mark and then at Margie, I'm not sure what he's expecting, but it's slightly odd.

He points at Margie. "It's in her bag."

"What?" I say.

"I was at the bar and happened to look back after I ordered and saw Mark grab it and give it to Margie, and she put it in her bag," Pete says.

The Maddens look perplexed.

Very calmly, Mark says, "I don't think that is what you saw, Pete."

Pete gestures to Margie's large tote bag, still sitting on its own stool next to Margie. "Rachel's phone is in that bag. Check it!"

A man in a large group knocks into us. Pete is rammed into the table. He rights himself and shoves the guy back.

"Whoa, chill out!" I say and stand between them before anything can escalate.

The man doesn't react and continues moving through the bar with his friends. Margie puts her bag on her lap and rummages through it.

"Oh," she exclaims and holds out my phone through the smoke of the cocktails. "It was in my bag!"

Pete folds his arms, satisfied.

Margie hands it to me. "It must've fallen in when someone knocked the table, or when that server came a moment ago and cleared the empty glasses."

"Bullshit!" Pete says. He sways. He's very drunk.

Margie frowns.

Mark stands taller.

I pocket my phone and put a hand on Pete's shoulder. "It's okay, Pete. I'm just pleased to have it back. It must've got knocked in there. No worries. Let's enjoy these cocktails."

But Pete snarls, turns, and storms towards the exit.

I chase after him. "Pete!"

He spins to face me. "I know what I saw, Rachel. They took your phone!"

I shake my head, and he leaves.

Why would the Maddens take my phone? I can't think of one reason. But why would Pete be so adamant about it? He's drunk, and maybe he saw Mark reaching for a napkin and Margie getting something out of her bag or adjusting it. He put two and two together and got five.

Or is he trying to alienate me from the only other friends I have in town? Maybe that's part of his and Kelvin's plan to isolate me and get me to leave the city. I'm completely alone with no Brandon now.

Margie's large bag has been wide open on that stool all night. It's highly likely the table was knocked and my phone skidded and fell into her bag. People have been bumping into us for the entire time we've been here. Thank goodness it fell in there and not on the floor where it would've got stamped on and broken.

I rest my hand over my phone in my trouser pocket and head back to the table. The Maddens are both frowning, clearly offended.

"I'm sorry about that," I say.

They both glower at me. That's it, the end of my friendship with them.

Eventually, Margie smiles. "I'm not too sure that Pete is a good egg!"

Mark snorts, amused, and shakes his head.

She points to the cocktails, no longer smoking, but still looking elaborate and delicious. "We shouldn't let them go to waste, should we?"

CHAPTER 15

The strange noise comes again. I glance at Margie. But she hasn't seemed to notice, too busy trying to open a sachet of wasabi.

We sit across from one another in a café in the middle of a busy shopping centre. It's not the kind of place that I would pick, but Margie said it had 'surprisingly good sushi'. And, surprisingly, it does. We're just finishing up our large sushi platter for two.

Pete and I were meant to be going out today to do some January sales shopping, but he messaged me this morning to say that he had lots of things he needed to do for his dad's party and couldn't make it. I know it's because he's still upset about last night's phone incident at the bar.

I messaged Margie to see if she fancied it. She did.

We've got a table right in the centre of the café, shopping bags tucked around us. Margie insisted on getting me a new outfit for my birthday, which is in a few days. But not just clothes, she got me shoes, makeup, and perfume – the same Dior one she was wearing last night.

"I love spending money on others, and it's for a special occasion so let me treat you," she'd insisted as we entered the first shop this morning. And treat me she has.

"Did you hear that?" I ask Margie, urgently.

Margie pauses her battle with the sachet and listens. "Hear what?"

THE NEW GIRL

I shake my head. "Oh, nothing," I say.

But it comes again. Laughter. Not any old laughter, it's *my* laughter. As if it's an echo of me laughing. Except I'm not laughing right now.

The open café sits in the atrium area of the vast shopping centre. It's a cavernous space with escalators, a glass lift, the open sides of three floors and a high glass roof. It's echoey and noisy. There are people everywhere. The café is full, and the shops are heaving with bargain hunters.

"My laughter. Can you hear it?" I ask Margie.

She frowns at me. "But you're not laughing, my dear."

I point upward. "There! Can you hear that? It sounds just like me."

Margie listens, but then shakes her head slowly. "No, I don't think I can hear your laughter."

I scan around us, and my skin crawls. Eyes are on me. Someone somewhere is watching me, I'm sure of it. I feel as if I'm in the middle of a fishbowl. The café is open on all sides. Exposed. Someone looking over the railing on the top floor could see us. We're surrounded by others eating, walking from shop to shop, chatting, waiting in queues at fresh juice or bubble tea counters. I search out ginger hair, two faces the same. But don't see anything. The entire vast space swirls in and out of focus.

Light-headed, I put down my chopsticks and nudge my plate away, no longer hungry. The soy sauce has left a salty film over my gums and tongue, and my mouth tastes vile. I gulp back some water, rub my eyes and shudder.

I'm hearing things now too?

"Are you okay?" Margie asks, concerned. "You've gone very pale."

"Yes, I think so. Just having a funny five minutes."

She nods, unconvinced.

I pick up my phone. "Shall we see what's on at the cinema?"

"Excellent idea."

A few hours later, after a lovely afternoon watching a hilarious rom-com with Sandra Bullock, I let myself into my flat loaded with shopping bags and pleased to be home. The movie was a great distraction, and I didn't hear anything weird again. I'm not entirely sure why my brain thought it was hearing myself laugh. Fingers crossed it doesn't do anything like that again. I kick off my shoes by the door and head through to the bedroom with my bags. I want to try on my new outfit.

But my foot squelches on the carpet, and water seeps through my socks.

WTF?

As I get closer to the kitchen, my footsteps splosh on the soaked carpet. I can hear running water. I open the door to my bedroom, throw the shopping bags on my bed and slowly push open the door to the kitchen.

It's flooded. Water ankle-high. The kitchen tap is on full whack, and water pours over the side of the sink, down the kitchen cabinet and onto the lino. The washing up bowl floats in the water on the floor.

I wade through as fast as I can, soaking my socks and the bottom of my jeans instantly, and reach for the tap, twisting it off. I roll up my sleeve and pull the plug out of the sink. The water in the basin drains away with a gurgle.

I must've left the tap on with the plug in. Everything in my gut says I didn't do that. But the truth is, I really can't remember. I've been operating on automatic. I made coffee and cereal this morning before I went out, like I do most mornings, but I was barely paying attention, my brain elsewhere while my body went through the familiar motions.

I grab a large mug from a top cupboard, bend to scoop up water and pour it down the sink. I do this a few times. The level is going down steadily, which means it must be draining somewhere. No doubt into the flat below.

I splash across the wet lino and stick my head out the

door. The water has seeped into the carpet in the hallway but the lounge and bedrooms look untouched. The water mark leads up to the front door but doesn't quite touch it.

There's something missing though from next to the front door. It takes me a moment before it twigs. The bin bag with Brandon's stuff in it is gone. Did I put that in the outside bin when I went out this morning? It's highly likely. I'm so distracted and stressed and forgetful at the moment I probably just did it out of habit. Saw a black bag by the front door and chucked it.

Or could the twins be messing with me? Flooding my flat and binning that bag is the kind of bizarre thing they'd do. I thought I saw them last night. But realistically, they can't be in Cardiff anymore. They must be back in Nottingham – otherwise where are they staying? They rarely have any money, unless they've had a windfall from a rich boyfriend, and their whole life is a three-hour drive away.

Has someone else got into my flat? Brandon? But I just don't think he'd do something like this. It's certainly not the best way to win me back.

Heavy banging on my front door makes me jump. No one has ever knocked directly on my door. There's a buzzer on the front door to the building that everyone visiting presses.

The thumping comes again. It's angry, urgent, determined.

I pad across the squelching carpet and open the door… to a fist in my face.

It's my downstairs neighbour, Dominic, just about to knock again. He drops his hand.

"I've been out all day, just got back, and there's a helluva lot of water coming through my kitchen ceiling!" he says in a rush.

"I've just got in too. My kitchen is flooded!"

"Where's it coming from?"

"It's my fault. I accidentally left the tap on and the plug

in," I say.

I don't know if I truly believe that's what happened. But there's no other explanation. It must've been me.

A flash of annoyance passes across his countenance.

"I'm guessing you've turned it off now?" he says through gritted teeth.

"Yes! Of course. I'm so sorry." I shake away the doubt and switch into action mode. "Let's get this sorted. I'll phone the landlord if you can find an emergency electrician? I'm assuming we don't want the electrics getting wet…"

On Sunday, I spend the morning cleaning up after the flood, drying carpet and lino and other stuff out, dealing with my irate neighbour, my even more irate landlord, my contents insurance company, the landlord's buildings insurance company, the emergency electrician, and an emergency plumber – who, it turned out, we didn't need in the end because there were no plumbing issues and no repairs required.

There's no food in the flat for lunch, so I drive to the nearby supermarket to stock up. As I'm unloading the trolley onto the till's conveyor belt, I notice the cashier.

My legs give way, and I collapse onto the cold floor.

Derek Forrester.

My pulse races. I can't catch my breath.

"Are you okay, love?" a man asks and puts his hands under my armpits to lift me up.

I brace myself. But the cashier, who is now standing and peering over the conveyor belt to see me, is an older, greying man who looks nothing like my father.

The man who fathered me is not anywhere to be seen. My mind is playing tricks on me.

After paying, I drive home in a daze and carry the food up my stairs. The flat is freezing. I left all the windows open to air the place. The electrics have to dry out for another twelve hours before we can switch back on, as recommended by the electrician. So, I have no power right now. And having no power always feels unnerving.

I close the front door and take the bags through to the kitchen, popping them on the counter and unloading slowly. I didn't get anything that needed to go in the fridge or freezer – both currently switched off. Everything is still damp, but not soaking wet anymore. The lino has all been pulled up so the electrician could get to the floorboards. It's drying off, but likely not salvageable.

My mouth gasps for a cup of tea, but I can't boil the kettle and didn't buy any more milk because I can't store it in the fridge. I take down a large glass and go to grab the cordial on the side next to my toaster. My hand grasps at air.

The cordial bottle isn't there. I rack my brains trying to remember if I moved it when I was cleaning up, but know I didn't. The counter wasn't affected. And I know I had a nearly full bottle before I left for the shop, because I checked if I needed to buy anymore.

I open a few cupboards in case I put it somewhere else. I check the fridge. And find the TV remote on the top shelf. *Huh?*

Holding the remote, I head into the lounge, drying my feet off on the towel outside the door, and see my shower gel on the coffee table on its side, where I'd usually put the TV remote. I switch them over and go to my ensuite bathroom.

And there, by my shampoo and conditioner, is my bottle of cordial. I put the shower gel back where it belongs and grab the cordial.

What the hell is going on with me?

This is nothing like when I was depressed before. I need to speak to my doctor. But he's back in Nottingham because I haven't got round to organising one in Cardiff yet. And I can't exactly nip back to see him. It's too far, and I can't take any time off work because I'm still on probation.

And what would my doctor say? He'd ask me what's happened recently and tell me that I'm under a lot of stress and need to take it easy, have a break, try to unwind.

I don't sleep a wink that night. Worries about my mind failing go round and round in circles, bounce up and down like a never-ending ball.

A feeling of teetering on the very edge of a cliff comes over me and, no matter how hard I try, it won't go away.

CHAPTER 16

The Monday morning work-in-progress meeting has gone really well. Thank goodness. Even though I feel massively out of sorts after the craziness of the weekend, I've held it together and forced myself to keep functioning. And, so far, nothing weird has happened.

There was a coffee waiting for me on reception again this morning. But I immediately binned it. Dealing with that every morning is wearing but I forced myself not to think anything more about it. Tyler can do one. I've got too many other things going on right now. He'll get the message soon enough, and it's his money he's throwing away on undrunk coffee. I don't imagine he gets it for free even though he does work there. If he does anything else then I'll involve the police, but he's not tried to contact me in any other way, just these coffee deliveries.

For the entire meeting, I fired up everyone to keep working hard on this large project for Arun. It's taken all my energy. The team files out of the meeting room, motivated and eager to face the week with clear tasks and deadlines. I, however, feel as if I could crawl under my desk and sleep for a week but at the same time run an ultra-marathon.

Pete hangs back. I hang back too.

"Rachel, please could I have a word?" he asks.

I nod, wait for the last team member to leave, and shut the door.

"Shall we?" I say and gesture to the conference table and chairs to sit back down again.

Pete takes a seat at the head of the table, and I take one to the side – still warm from when Kalisha was sitting in it a moment ago. *Eww.*

"Everything okay?" I ask.

"This isn't work related," he says.

I place my pen on top of my notebook and fold my hands in my lap. I'm upset with Pete for stomping out of the bar on Friday night and cancelling on me at the last minute on Saturday, but I want to remain completely professional while we're at work. No point getting emotional and making it even weirder between us. I'm still his boss, after all.

"Go on."

"I've heard some things… about the Maddens."

"I see."

"After what happened on Friday night when they took your phone, and then pretended they didn't, I asked around. I'm mates with a lot of people in Cardiff and thought someone must know someone who knows them. They're quite distinctive, aren't they? Rich, older couple. She looks like a supermodel, and he looks like an ageing rocker from the sixties."

I nod, refusing to get drawn into gossip, treating the Maddens as if they were work colleagues, and gesture for Pete to continue, as if he was giving feedback on a teammate's performance while I remain completely neutral.

"Apparently, they like to pick up waifs and strays and sad cases."

"Is that what you think I am? A sad case?"

"No! Sorry. I just mean that they pick up people, are seen around town with them for a while, and then those people get dropped and aren't seen with them again."

"What exactly are you trying to say, Pete?"

"They're not to be trusted. Be careful with them."

I consider him for a moment. He looks genuine. And perhaps someone has passed this gossip onto him, and he's believed it without considering where it came from or what it might mean and feels he's doing me a favour by letting me know about it.

The Maddens have been nothing but nice to me from the moment I met them. They had a large number of friends at their New Year's Eve party. They knew everyone's names – well, apart from mine – and everyone clearly adored them.

Could this be personal? I sensed he was jealous of my new friends when I first mentioned them to him at the coffee shop on the day I met Tyler. Could Pete be doing his best to break up our friendship?

Pete has worked his arse off on the big project, mentoring the more junior team members and coming out with some excellent ideas. But is he hoodwinking me by being a great employee, only to derail the project in spectacular fashion as part of Kelvin's 'plan' when I'm least expecting it?

Or maybe this is another attempt to make sure I'm alone and vulnerable in my personal life by wrenching me apart from my only friends in the city. He tried before by accusing them of taking my phone. That failed, so he's trying again.

Whatever the reason, I don't believe what he's telling me is the truth. Perhaps the Maddens did have a friend who they are no longer friends with anymore – that's got nothing to do with me and my relationship with them, has it? Maybe people are jealous that they're not closer to the Maddens, so make up vicious rumours. As Pete said, they are a couple that stand out, and they are a couple that everyone wants to be friends with.

On the tip of my tongue is a question about the conversation I overheard, but I bite it back. There's a lot of work that needs to be done, and I need Pete to continue in the way he's been working. I'll keep a very close eye on him.

And on Kelvin.

So far, Kelvin has been staying out of my way, hasn't mentioned this big project or asked me about it. He also chose not to come to the work-in-progress meeting, even though he's invited. He's meant to be the head of the team but has no idea what we're doing.

I smile at Pete. But it's not warm. It's aloof, professional. From herein, I'm his boss, and we're no longer friends. That makes me sad, but it is what it is.

"Thank you for this information. I shall take it into consideration. Let's get back to work. We've got lots to do."

I stand, indicating that the chat is closed, and open the door for him.

He stands too. As he passes me, he says, "Just watch your back with them, Rach."

I scrutinise him from behind as he heads to his desk. *Oh, I'll be watching backs, Pete. Yours and Kelvin's. Don't you worry.*

I get to my desk. It's almost midday. The meeting was unusually long, going over everything that needs to be accomplished for Arun in such a short space of time. My stomach grumbles.

Kalisha appears at my desk and crouches beside me so she can talk to me discreetly.

"Rachel, I'm sorry, but can I work from home this afternoon? My sofa broke, and I ordered a new one, but they can only deliver it this afternoon. So annoying! Is that all right? I'll log on as soon as I get in and work late. I promise I'll get everything done today that I need to."

She looks at me with pleading eyes. She's avoiding her one-to-one Monday afternoon catch up with Kelvin again.

"Of course, not a problem."

She hurries away, grabs her bag and coat from her desk and exits swiftly. I open the Notes app on my phone and add this to the evidence I'm compiling about Kelvin.

It's a dry evening, so I decide to walk to my belly dancing class from the office. I worked late and had dinner at my desk. I picked up my exercise gear at lunchtime when I had to dash home to meet the landlord and the buildings insurance inspector to assess the water damage and discuss what I can claim and what the landlord can claim, *blah blah blah*. It's a headache dealing with all that admin on top of everything at work. I really don't have the headspace for it.

Margie messaged to ask if I wanted a lift from home, but I explained I was coming from work and would probably walk, so would see her there. My body is rammed tight with too much energy. I need the exercise and the fresh air to help me let off some steam.

After our morning chat, I paid close attention to Pete. But he did a sterling job all day and stayed late too, just finishing up when I left for the night.

I walk past Cardiff Castle, across the River Taff and into Bute Park, taking the riverside path towards Pontcanna Fields. Although it's 7.30 p.m. and dark, it's still busy everywhere with commuters, dogwalkers, joggers and people taking advantage of the mild evening to go for a stroll after being cooped up with rainy weather for the past few days.

It's a pleasant walk. I force myself to take in my surroundings, be mindful, and not spend the entire time in my head going over and over everything that has happened recently.

That lasts for about five minutes.

I drift off into Rachel's World. Preoccupied and not paying much attention, I walk further and further away from the city centre.

My body sounds an alarm: a chill creeps across my shoulders; my skin crawls.

I dial into my surroundings. There's nobody else about. The path I'm on is the main path along the river and slightly raised. But there's a second, lower, unofficial trail right next to the river where dogs and more adventurous humans go. It's lined with tall trees and thick undergrowth. On the other side of the main path, the bank drops down to a dark, open space. Perfect for picnics in the summer, but now deserted and muddy. My footsteps crunch on the gravel. Something moves in the undergrowth... animals? Birds? Wind rustles through the tree tops and branches creak.

There are street lights dotted along the path, but the trees have grown up around them and cast long shadows that are perfect hiding places. I speed up. This is a prime place to get attacked. What was I thinking walking along here? Stupid idea. It was bustling a moment ago, but it's as if I've wandered into the middle of nowhere and am no longer in the city. I fumble in my handbag, find my house keys, and put them between my fingers.

Footsteps crunch behind me. They're faster than mine and getting closer. My blood freezes in my veins.

I spin around. I refuse to be jumped from behind, I'd rather face what's coming.

But there's no one there.

I carry on along the path. The footsteps start up again, but this time they're keeping pace with me. I'm definitely being followed.

On the left there's a turning towards another path that goes through the picnic fields. Should I turn down there? I don't know where it leads. I need to get somewhere busy fast, but the path looks as if it goes into an even gloomier area of the park. I pass it and keep straight. Do I run? I know where I need to leave the park to get to the community hall, but it's not for another ten minutes or so.

A cackle cuts through the silence.

Up ahead there's another path joining mine. Three dogwalkers come up the little hill and onto the main path. One sees me and smiles. Three women, each with a dog, chatting merrily and laughing raucously.

I speed up to reach them. "I'm sorry to intrude, but do

you mind if I join you? I felt a bit vulnerable on my own there."

"Please do," the one nearest me says.

"Thank you, I had a creepy feeling I was being followed."

I glance back behind us; the path appears empty. But to either side, anyone could be hiding in the darkness.

"Did you really? Well, if anyone unsavoury comes near us, we'll set the hounds on them!" She indicates the three dogs.

I take in the 'hounds': a sausage dog, a pug, and a tiny white fluffy thing. I doubt they'd do much damage but am pleased to be with this group nonetheless.

The white fluffy dog sniffs at my feet and looks up at me.

"She's asking for a lift. Can't go as far as the other two." The woman scoops up the dog and hands her to me.

I hold the little body. Her weight, her warmth, her soft fur, and the feel of her little heartbeat soothes me immediately.

"What kind of dog is she?"

"A Maltese and chihuahua mix. Her name is Crumpet."

"Crumpet is very, very cute," I reply, holding the dog up to my face so I can see her better.

I tuck her under my arm and glance behind us again, but no one is there. Did I imagine those footsteps? Possibly. But the hairs on the back of my neck prickle, and I can't shake the feeling that someone is still there, still watching me.

Later that evening, I sit in bed and set my alarm. The three lovely dogwalkers walked me all the way to the community hall, saying they had to go that way anyway. I carried Crumpet for the entire journey, and when I put her down, she rubbed herself against my leg briefly as if to say thank you.

The belly dancing class was brilliant, and Margie was on

top form. She gave me a lift home, and I filled her in on Saturday night's flood drama.

My flat stinks of damp. Now the power is back on, I've got the heating on full blast to dry out the place, but it's taking too long. The last thing I need is mould everywhere. The lino in the kitchen is still all pulled up and beginning to whiff, and the floorboards underneath give off a musty, old-dust smell.

I still have no idea where Brandon's stuff went. The large wheelie bin outside is a communal one and full of black bags. I wasn't about to go searching through it to find Brandon's bag. I must've binned it. Even though I don't remember doing it.

My heart twinges. I miss him. With everything else that's happened I've been suppressing it, but it's still there. It feels very final with his stuff gone. I miss being in a romantic relationship. I desperately want him here to hug me and tell me everything is going to be all right.

But I haven't heard from him in a while. Maybe it was him who sent the teddy, poem, and roses, but why not put his name on the card? And I won't take him back. I'd be doing myself a disservice by allowing him to treat me badly, drop me and pick me up again. But I'm still heartbroken.

My phone lights up in my hand with a message from Mum:

Happy Birthday, NZ time!!

I reply to say thanks. She's typing. I nestle under the duvet and get comfy on the pillow, holding my phone at an angle so I can read it lying down.

Finally, her message arrives:

I'm so sorry to have to say this, but I don't want to keep it from you, even on your birthday. I debated about telling you later in the week, but I know you'd want to know and that it would upset you that I hadn't said immediately. So here goes, I got some test results back. And it's not looking good.

She goes on to tell me the results, what type of breast cancer she has, the stage and prognosis. My world cleaves in two. I'm frozen in bed, but it's no longer comfortable, it's as if I'm lying on a bed of nails that are pushing through my skin all over my body. The pain is unbearable. I heave but manage to swallow back the vomit.

I type a reply:

I'm so, so sorry, Mum. I love you. Can I do anything?

The response is almost instant:

Just get here soon. I think we should be together.

Through a deluge of tears, I type back:

I'll be there as fast as I can.

She reads my message, and the app tells me she's no longer online, off to get on with her day. I cry and cry, floods of it like the sink overflowing in the kitchen the other day. Tears gush from my eyes and soak my pillow.

CHAPTER 17

On Tuesday morning, I step out of my building's main door and wander down the driveway to the street.

Dazed, I debate the best way to ask Kelvin about taking compassionate leave and a holiday sooner than March. And whether I should bypass Kelvin altogether and speak to Arun. But he's relying on me to get this big project completed. I doubt he'd let me take holiday either.

Parked on double yellows on the road right in front of my building with a huge white bow and a large handwritten sign propped against it, is a silver SUV. The sign reads: 'Happy Birthday, Rachel'.

Traffic swerves around the car. It shouldn't be parked there. It's a no stopping and no parking zone.

I stare at the car, the sign, the bow, and it takes a while for my grief-muddled brain to process what I'm seeing. I walk towards it and hold my hand out to it, as if it's a mirage. But it's very much real.

Who left this here?

"Surprise!" a figure jumps out at me.

"Fucking hell!" I fall into the car, knocking the sign onto the pavement. I clutch at my heart as I right myself.

"That's no way to talk to your old man, now, is it?"

And there he stands. My father.

His short red hair is slowly going a bright white, not grey, but he still has red eyebrows and stubble. He's old and saggy looking, no doubt due to his heavy drinking habit and unwavering avoidance of wearing any SPF. He also smoked for most of his adult life but managed to kick that habit a few years ago when a smoker friend passed away from chronic obstructive pulmonary disease. Dad's a similar age to Mark, but looks ten years older.

He's still chunky and broad with a large belly and thick arms. He's the same height as me, but a lifetime of manual jobs in predominantly male environments has made his body stocky and given his bearing a hard edge. He has an alpha-male, leader-of-the-pack vibe about him. Nobody messes with him if they can help it.

He slaps my bicep, a little too hard, so I know he's definitely real and sadly not an illusion.

Anxiety explodes. My pulse hammers, hands shake, teeth chatter. I can feel it rushing around my body like a hunter chasing prey.

"Hi, Dad. You scared me."

"It's a surprise. That's what's meant to happen." He thrusts the car keys at me. "Here you are. Take it for a spin."

"Thank you, but I've already got a car."

I gesture at my small Toyota Yaris that's parked in my tight designated space outside my flat. This is just like my father – completely unpredictable. Some years, I never receive a birthday message, others, like this year obviously, I get completely over-the-top gifts that he's not considered if I actually want or need. He's probably got this car cheap from a friend of a friend or someone down the pub he started talking to who owns a second-hand car shop. He won't have considered me at all when choosing this. It's a huge car that is completely impractical in a busy city and wouldn't fit in my parking space.

And not to mention all the hassle I'd need to go through to change over insurance and car tax, as well as selling my existing car. He doesn't think stuff through. Never has, never will.

His face screws up and eyes narrow.

I swallow back the anxiety that threatens to burst from my body.

He continues to hold out the car keys, which I refuse to take.

"Take the damn keys, Rachel," he says, his voice rising. "And show a bit of gratitude."

Pedestrians watch us as they walk past. My father has never cared if people can hear or see him or what anyone thinks. He's perfectly comfortable with making a scene in public. I, however, feel like I'm on a stage with an audience hanging on to my every move.

I weigh up my options. And take the keys. Accepting the gift will cause the least fuss.

"Thank you. What a lovely gift."

My bus whizzes past and slows to pull in at the bus stop a few paces up the road. "I need to go, Dad. That's my bus for work."

"What? You're not going to take your new toy for a spin?"

"No. Maybe later. I can't be late for work."

I attempt to edge past him and run for the bus, thankful there's a queue of people waiting to get on, but he grabs my wrist.

"Drive the car in."

"I don't have a parking space. I need to get that bus."

"I'll meet you for lunch."

"Dad... I've got a really busy day at work."

His grip tightens uncomfortably. "I don't give a shit. You can spare some time for your old man on your birthday. Tell me where you work, and I'll meet you there at 1 p.m."

I don't want to tell him where I work. I don't want to meet him for lunch. And I really don't want this fucking car. But I know he won't let me go until he gets what he wants, so I say, "Sure," and tell him my work address. Hopefully, this car will have been towed by the time I get back this evening for being parked where it shouldn't so I won't have to deal with it.

He releases my wrist, and I sprint for the bus, jumping on just as the doors are closing. There are seats free, but I cling onto the handrail by the front, near the driver, panting as if I've just sprinted one hundred metres. I suck back the cold air whenever the bus stops and the doors open. The panic attack that comes on whenever I see my father kicks into gear. Sweat streams down my back, my cheeks burn, my chest constricts, and I struggle to breathe. My insides contort painfully, and a light-headedness comes over me, turning my legs to water. Trembles hit me from head to toe. I think I'm going to pass out. I've never had one so bad.

Frantically, I pull off my scarf and hat, open my coat – anything to cool me down. I focus on steadying my breathing, the movement of the bus, clinging onto the handrail to keep me upright.

By the time I reach work, I've calmed down, but I'm numb, as if I'm not part of reality but am one or two levels of consciousness removed. Everything is slightly blurry around the edges, not quite fixed, hazy. It's as if I'm operating a few seconds behind everyone else. There's another coffee waiting for me on reception. The receptionist just holds it up for me and doesn't say anything.

Automatically, I pour it down the sink and bin the cup before heading to my desk. I'm so jittery and out of sorts that I decide not to go and talk to Arun or Kelvin about taking leave during my probation period. I'm not sure I'd get the words out in the right order.

I keep my head down all morning. A few team mates wish me a happy birthday, but otherwise I don't feel like chatting. Dread at seeing Dad again at lunch eats me up and sucks all cheerfulness right out of my bones. I can't focus on work so check emails obsessively and reply when I don't need to just to look as if I'm doing something. I flit from inbox, to an open document that I should be working on, to a white paper that Arun has sent me that I need to read, to the homepage of BBC News, to my to-do list, and back again.

I smell him before I see him. Kelvin. Just as his overpowering aftershave drapes itself over me, he drapes his top half across the shelving units at the end of our pod of desks like he owns the place. He switches between eyeing us and playing with his phone. Nobody acknowledges him. Even I can't muster the will to be politely professional by saying something. I ignore him. And he lingers. Is he waiting for something?

The receptionist walks in with a parcel and hands it to me.

"Not coffee this time," she jokes and leaves.

Kelvin's attention pricks. "Go on then, open it," he eggs me on.

Has Kelvin got me a birthday gift? Perhaps everyone chipped in to get me something?

The team all look up from their monitors to watch me. I look at the front and back of the brown parcel, but it only has my name on it and nothing else.

I run a pen along the tape to open it. Inside is another. It's blue and obviously a jewellery box. The team got me jewellery? An odd choice.

I tip the brown box upside down but there's no card or indication of who sent this. I open the blue one.

A dazzling necklace sparkles. I touch it, hold it up. Is it real diamonds? It can't be. It's heavy and cold to the touch.

"Ooh," Kelvin drones. "What are you doing working here if your beau sends you diamond necklaces, eh? You should be a woman of leisure living off your rich man." He laughs.

There are a few tentative chuckles from the rest of the team.

I stare at him. Once again, he's attempting to embarrass me in front of everyone. He's making it a habit to materialise when I get gifts – now, and when the teddy and poetry arrived. Did he send it? Is this part of his plan to make me feel uncomfortable at work and get me to leave?

"Did you get me this?" I blurt.

It comes out all wrong and sounds as if I'm asking if he gave it to me as a romantic gesture.

"What?" Kelvin howls with laughter, pointing at me and then to himself. "As if!" He does an over-the-top grimace like he can't think of anything worse than dating me.

He saunters back to his office with a smirk on his face.

Cringing, I glance at my team's faces. Confusion is writ large across their wide-eyed expressions. They all quickly look away from me and back to their monitors.

The necklace weighs down my hand. I put it back in the box. It's a choker-style necklace. Not something I'd ever wear. Who the hell got me this? Was it my father? Does he expect me to wear this to lunch? Not a chance.

The glittering stones both awe and worry me. I touch my neck, and the image of someone's hands around it, choking me, flashes behind my eyes.

In my grief-stricken, panicky state, my brain immediately conjures up sinister reasons for this necklace being gifted to me. Hidden in it is a tracker or an audio recorder or a camera. It'll slowly ooze poison that seeps into my skin and kills me. Or it'll explode in my face as soon as I open the clasp to put it on.

I snap shut the box. I'm being ridiculous. It's just a necklace. I put it in the top drawer of my desk. And there it will stay until I can figure out who gave it to me and give it back. It'll never, ever, go around my neck.

CHAPTER 18

Gusty wind whips at my face, lifts up my hair and tugs at my clothes. At a few minutes to one, I headed outside my office building. I did not want Dad to come in. He would've found a way to get through security and surprise me at my desk. Better to meet him on the street.

My phone dings. I pray it's Dad saying he's changed his mind about lunch. But it's a message from Heather. It says:

Happy Birthday.

And that's it. No conversation-starting question or general chit-chat. It's clear she's still in a mood with me. I sigh. I don't want to become distanced from Heather now that we're not living near one another. If I'd still been in Nottingham, I would've popped to hers. This is the first time we've not been living within a ten-minute drive of one another.

I spot Dad striding towards me and put my phone away. As he gets closer, anxiety ratchets up and up until it pushes on the top of my head. I imagine my skull bulging and distorting with the pressure.

I shiver and burn at the same time. My armpits dampen. I take long, deep breaths to stave off another panic attack.

"Rachel," Dad shouts too loudly from a few steps away. He reaches me and ushers me to the left. "What's with the long face?"

"Just a bit of a headache," I reply. "Busy morning. Better now for some air." I plaster on a smile.

He grunts. "I've been walking around, and Cardiff's a decent enough city."

I can smell the beer on his breath, so what he means is, he found a good pub where they were friendly to him and the beer was cheap, so now he likes Cardiff.

"Yes, I love it," I reply.

But he doesn't hear me, guiding me with a firm hand on my elbow. "I've found us a place for lunch."

We turn a corner, and he points to the coffee shop where Tyler works.

I stop dead in my tracks. "No, Dad. I'm not keen on that place. Let's find somewhere else."

He drags me on. "Nonsense. We're going here. Looks all right to me."

I know not to argue, and I also know not to mention Tyler to Dad. When I was growing up, there were quite a few occasions when if a boy so much as glanced my way, Dad would threaten them with castration. I cross my fingers that Tyler isn't working today.

We go through the doors and join the short queue. Tyler's behind the counter with his back to me. Because, of course he is. That's just my luck at the moment. He's busy making coffee orders while another server operates the till.

I cross my fingers again, this time praying Tyler doesn't say or do anything in front of Dad.

"What you having?" Dad asks. "That weird mint-mocha-with-extra-coffee-shot crap?"

I'm surprised Dad has remembered my coffee order; he doesn't usually remember anything specific about me or my life. I glance at Tyler's back and grab a can of fizzy lemon, which can't in any way be tampered with or spat in or messed up on purpose.

"No, I'll just have this today, I think. Too much coffee

this morning."

Dad looks at the can in my hand, and then at me. "Don't be daft. We're in a *coffee* shop. Put that back."

I smile sweetly, calmly, not wanting this to look as if I'm being disagreeable. "No, thank you. I'd really like this, if that's okay?"

Dad purses his lips, but lets it go. "And to eat? My shout." He studies the fridge with sandwiches and salad boxes. He points at a tuna panini. "Grab me that one, would you?"

I grab the panini and pick up the chicken salad wrap for me, think better of it, and switch it for the ham and cheese sandwich.

We get to the counter, and just as Dad is distracted ordering a 'normal coffee with normal milk', Tyler turns. We lock eyes. He glares at me. His nostrils flare, mouth clamps shut and jaw clenches. I look away before he does, but his stare chisels into me until he turns to make Dad's drink.

I take the tray with my lunch. "I'll find us a table while you wait for your coffee and panini to be heated up."

Dad grunts his agreement.

There's only one table free, right in the middle of the coffee shop. I put the tray down and slide onto a seat. Almost everyone here is from work. I spot Arun and two VIP clients in the corner, having an intense conversation. I look away. I can't risk Dad seeing me looking at them. He'd want to know who they are, and then he'd go over, disrupt their meeting, shake Arun's hand, pat him too hard on the back and thank him for giving me a job, or something similar.

I take off my coat and unwrap Margie's scarf and put them on the back of the chair. Dad arrives with his drink and food and sits too. He doesn't look at my neck or make any comment about the lack of a necklace, so I know he didn't send me that gift.

He takes a sip of his coffee. There's a moment while he

assesses. A smile slowly spreads.

"Decent." He lowers the cup. "So then," he says in his overly loud voice, "why didn't you tell your old man you were moving to Cardiff? Anyone would think you were trying to shake me off." He glares and thumps the table, everything on it jumps. "Can't imagine that you did that on purpose. I expect you forgot, eh? A slip-up in all the excitement of the move, *eh*?"

He leans forward and jabs a finger at me. It connects sharply with the top of my arm.

Panic blasts through my body. Unlike the twins on New Year's Day, he is *not* in an agreeable mood. This is bad. Very bad.

My relationship with my father has been 'mostly estranged' since I was sixteen, although he's oblivious to that. I tried to escape him, thought the move to Cardiff would be the final severance. My father is mostly a nice person. He worked his arse off to provide for us when I was growing up and used to ferry me around everywhere when Mum was doing twelve-hour shifts.

It's his temper that concerns me, has always concerned me.

Because it's not like any normal temper.

My father could be having the most wonderful time, but something – anything, there's no distinguishable trigger that I can tell – will tip him over the edge, and a bomb goes off. He explodes. He will scream, shout, shove tables over, punch things, smash stuff up, threaten others, get into fights, need to be restrained. And then, just as fast as the rage arrives, it disappears quicker than I can click my fingers, and he acts as if the rage never happened, not understanding why everyone around him is shocked, muted, on edge, scared.

He's been like this for as long as I can remember. The rage is random, unpredictable. Since an early age, I've obsessively watched him for a sign that might suggest he's about to detonate – but I've never found one. And it's this not knowing that sends my brain into overdrive. It's why I can't be around him. I can't be myself. I try to be the most amenable person in an attempt to ward off a rage. But I know it's no use. The monster comes out when I'm least expecting it.

My earliest childhood memory, when I still had the little finger on my left hand and my parents were still together, was when we were at our local KFC. I was sitting next to Mum, the twins on the other side of the table next to Dad. He opened the family bucket, saw there were seven bits of chicken instead of eight and flew into an almighty rage. He threw our entire dinner against the window — chips, chicken, milkshakes, baked beans. Then he stood, stomped to the condiment stand and swiped everything that wasn't fastened down onto the floor. He leaped over the counter, stormed into the kitchen area and either smashed up or chucked on the floor everything he could get his hands on. He screamed and yelled. Mum attempted to pacify him but he ignored her. The police were called.

Another time was at my school play. A tall man sat in front of Dad and blocked Dad's view of the stage. Dad went mad and had to be bundled out by a science teacher who was also into bodybuilding. And then there was a road rage incident when we were on holiday in France. A Danish man happened to be towing a caravan that Dad considered too long and too annoying to overtake. The list goes on. He's always narrowly missed prison sentences.

The last thing I need is for Dad's temper to flick on now. He'd smash the shit out of this coffee shop. There's too many chairs and tables to shove over, too much crockery to break, too many packaged sandwiches that could be thrown at the windows.

But this time he's angry at *me*. His rage has never been directed my way before. Yes, he's heavy-handed when he touches me, but he's never been physically violent to me, only ever in front of me. I've never done anything to upset him, until now. What would he do? What is he capable of? An image of him pulling me apart and throwing my limbs at the windows surges across my brain.

Dad has always made me anxious. But now I'm frightened.

I need to handle this situation delicately. Unlike my sisters, Dad is not a lie detector. So, I tell a fib.

"Yes, I was so busy with the move that it completely slipped my mind." I slap my forehead to indicate forgetfulness. "I'm so ridiculously sorry! Stupid, awful daughter. Forgive me, please?"

His eyes narrow and nostrils flare. His hands slowly form fists.

I brace myself. He's about to blow up, rip me into pieces, tear this coffee shop apart...

But he takes a sip of coffee. The danger passes.

I let out a long silent breath through my nose so he doesn't notice and tamp down the adrenalized flight signals telling me to RUN.

"Thank goodness you got my address," I say. "How did you get it?"

He shrugs. "From the twins."

And I know he won't elaborate. My father's relationship with his eldest children is another reason I want to distance myself from him. He is blind to their misbehaviour. In his eyes, they can do no wrong. I realised a long time ago that he should've done more to protect me from the twins when I was a child, especially on the day of my accident. Dad shouldn't have left me with them unsupervised. He was in the other room watching telly while the eleven-year-old twins took seven-year-old me into the kitchen. After, he insisted it was an accident. It was the final straw for Mum, and, later, when I was older and able to process what had happened, I realised he was partly to blame.

He always makes excuses for them. The peanut butter incident was the end for me. The twins won't let me go because they get a kick out of screwing with me and are just waiting for the right moment to hurt their hated little sister again. Dad won't let me go because I'm his offspring and, in his world, blood ties are sacred. I attempted once to tell them I didn't want to see them anymore. They ignored me.

Disappearing from Nottingham was the only thing I could think of. And it failed.

I eat one side of my sandwich very carefully. The last apoplectic episode I witnessed from Dad was when a bit of lettuce fell out of a wrap that Caroline was eating. My mouth is dry, and chewing is difficult. I swig my can of fizzy lemon, but it doesn't make a difference. I swallow with an effort and decide not to eat the second half.

"How's your mother?" Dad asks.

Mum wouldn't want me to say anything about her cancer to Dad. If she wanted him to know then she'd tell him. So I keep it vague. "I speak to her regularly."

"She still with that bastard?"

Dad hates Mum's second husband, even though Mum met Stuart years after she'd left Dad, and Dad has never met him. Dad refers to Stuart as if he stole Mum off him. Dad's still very much in love with Mum and hasn't been with anyone, as far as I know, since.

"Yes," I reply cautiously, bracing for a negative reaction.

He snorts and takes another bite of his panini. "I want you and me to be close. You're my baby girl. I want you to need me."

"Sure, Dad," I reply with a smile.

Anger flashes across his face again. "I should've helped you move. That's what dads do."

"I used a moving company. It was really easy. They did everything. I'm so sorry for not telling you." I apologise again. I'm just going to have to keep saying sorry forever to appease him.

"How's that fella of yours?" He grasps at air,

attempting to remember the name. "Ben."

"Brandon," I say.

"Yeah. Him."

"Brandon and I split up not long ago."

Dad reaches into his pocket and pulls out his phone, presses a few buttons on it and scrolls. This is typical Dad. He says he wants to be close, but doesn't pay any attention whatsoever to what I say. It's as if he's ticking a box in his head marked 'engage with youngest daughter', but there's no genuine interest.

He lifts up his phone, says, "Smile," and takes a photo of me with my mouth full of fizzy pop.

"Oh! I wasn't expecting that," I say.

"Can't a man take a photo of his own flesh and blood now?"

"Yes, of course."

He puts his phone back in his pocket.

"How's Mick Jagger?" I ask, steering us onto safer ground.

Dad smiles fondly, remembering his ancient tortoise. "Still going, the old bugger."

"Are dandelion leaves still his favourite?"

"Yup. Goes mad for them."

We both finish up our food and drinks.

Dad stands. "Need a tinkle."

He heads towards the toilets at the back of the coffee shop.

"Bitch," is hissed behind me.

I turn. Tyler cleans the next table along, staring right at me with a scowl on his face.

Perhaps it's all the stress from being around Dad, but I'm ready to explode. This must be the feeling Dad has before one of his rages. I stand and approach Tyler. He fronts up to me as if I'm about to start a fight and he needs to protect himself.

But I don't explode.

Very calmly I say, "You need to stop dropping off

coffees every morning to my work. I told you to stay away from me."

His face screws up. "You what? I haven't brought in any more coffees for you since last Tuesday when you told me not to. I gave you two, total."

I frown. He's lying.

He continues, "You're the one who has come here to *my* workplace and made up some shite to talk to me. What are you doing? Are you trying to rub it in my face that you're not interested? Or make me ask you out again so you can tell me no? Is this a power thing? You're pathetic."

He stomps off. A second later, Dad comes back. His eyes on his phone. He can't have seen that altercation, or Tyler would've had two black eyes by now.

"We're done here," Dad says and strides towards the exit.

I grab my stuff and follow behind.

Outside, he turns to me and opens his arms for a hug. I embrace him reluctantly and pull away fast. He looks at me. It's no longer the look of parental love that he's given me for thirty-five years. He's mad at me. It's frightening.

"What are your plans for the rest of the day?" I ask.

"Dunno. Bit of sightseeing. Hear there's a castle."

"Yes." I point in the direction of the castle. "It's that way."

He grunts in acknowledgement.

I continue, "Are you staying in Cardiff?"

He shrugs. "Not sure yet. Might go for a few days into the countryside. Bit of a holiday, you know? Meant to be beautiful round here." He puts one of his bear-paw hands around the back of my neck and gives me a shake. All my bones rattle. "Don't you go forgetting about your old pa again, understood?"

"I understand," I reply quickly.

He releases me roughly. "You'll see me when you see me." He doffs an imaginary hat at me and strides off.

I watch him turn a corner out of sight, hurry to a bin and vomit in it. His fury has turned on me. The bomb didn't go off this time, but it's ticking. Panic jangles every one of my nerves. I take a long, deep breath to steady myself and head back into work.

I go straight to the reception desk. There's a bored-looking man I don't recognise behind the counter.

"Hi, is the usual receptionist here? Tracey, I think her name is."

His face brightens. "Hi. No, sorry. Tracey had to head home earlier. She's got the flu. I'm from the agency and am covering while she's away. She's not likely to be back this week. Can I help with anything?" he asks hopefully.

I debate momentarily whether to ask if there's CCTV footage of the reception area and whether I can review the past few mornings to see Tyler drop off coffee, but I don't. It feels a bit over the top. And what would I do with the footage – go and show it to Tyler to prove that he was lying? No, I'm better than that. He's the arsehole.

I thank the temp and head to my desk.

"Rachel, can I have a word? In my office," Kelvin says at around half five.

But it doesn't really register, and I continue to stare at my monitor. I've been distracted all afternoon – panicking about what Dad might do to me the next time he shows up, and stewing over Tyler's lie about not dropping off all those coffees so he could make out that *I* was hassling *him*.

"Rachel!"

Kelvin's voice cuts through loud and clear this time.

I jolt, grab up my notebook and pen like a shield and sword and follow him back to his office. Why does he want to chat to me in private? What is going to happen in his office that he can't say – or do – in front of other people? I watch his back suspiciously all down the corridor to his office at the end.

If I screamed from within his office, would anyone

hear me? I shake off that thought. I need to focus and remain professional.

In his tiny office, we squeeze around each other. He shuts the door, makes his way to his chair, and sits. He gestures for me to sit too.

I do. He turns his monitor so we can both see it.

"This is the weekly planning data you send every Tuesday, right?"

"Yes."

I emailed it about half an hour ago to Arun and Kelvin, copying in the entire team.

He taps at a figure on the spreadsheet. "Notice anything wrong here?"

I see it immediately, and my hand goes to my mouth.

"Yep," he says smugly.

He leans back in his chair and puts his hands behind his head with his elbows up like he's just solved a mystery and is deeply satisfied with his detective work.

I've made the most basic of errors with the formula in the spreadsheet; it's not showing a figure but a load of random symbols indicating a mistake. It's the kind of thing a junior colleague might do on a planning spreadsheet. Ridiculously embarrassing for someone at my level.

Kelvin smirks. "You'd better go fix that pronto."

"Thank you," I say and stand up.

"You owe me a favour now."

I stare at him. He's truly repulsive. This is not how a boss should act. I don't want to be indebted to him. What favour is he going to ask of me?

He winks at me. I grimace at the sleaziness and sprint from his office to fix the spreadsheet and resend it to everyone before anyone else can notice.

I can't believe I made that mistake. My mind is unravelling fast. I'm worried what it might do next.

CHAPTER 19

Rain hammers on my hood. It's a miserable evening. The bus stop is packed, and there are too many people crammed under the row of shelters. There's no room for me, so I stand in the rain just next to the shelter that my bus stops at. It's too windy for umbrellas. I hunker down into my coat. Only my eyes are on show. My beanie is pulled down to my eyebrows, my hood is up and tightly cinched, and my scarf is wrapped around my neck twice, covering my nose.

Everyone around me is the same: bundled up in winter coats, braced against the elements. Usually, I recognise one or two fellow commuters on their way home from work. But not today, we're all strangers here.

And competitors.

I'm standing too close to the kerb. Busy traffic trundles past. Thankfully, there are no puddles collecting in the road so I'm not being splashed by vehicles travelling too near to the pavement. But I'm closer to the road than I'd like to be. I'd move back, but there isn't any kind of queue due to the rain. Everyone wants to get on the next bus, and we all huddle under the shelter and next to it. I'm sticking to my spot like glue. I can't give way and let anyone else in front of me, otherwise I won't get on the bus.

The atmosphere is tense.

Everyone knows there are too many people waiting.

Everyone knows that as soon as the bus pulls up, they need to be quick to secure a position close to the doors and jump on as soon as they open, otherwise it's another twenty-minute wait until the next one.

I just want to get home, wash the day off with a hot shower and celebrate what's left of my birthday. I'm right by the road, feet planted, elbows out, not allowing the crush of people to edge me into the path of traffic or further away from where the bus pulls in. I yank my work laptop bag higher up on my shoulder, thankful it's waterproof so my work laptop isn't getting soaked.

A bus turns into the road; I strain to see the number on it. The crowd bristles, all eyes focused on the bus. But it's not ours. It's one that stops at the next bus stop along, a few metres up the road. It hurtles towards us, towards me. I brace myself for the inevitable gust of air as it passes.

Strong hands grip my shoulders. A queue-jumper trying to get past. I refuse to give up my position, twisting from side to side to shake them off.

But the hands shove.

I tip forward into the path of the oncoming bus. I hang suspended, staring at the headlights of the double-decker. My feet are planted, and the hands still grip my shoulders.

The bus honks. I'm seconds away from getting splattered across the windscreen and crushed under wheels. My vision swims.

I'm yanked back. The bus zooms past. The displaced air makes my eyes sting.

Before I can catch my breath or scream, the hands leave my shoulders and reach around my neck. They squeeze, tighter and tighter. My hands grab, wrench, fight against this grip strangling me.

The pressure eases, and I'm spun around.

It's him.

He's grinning.

I suck down great wads of cold air. "What the fuck, Brandon! I thought I was about to die!"

"Whoa. Chill. Just trying to be funny."

My ex-boyfriend, all six feet one of him, stands in front of me. I haven't seen him since the day before New Year's Eve. He's got an athletic build and has a ridiculously strong grip due to his passion for rock climbing. His wide, charming smile is plastered across his face. It's a smile that everyone falls immediately in love with. But it's not endearing today. It's infuriating.

He continues, "I can't see, but I could *feel* that you're not wearing your birthday jewellery."

I glower at him, angry that he thought it would be funny to make me think I was about to get run over or strangled.

He cocks his head to one side. "I sent you a necklace today. Did you get it?"

"Yes, I got it. A diamond choker."

"Definitely *not* diamonds. Did you get my other gifts – the teddy, roses, poetry?"

"I did."

"I want you back, Rach. I'm deadly serious."

The crowd bristles once again, presses closer together. I glance up the road. Our bus is on the way.

"My bus is coming," I reply.

"Ooh, I like that you're playing hard to get. It's like you're a whole new girl I'm chasing and not the boring Rachel you'd become."

I frown.

He keeps going. "I've booked us a weekend away this weekend in a remote house in the countryside. Just the two of us and the hills. I'll pick you up from work on Friday, and we'll head straight there, okay?"

"Piss off, Brandon."

A flash of anger crosses his countenance but almost immediately mellows.

"So you're mean now, too? I like it. I can also be mean, you know." He waggles an eyebrow at me.

My bus pulls in, and the crowd surges forward.

"I need to get on this bus. Get out of my way." I barge past Brandon.

From behind, he says in my ear, "You'll be mine again soon, Rachel. Don't you worry."

I'm swept away from him by everyone eager to get on the bus. The flow moves fast, and I step on and make my way through to the back of the downstairs, the upstairs already full. It's standing room only, and I grab hold of a handrail.

I was lucky to get on. There's still a large crowd of people waiting on the pavement. But the doors close.

As the driver pulls away, I see Brandon next to the shelter, arms folded. People dart and swerve around him. He's staring straight at me. He has a smirk on his face that I've never seen before.

I jump off at my stop and attempt to ignore the SUV with a massive bow around it still parked outside my flat. But the new, bright-yellow packet stuck to the windscreen catches my eye. There's no chance I'm dealing with a parking ticket this evening so it can stay right there.

Hesitantly, I head inside. Relief sweeps me up when neither my father nor the twins, or even worse – all three – are waiting for me for a family birthday 'treat'. But panic soon replaces the sweet relief: the next encounter is coming. They won't leave me alone now that they have my address.

It takes all my strength to block that thought along with the reeking damp smell. I shower quickly, dress in the outfit and spritz on the perfume that Margie kindly got for me and drive to theirs, parking in their spare allocated space.

Margie insisted we do something for my birthday. I was pleased. I love celebrating my birthday. But it's a rubbish date. Everyone is either too broke or all partied out or both after Christmas and New Year to do something on the seventeenth of January. And this year, it's on a

THE NEW GIRL

Tuesday, which sucks, but I have no one else in Cardiff and enjoy their company, so I suggested a quiet dinner, and Margie said she'd host.

I knock on the Maddens' front door.

Mark opens the door, dressed in his usual impeccable smart-casual attire. He beckons me in, closes the door behind me and hands me a glass of champagne.

"Happy birthday!" He kisses me on the cheek. "Now, I know you're driving because you've got work tomorrow, so we thought we'd have one glass of champagne, and then I've got in some non-alcoholic beers for after. Margie's ordered a curry from – in our opinion – the best curry joint in town."

He picks up his own glass of champagne from the side table in the hallway and clinks his glass to mine. We both take a sip.

It's delicious, but tastes slightly strange. I can't really tell. I don't drink champagne that often, so am no connoisseur. But I know the Maddens will be drinking the finest brand.

Mark leads me through to the lounge. Margie stands and clinks her flute to mine, and I take another sip.

"Happy birthday," she echoes her husband and gives me a hug. "I love, love, love that outfit on you!"

"Thank you. Ditto," I say and gesture at her red, sparkly, flared jumpsuit like something out of a disco music video from the seventies.

She twirls, giggles and swigs half of her champagne in one go, and I guess this isn't her first glass. She's giddier than usual. Come to think of it, Mark is also in high spirits. How sweet of them to get so excited for my birthday, to make such a fuss of me.

"We thought we'd make the effort on this *special* day. Takeaway should be here any minute. Let's take some photos! Well, that's if you don't mind?"

"Not at all."

She claps her hands. "Outside! With the bay in the

background!"

Margie ushers us through the door. The rain has stopped, but the terrace is still wet and slippery.

"Mark, darling, would you get the champers? I need a top up!"

"Will do." Mark heads inside to get the bottle out of the fridge.

"I've forgotten my earrings! Give me two secs." Margie dashes back into the flat and scoops her earrings off the coffee table and puts them in.

Left alone on the terrace, I drink my champagne and walk to the railing to look out at the view. I feel woozy already, the champagne going straight to my head. Unsurprising. I've barely eaten today. Half a sandwich at lunch, and that's it.

I grip the railing with the hand not holding my flute. It's a long way down to the car park below. The ground lurches up, and my perfume intensifies.

Am I falling?

Margie's arm around my shoulders brings me back to myself. It's her perfume I can smell. We're wearing the same stuff.

She steers me away from the edge and turns me around, giving Mark her phone so he can take a few photos of the two of us – standing, sitting, hugging. Margie insists we do some silly poses, and I go with it, laughing. Mark joins in, and we take selfies of the three of us. Margie snaps some of me and Mark, and then I use her phone to get a few of the two of them. Margie records a couple of videos.

I finish my champagne. Mark tops up his and Margie's glasses from the bottle. Fat raindrops splash on our faces, and we hurry inside.

"Do you fancy a non-alc beer?" Mark asks me, reaching into the fridge and pulling out a bottle, studying the label closely. "Apparently these are the best, according to the chap at the off-licence, anyway."

"Yes, please," I say.

My balance spins out of control so I plonk myself down on the lips sofa.

There's a firm rapping on the front door. Each thud bounces around my head and echoes endlessly.

"That's the curry. I'll go," Margie says, but her voice sounds very far away.

I'm drunk after one glass of champagne. But I'm not going to fight it, I'm going to roll with it. Especially after the shit day I've had. The zero per cent beer and some food will soon sober me up. I might as well enjoy this brief tipsy moment.

CHAPTER 20

I come to with a cracking pain in my forehead. I'm disorientated. Nauseous.

Where am I? What happened to me?

I check in with all my senses. I'm in bed, yes. But what bed? I blink a few times for my eyes to adjust to the gloom. Then I get a whiff of damp, of sodden wooden floorboards that haven't dried out quick enough. My fleece duvet cover rests under my palms. It's my bed, in my bedroom, in my Cardiff flat.

But I'm on the wrong side. That must be why something feels so off.

A snore that ends in a little snort turns my blood to ice.

I'm not alone. And I'm naked.

There's someone lying beside me.

My phone alarm screeches, piercing my foggy head like an arrow. Without thinking, I reach out to grab my phone, but my hand hits the wall. The nightstand is on the other side. I haul myself up to a sitting position and scan the room to pinpoint the location of my phone.

A groan comes from the person in my bed. A man, very definitely.

Did I do something stupid last night and call Brandon? Or – *shit* – Tyler? Who else could this be? I've never had a one-night stand before. It is simply not my thing.

Keeping a bit of the duvet covering me, I hang over the edge of the bed and find my handbag. My clothes and underwear are strewn everywhere. His clothes and underwear are tangled up with mine.

Fuck.

He sits up. Rubs his head and hair.

"Morning," he says groggily.

I stare. Gulp.

Oh fuck, oh fuck.

I have absolutely no idea who this man is. I've never seen him before in my life.

I yank my phone out of my handbag and switch off my alarm, then tap out a message to Margie.

WTF happened last night? There's a man in my bed!

In my brain, a teeming cluster of spiders crawl through all my memories of last night, but come back blank. The last thing I remember is having a glass of champagne at the Maddens' apartment and sitting on their sofa.

I don't know his name. Did we have sex? I have no idea. The swirling in my belly explodes – if we did, then did I consent? What the hell happened in this bed? My body knows but my mind doesn't. It's an unsettling disconnect. I have an overwhelming urge to rip off the bedsheets and throw them in a pile in the garden and set them alight. But I don't move. I'm frozen with that morning-after-a-very-drunken-night lethargy.

"I think you should leave," I say.

"Yep," he says.

And with a vigour I definitely don't have, he jumps out of bed, throws on his boxers, clothes, coat and beanie hat, puts his wallet and phone from the bedside cabinet into his jeans pocket and says, "I'll let myself out."

I nod.

He hurries out the bedroom, and the front door opens and closes.

My phone lights up with a message from Margie.

Wild night! You decided to have some more champers and

> insisted on going to JJs after curry. We had far too many cocktails. You pulled a guy! We had the best time!

JJs is the Cardiff Bay bar we went to with Pete, just down the road from the Maddens'. I don't remember any of it.

My phone dings. A slew of photos come through from Margie. All from JJs: me on my own holding up a cocktail, me with Margie, me with Mark, a selfie of the three of us, me with my arm around the random guy who just vacated my flat, the four of us looking like we're on the best double date ever. I put my phone down. All of last night is a blank.

Wild night, indeed. And I think I'm still drunk. The last time I got sozzled on a weeknight was when I was a student. This is completely out of character for me. This behaviour is, well, alarming.

I'm on the contraceptive pill but should I organise a sexual health check? That stranger could've shagged half of Cardiff for all I know. Yes, it's probably wise. There's perhaps a drop-in clinic I can go to in Cardiff. I'll check later because, right now, I need to put aside last night and get ready for work. I have a busy day today. And it's starting at 8 a.m. rather than 9 a.m., so I need to get a wriggle on. I wanted to have a clear head, to be focused, to be on top form today – but I'm not sure that's going to happen now. I peel myself off the mattress and head to the bathroom.

After a hurried shower, I scrape back my unwashed hair into a ponytail, dab blusher on my pallid cheeks and smear concealer under my eyes to hide the dark circles. My eyes squint, apparently unable to open properly, and I make a mess of my mascara. But no time to fix it right now.

I'm running well behind schedule.

I chuck on some clothes, gather up my things and head into the hallway to pick up my work laptop and car keys. Neither of which are there.

I rummage in my handbag and find my car keys. But I remember my car isn't parked outside. It's still at the Maddens'. There's no way I drove it home last night; if I had, then I would've woken up in a police cell, arrested for driving under the influence, and not in my bed.

But my work laptop I'm certain I left by the door when I got in from work.

I quickly scour the apartment but can't find it.

My stomach sinks. Did that random guy pinch it on his way out?

I should call the police and report it missing. And also inform my IT department. There's a whole protocol to follow when you lose work phones and laptops. My hungover brain aches with it all. And I don't know for certain that it's been stolen. It's not where I put it, and I can't find it – just like my Kindle, which showed up eventually.

Urgh. I can't decide what to do…

I'll deal with it later, when I have more time to look properly. I'm extremely behind now. I book a taxi. I message Pete to apologise profusely that I'm going to be late. I'm mortified. It's unprofessional and not like me at all.

We have a packed day visiting various railway track maintenance sites. I'm meeting him at the Cardiff station depot to collect a work pick-up truck because some of the sites are off-road or down rarely used tracks in remote countryside, and work prefers we use work vehicles in case private cars get damaged. I'm doing the driving. Pete is coming with me this time to help direct me to some of the harder-to-find sites, but, going forwards, I'll do these kinds of visits on my own.

I hope Pete has brought his laptop. I emailed him yesterday with the itinerary and all the addresses. I'll have to take notes on my phone. Not ideal, but better than nothing.

The taxi finally arrives, but we get stuck in traffic. On

the plus side, I use the time to clean up my mascara and to book an appointment for next week at a sexual health clinic. But on the downside, I get to the depot almost an hour late.

Pete waits by the depot's large metal gates, his laptop bag over his shoulder. His car is parked in a visitor's spot outside the gates. There's nobody else around. The depot is next to the rail tracks and is mostly used to store company vehicles. There's only a handful of people who work here.

I stumble out of the taxi, zigzag over to him, unsteady on my feet like I'm still drunk.

"You look hanging," Pete says as I near him. "Big birthday night out, was it?"

Blood rushes to burn my cheeks. It's not good Pete seeing his boss like this. What kind of impression must I be giving?

I feel the need to explain. "I'm never usually late. I'm always early. Just a rotten morning one way or another."

He shrugs, looks at his shoes, looks everywhere but at me. Shifty. He gestures towards the gates.

"Shall we? We're going to be very late for the first appointment."

From a lone man in a portacabin, I sign out the heavily branded pick-up and get the keys. We find the vehicle, jump in, and I start the engine. There are quite a few differences to my little car: the indicators are on the other side, reverse is on the left of the gearstick instead of on the right, and the dashboard has additional gadgets fitted, which monitor speed and journey duration and bleep sporadically. It's also much, much bigger than my Yaris. This wouldn't faze me normally, but I'm still queasy, flustered. Hungover.

Pete texts on his phone. He's barely looked up from it and barely said more than two words to me. I explained earlier about not having my laptop, so he logs on to his, opens the itinerary and shows the screen to me. I put the address of the first site we're visiting into the built-in sat nav in the dashboard. I wonder briefly if it was Mark's company who designed and made the on-board computer.

I grind the gears, stall the engine, find reverse, and, eventually, we leave the depot. I pull onto a busy road. A car swerves out of a side road right in front of me and immediately brakes. I slam on the brakes too, but my reaction is slower than usual.

Pete and I jerk forward. The edge of my seat belt digs into my neck. I brace myself to hit the car in front.

But the pick-up doesn't connect, stopping millimetres away. We lurch back.

The van behind me honks angrily.

My heart pounds. I've never had a crash, not even a little ding. I've never had points for speeding or ever been pulled over by the police. I'm usually a very careful and patient driver.

"Bloody hell!" Pete shouts. "You nearly went in the back of them! Are you still drunk?"

The car in front speeds away. But I'm shaking so much I can't function quick enough to get moving. Impatient drivers stuck behind me blare their horns.

Pete is immediately back on his mobile, frantically tapping out a message.

I finally get the pick-up started, and we pull away, but my hands are clammy on the steering wheel, and sweat streams under my armpits. I really don't think I should be driving. I can't ask Pete to drive because the vehicle is signed out under my name, so he's not permitted to. I drive slowly and carefully and am thankful we're in slow-moving traffic so I can familiarise myself with this vehicle and not have any more near misses.

My phone rings, and I jump. "Do you mind seeing who that is?"

Pete picks my phone up from the tray behind the handbrake.

"It's Kelvin," he says. "You want me to answer it?"

I saved Kelvin's number in my phone when I first started at work, as I did with all my team's numbers. He's never rung me before, and I've never called him.

"Yes, please."

Pete answers, there are a few words exchanged, and he hangs up. "Kelvin says we need to go back to the office immediately."

"What? Why? He knows we're on visits all day."

"I don't know. He didn't say," Pete replies.

He shifts in the passenger seat and clears his throat. He's acting… guilty.

He continues, "I can direct us from here. Take the next left."

CHAPTER 21

"Rachel, please can you come with me." Yvonne from HR stands next to my desk waiting for me.

Kelvin has shifted my chair to one side and perches against the desk. His bum touches my keyboard, which fills me with disgust and doesn't do my nausea any favours.

I blink at her.

She continues, "And please can you hand the keys to the work vehicle to Kelvin."

He eyes me smugly as I drop the keys in his palm. Yvonne ushers me towards the corridor, a concerned look on her face.

Kelvin stands to follow us and gestures to Pete. "Cancel all the visits for today."

Pete nods, sits, and sets up his laptop.

Yvonne pushes the elevator button, and the three of us wait for its arrival. Kelvin can't wipe the glee from his face.

"What's all this about?" I ask.

But the sinking feeling in the pit of my stomach tells me it's not good.

"Let's wait until we're in my office," Yvonne replies.

The lift doors open, and we shuffle in, finding space between the three people already in there.

We go up three floors and make our way to Yvonne's office in silence. Kelvin gawps at the size of it, with ample room for desk, sofa, printer, and large cabinet. It also has two windows. Yvonne motions for me to sit – on a comfy-looking chair, not like Kelvin's plastic garden chair.

"Kelvin, please wait outside," Yvonne says briskly.

He huffs but goes out, deliberately leaving the door open to eavesdrop.

"And shut the door," Yvonne adds.

The door closes. Yvonne sits behind her desk.

"Rachel, as per your contract, we are permitted to do immediate response urine tests if we have any reason to believe an employee may be under the influence. We would like to do one now, if you are in agreement. Please note, if you do not agree, this can lead to your employment being terminated."

"It's fine. I'll do it."

I just have to hope all the booze from last night has made its way out of my system. If I refuse, I'll get fired. I'm still on my probation period, and it's an immediate dismissal.

Yvonne retrieves a test from her cabinet, talks through all the official stuff, and leads me past a lurking Kelvin to a designated toilet. She takes the test out of the packaging and hands it to me. I head into a cubicle, and she positions herself outside.

"Sorry, I have to stand here to ensure the test isn't tampered with," she explains.

I lock the cubicle door and do what I need to do. When I come out, Yvonne has donned plastic gloves and takes my urine sample from me, heads to the sink and uses a pipette to take a small amount of my sample and drop it onto a small plastic test strip.

Satisfied she's done what is required for the test, she bins the sample and her gloves.

"This won't take long. Let's head back to my office."

Kelvin still loiters outside her door. He looks hopefully at Yvonne, but she ignores him and follows me into her office, closing the door in his face.

She sits at her desk and points to the water dispenser in the corner. "Help yourself."

I stand, fill a paper cup, and take a sip. It tastes plasticky and makes me gag. I politely leave the cup next to the dispenser and sit back down on the chair in front of Yvonne's desk.

She studies the test strip. "This is showing alcohol and other substances in your system."

My world turns inside out. Other substances? What does that mean? Did I take drugs last night? I've never taken drugs before. I've never even smoked a cigarette. But is that why I can't remember? Was it with that guy? Did I do it willingly? Did my drink get spiked at that bar? Was it the Maddens? I shake my head at that ridiculous thought – of course my friends wouldn't do that.

Yvonne continues, "As per your contract, it is not permitted to be drunk or on illegal drugs at work. And because you're on probation, this is an instant dismissal. I'm sorry, Rachel."

I'm too numb to reply.

Yvonne looks sad. She was the first person to interview me when I applied for this job. We'd got on so well. She said she was confident that I was a great candidate. How disappointed she must be.

She stands, gestures for me to do the same. We walk to the door, and she opens it. Kelvin almost falls through. She glares at him as he clears his throat and steps aside.

"Well?" he asks eagerly.

"I'm going to find Arun," Yvonne says. "Rachel, please gather your belongings from your desk. We'll be there shortly."

She strides off down the corridor to find my big boss. In silence, Kelvin ushers me to the lift and back to our floor. He walks and stands a step behind me, like a prison guard escorting an inmate.

I get to my desk and open drawers. I haven't been here long enough to fill them with many personal belongings. A few granola bars, my headphones and Brandon's awful necklace go into my bag, which I fling over my shoulder.

"What's going on?" Pete asks me.

"Rachel's been fired!" Kelvin bursts out, too loudly, too happily, completely unprofessionally. "She failed a urine test. She's been on the piss and come into work still drunk. She almost crashed a work vehicle this morning!"

The team freeze and stare at me and at Kelvin. Pete's mouth hangs open, shocked. Arun and Yvonne arrive and stand behind Kelvin, but he doesn't notice.

He continues, "A concerned member of the public called in anonymously to complain about Rachel's driving. She almost caused an accident!"

Anonymous caller, my arse! I look at Pete. He looks away.

Arun clears his throat and shoots a furious look at Kelvin. Yvonne purses her lips. All this should've been done privately and definitely not in front of the team. It's a confidential matter. Kelvin quietens down with a self-satisfied smirk.

"I'll take your work laptop. You won't be needing that anymore," Kelvin blurts, not able to contain himself from humiliating me even with his boss and HR present.

"I've not got it with me. It was potentially stolen this morning," I reply.

"Stolen! Did you report that to the police? To the IT department? You certainly didn't report that to me, as per guidelines!"

I shake my head, no. I'm not sure this morning can get any worse.

But Kelvin continues, "Another firing offence! A huge breach of security. You really were a disastrous hire!"

"Enough, Kelvin," Yvonne says.

"Can the four of us go somewhere private, please?" I ask, keeping my cool, attempting to remain professional in the face of Kelvin's highly unprofessional behaviour.

Yvonne nods curtly and leads us to a small meeting room. Once we're in, she closes the door. We remain standing. Kelvin beams and fidgets like an excited child on Christmas morning.

"I'm going to head home now," I say. "I will search again for my work laptop and send you, Yvonne, an email once I know what the situation is, and then you can inform me of the appropriate action to take."

She nods.

I continue, "However, Arun, Yvonne, before I go, I want to bring something urgent to your attention that I was closely monitoring. But now I'm no longer employed, it will need to be investigated further. Kelvin has been acting inappropriately towards Kalisha Jenkins on the team. I'm not aware of the full extent of this, however Kalisha is very uncomfortable in Kelvin's presence, even taking time off sick to avoid one-to-one meetings with him. She deserves to feel safe in the workplace, and I don't believe that is currently happening."

Arun's eyes widen. A deep frown creases Yvonne's forehead. She glares at Kelvin.

Kelvin is livid. He clenches his fists and takes a menacing step towards me. His entire body language screams: *I want you dead, Rachel, and I'm the one who's going to do it.*

"Kelvin," Arun warns.

It's enough. Kelvin's raging bull doesn't charge. Instead of twisting my head off my body, which he so clearly wants to do, he raises a finger and jabs it at me, not quite connecting with my collarbone.

"Don't come to me for a reference. I'll be sure to let my network know not to employ you. You'll never get a job in this industry again."

"Kelvin!" Arun shouts.

"I'll be heading off now," I say, still calm.

Ignoring Kelvin, I nod briefly to Arun and Yvonne and leave the room.

"This isn't over," Kelvin hisses at my back.

I hurry to the stairs, fly down them, through the lobby and out onto the street. My emotions are just about to break and crash when I hear my name.

Pete runs up to me.

Even though he's the last person I want to see, I need to say something to him.

"Pete, I'm so, so sorry. I shouldn't have been driving earlier. I woke up still feeling drunk and should've called in sick or asked if you could drive, no matter if it looked unprofessional. I shouldn't have put you in danger. I've been making some terrible decisions recently and really not acting like myself."

He waves his hand at me. "That's okay, don't worry. I need to tell you about the Maddens."

"What?"

He moves closer and glances to either side like he's about to impart some juicy gossip that he's not meant to be sharing.

"I've been doing some digging. There are more rumours about them. You know I told you they pick up new friends, use them for a while and then ditch them. Well, about a year ago, they were friends with this young woman, Carrie, and then she suddenly just disappeared, and no one has seen her in Cardiff again."

He rubs his hands together in obvious pleasure at this gossip-mongering. I have zero patience for people who enjoy talking about other people's private lives and spread scandalous tittle-tattle for fun.

All my pent-up emotions burst forth. "Stop with the Madden-bashing! You got what you wanted. What Kelvin wanted. I know you were the anonymous caller, okay? You texted Kelvin after my near miss this morning to suggest the urine test. A while ago, I overheard you two talking in his office. You want my job. Kelvin wants you to have it so he can continue coasting. You've got rid of me. You won. So, please, keep my friends out of this."

He gawps at me, blinks a few times. Perhaps he thought talking about the Maddens would distract me from what just happened. Perhaps he had no idea whatsoever that I was onto him and knew about his and

Kelvin's little plan.

Finally, he replies, "I was texting my mum this morning about clearing out my great aunt's flat now that she's in a rest home..."

He trails off unconvincingly.

I hold up a hand. "The lies can stop now. This is my bus. Good luck with everything."

I jog towards the bus stop, flag down the bus, hop on and take a seat.

And then, I cry.

CHAPTER 22

Something in my brain snaps. I've been in a waking trance for hours, eyes open and sitting on the sofa.

Slowly, my senses come back online. Dry mouth. Rank taste. Stomach complaining after no breakfast and demanding lunch. Outside noises dial up again: traffic, birds, people talking. And the damp odour invades my nostrils.

I got home from work earlier and sat on the sofa, stunned. Fired. Jobless. Never in a million years would I have thought that would happen. I'm always so conscientious at work, always want to do my best. But today I did my worst, and now I'm unemployed. It still hasn't quite sunk in. It's taken my brain hours to process. And in that time, I haven't moved. I blink and roll my stiff shoulders.

My left hand clutches my post, which I don't remember picking up from the hallway on the way in, and I see a letter for the previous resident, a pizza takeaway flyer and a handwritten envelope with just my name and flat number on it, no stamp.

I drop the flyer and letter on the floor and open the envelope addressed to me. It's a printed letter from my landlord. In normal circumstances he'd give me a month's notice to move out, but as per the contract that I signed, he's giving me ten days' notice to vacate the property in order to do emergency repairs following the leak and flooded kitchen.

My brain threatens to shut down again. My life has been upended on the floor and is getting stomped on. Soon I'll have nowhere to live. Jobless and now homeless. My chest constricts so tight that I pant to take in air. My cheeks flush, and I realise I'm still in my heavy winter coat and boots.

I stand, pull off my coat as I walk to the hallway and hang the coat on the hooks by the front door. As I kick off my boots, I see my work laptop bag propped against the wall near the front door – exactly where I left it, and exactly where it wasn't this morning. I open the bag frantically and confirm the work laptop is inside with nothing missing. I don't know why I couldn't find this earlier. It must've been there all along and I just didn't see it.

I'm going mad. It's happened – my mind has fallen apart.

Dizziness sweeps through me. I fall against the wall and hold onto it to stay upright. The unsteadiness on my feet is replaced with an overwhelming exhaustion. A nap. That's what I need. The blissful ignorance of sleep for a couple of hours, and then I'll feel able to deal with all this. I open the door to my bedroom and am hit with a smell of bodies and sweat and a scene of tangled bedsheets and clothes flung on the floor. I usually make my bed every morning, keep my space tidy. But the disarray is like a slap in the face.

What happened in this room? Was I force-fed drugs? Was I raped? Or did I willingly take the illegal substances that showed up in my urine test and consent wholeheartedly to sex with a stranger? Both things I've never done before and would never consider doing if I was in my right mind. But that's the problem, isn't it – I'm not in my right mind. A dark, slimy sensation brews in the pit of my gut. I close the door and head back to the sofa.

I should call the police. But I don't remember a thing. I

don't know if something bad happened or not. I couldn't tell them the name of the man or anything about him. I've got photos of him on my phone that Margie took – could the police identify him from them? But the photos look like we're having the best time. I'm not in any pain or bruised, and there's no used condoms or anything else anywhere, from what I can tell. I decide to leave it. I have no evidence. Just a bad feeling.

I was hoping bits of last night would come back to me during the course of the day. But they haven't. It's a big black hole. The last thing I remember is eating curry. No. I don't actually remember eating it, just talking about eating it.

My stomach grumbles loudly. I head into the kitchen and eat some buttered toast standing up. I immediately feel a little better. I need to make the most of this situation. I have some savings that will tide me over for a little while. I can put my stuff into storage and go to New Zealand to see Mum next week and not have to wait until March.

Yes. Silver linings and all that. I always feel better when I'm taking action. I grab my phone and, pushing down the fear of flying that raises its ugly head, cancel the March flight. I can't let that phobia overwhelm me right now. I look for flights leaving next week, to give myself a few days to pack up the flat. I find one for next Thursday. Perfect.

I click to book it and put in all my details. Unlike the last flight I booked, this airline asks for my passport number. My passport is in a drawer in my bedside cabinet. I jump up and head to my bedroom but pause on the threshold. The dark, slimy sensation comes over me again. Lost memories haunt the room. I take a deep breath, attempt to squash the feeling, and head in. I search around in the drawer. No passport.

Not this again.

That is where I *always* keep it, along with some other important paperwork and documents.

I use my hand to feel for the passport, not trusting my eyes. I tip everything out of the drawer onto the messy bed and sift through it all. It's not there.

A frustrated yell bursts from my mouth.

I know I put it there the last time I had it. A little voice tells me to look around the flat for it, but that's pointless. I always replace it in this drawer. Always.

I smack my forehead. I need to think. To problem-solve.

Back on the sofa, out of my awful bedroom, I bring up the government website all about passports on my phone. I'll just get a new one. Report the old one as lost. I can use a fast-track service for a large fee. I have to get to London though, a two-hour train journey from Cardiff. That's fine, I can manage that. I book an appointment for Monday afternoon.

And feel better.

I have a purpose. I have things to do now. Pack. Find a storage facility. Sell my car?

It's only half three in the afternoon but it's already getting dark. I switch on the light and go to close the lounge curtains.

The first thing I see is a traffic warden hovering around Dad's gifted car and placing another yellow ticket bag on the windscreen next to the others. The second thing I see is someone across the road staring right at me, right into my flat.

When our eyes meet, they scarper down the lane between two large houses opposite. A hooded figure dressed in black.

Someone's out there watching me. Watching my flat. Wait. Is my imagination playing tricks on me again? No, I'm certain I saw them.

I whip the curtains closed. A pain in the centre of my chest forces me to bend over, to catch my breath, to avoid fainting.

Kelvin's furious face from earlier flashes behind my

eyes. He wanted me dead. I shiver uncontrollably, my fleeting feeling of being more in control from moments earlier is squished like a gnat and replaced with sheer panic. I grab my phone and call Margie.

The Maddens are my only friends now in Cardiff. I have no one else to call. Mum is so far away and has her own things to deal with. Heather has no time for me right now. And Pete is no longer a friend.

Margie answers with a cheery, "Hello! How's the head now?"

I sob into the phone, attempt to tell Margie what has happened with work, with the flat, with the person outside, with the lost passport, but I ramble, blub, choke on my own tears.

"Rachel, you're distraught! I'm seriously worried about you. Come round here, immediately. Your car is still here so I'll send Mark to come and get you. I had to do hair of the dog to feel better so can't drive... Do you hear me? Mark is on his way, okay? I don't think you should be alone right now."

"I don't want to be alone right now," I sob. I want my mother. But she's on the other side of the world. "I'm in a bit of a state."

I hear Margie shout, "Mark! Rachel needs picking up, right now. Yes, *now*!" There are a few muffled words I can't hear, and she comes back on the phone. "He'll be twenty minutes."

"Thank you so much," I reply and that heady feeling from the fish restaurant of being cared for by wonderful parents comes back to me like a soothing balm.

"I'll stay on the phone until he arrives, okay?"

"Thank you, but I'll be okay. I'm going to hang up and pack a few things. And get changed out of my work clothes."

"Sure. Message me the moment you get in the car, okay? I'll go and make up your bedroom."

We say goodbye, and I wipe my eyes. I head back into

my bedroom, find my overnight suitcase and throw in a few things including a change of clothes for tomorrow, some toiletries and my fleece pyjamas, which I always find comforting to wear. I get changed, chucking my work outfit on top of the pile of clothes already on the floor from my birthday night out.

A few moments later, I leave my flat, closing Ralph's door on the way out. I'm not entirely sure how much time has passed, but I'll wait for Mark outside. I don't want to be in my flat anymore. It's not even *my* flat now. Just a place I lived in briefly and now need to leave in ten days' time.

Downstairs, I open the main front door. But my way is blocked. By a hooded figure dressed in black. Their back is turned to me. It's a man. It's who was watching me earlier, I'm certain.

All the breath leaves my lungs.

The man spins around.

"Brandon? What are you doing here?"

Brandon's entire appearance is unkempt. Usually meticulously clean-shaven, today he has stubble. Over his hoodie he wears a long black trench coat that I've never seen before and which is definitely not his usual style. It's tatty and ill-fitting, as if he's bought it from a second-hand clothes shop. It hangs off him unfastened. Big purple puffy bags sit heavy under his tired eyes.

"Oh!" he says, surprised to see me. "I thought you'd be at work."

I frown.

He quickly adds, "You know you said you threw out my things, well I thought I'd come and see if they were still here…"

My frown deepens. "That was ages ago."

He shifts from foot to foot. Eyes darting everywhere. He rambles, "I left my favourite pair of boxers at yours… It was just on the off-chance that your bins hadn't been emptied… I was going to see if they were still there…"

I glare at him. He shouldn't be here. He knows it. He squirms under the weight of my obvious suspicion.

But a flick switches.

His eyes narrow. His body straightens and tenses. A dark look comes over his face that I've never seen before. No. I have seen it. But not on Brandon's face. On Kelvin's.

Brandon leans forward, hands up, about to shove me back into the hallway of my building.

A car horn blares.

"Rachel," a man's voice shouts.

Whatever Brandon had planned shifts in an instant. His hands drop, and he turns to see who shouted.

"Mark," I yell.

Mark has pulled over right where Dad's gifted car had been parked. The SUV is no longer there – towed? Did Dad come and get it between when I arrived home earlier and now? But I have no time to ponder this. I slam shut the front door, push past Brandon and hurry to Mark's car.

I throw my suitcase and bag onto the back seat and jump in the front.

"Everything okay?" Mark asks, nodding towards Brandon.

"Just drive, please!" I say urgently.

All the cells in my body pulsate. I've just had a very lucky escape, I know it.

Mark doesn't need to be told twice. He pulls out into traffic and hurtles away.

I glance back. Brandon sprints down the street in the opposite direction, his long trench coat flapping behind him.

CHAPTER 23

"Thank you," I say to Margie and Mark.

We're sitting at their dining table, listening to the ambient jazz music that Mark put on earlier and digesting after a delicious meal cooked by Mark. Bangers and mash with onion gravy and broccoli. A 'wholesome meal for this time of year', according to Margie.

Margie and I are both in our pyjamas. When I arrived earlier, Margie ran me a bath with lavender foam in the ensuite of the spare bedroom and insisted I relax in it for as long as I wanted. It was bliss, and when I finally got out, she'd laid my fleecy pyjamas on the bed to wear and had left a pair of her fluffy slippers and a super soft dressing gown for me.

I'd headed to the lounge wearing pyjamas, slippers, and gown – clothes that felt like a warm hug – and Margie had hers on too. We snuggled up under blankets and watched light-hearted rom-coms while Mark pottered and made dinner. While we ate, they listened as I told them all about what had happened with the pick-up, the failed urine test, the instant dismissal.

I continue, "You've been so kind."

"You're most welcome," Margie replies.

"I'm feeling much better," I say with a smile. And it's true. The tight knot in my chest has loosened.

"That's good. We were very worried about you."

"I really don't remember anything from last night. I

need to ask… did we do drugs together?"

They both shake their head.

Mark replies, "No. We haven't done any kind of illegal substances since we were in our twenties. And that was a while ago now."

I nod. "I guess it was when I was alone with that guy. I don't suppose you remember his name, do you?"

Margie immediately says, "No."

But Mark thinks for a while. Eventually, he shakes his head too. "No, I don't. I'm sure he introduced himself to us, but we were both very drunk."

Margie indicates her phone, which rests on the coffee table. "I took a couple of photos. I shared them with you this morning. Did you get them?"

"Yes, I did. And they don't jog any memories. In fact, I think I'm going to delete them. I just want to forget about the whole thing. I don't ever want to look at them again." My phone is in the bedroom, so I'll do it later.

"A good idea, I think," Mark says. He stands and clears the table.

"Allow me," I say and stand to help. "I'll tidy up. It's the least I can do after such a delicious meal."

Mark waves me away. "I'll do it, don't you worry. Anyway, I was going to get dessert first. Sticky toffee pudding and custard."

"Wow, can't wait," I reply, rubbing my belly. "I'm sure I still have some room for pudding."

"I certainly do," Margie says.

Mark kisses the top of her forehead. Margie puts her arm around his waist and gives him a brief squeeze. He heads from the table to the kitchen area.

I sit again. They are always affectionate with one another. But tonight, particularly so. It's clear they really love each other – even after all this time together. I sigh. It wasn't long ago that I thought I had something similar with Brandon. I was so convinced he was about to propose. That was the night I met the Maddens, when I should've been going to a party with Pete…

My final conversation with Pete comes back to me. I doubt I'll ever talk to him again.

"You look glum all of a sudden," Margie observes. "What are you thinking about?"

"Pete."

"Ah," she replies supportively.

I'd told them over dinner about Pete's involvement and my disappointment and sadness because I'd truly believed he was my friend.

"I forgot to mention this earlier, but after it all happened with the dismissal, he tried to deflect attention away from his part in it by making up an outrageous lie about you two."

Margie looks curious. "Ooh, what kind of outrageous lie?"

"He said something about a woman called Carrie. He told me he'd done some digging, and apparently she hung out with you for a while and then was never seen in Cardiff again."

Mark moves about the kitchen preparing the custard. He can't have heard me.

But Margie raises her eyebrows. "Well, poor Carrie. I do hope she's all right." She laughs. "But in all honesty, I don't recall us having a friend called Carrie. But we do know a lot of people. And it's a sad truth that people do come and go in our lives. Some friends have unfortunately used us and taken advantage of our wealth and generosity." She waves to catch her husband's attention. "Mark, dearest, do you remember a Carrie?"

Mark brings over a steaming dish and places it on the table. "Um, no, not that I immediately recall… There was a Carrie who was the wife of your marketing director at one point, do you remember?"

He walks back to the kitchen and grabs a jug of custard and brings it to the table. He sits.

Margie chews the inside of her cheek. "Ah, yes! I do

remember that Carrie! But that was a long while ago. And they lived in London." She shrugs.

"It's not important," I say with a smile. "I don't believe there's any shred of truth in Pete's gossip. It was so obvious he was in cahoots with Kelvin. He was trying to throw me off the scent and it didn't work."

Mark dishes up the pudding and hands a bowl to me and one to Margie.

"Smells divine," I say as the treacly aroma engulfs me.

"Thank you, my love," Margie says and leans across the table to kiss Mark.

As the three of us tuck into dessert, Margie continues, "We're planning on heading to Crimble tomorrow for a long weekend. It's our country estate in Powys. It's very peaceful and we feel like a break from the city."

I nod. Even though I have plenty I need to do, the thought of being alone all weekend fills me with panic. I'm worried for myself.

Margie takes a bite of dessert and swallows. She glances at Mark, puts down her spoon and touches my arm.

"We were wondering if you'd care to join us? We'll be back on Sunday evening so it won't change your plans for Monday. You'll still be able to head to London to get a new passport. We can sit for the next four days by a cosy fire, go for some bracing walks in the grounds – it has its own forest – and play board games. We'll lounge and eat plenty of food and drink and de-stress."

Yes! I want to shout immediately. The idea of relaxing in the countryside and giving myself some much-needed TLC tugs at every fibre of my being. It would be just what the doctor ordered, if I'd gone to see him in Nottingham, that is. But my sensible head resists.

"Thank you so much for the invite. But I should probably stay in Cardiff to pack up the flat and sort everything out."

"We know a company that'll help you with all that," Mark says. "And it will only take you a day. You're not leaving until next Thursday. What will you do for the rest of the time?"

What would I do? Overthink. Sit in a trance. Make bad choices. My brain might implode. If I don't rest, I don't know what the next stage of whatever is going on with me would be. Would I harm myself? Wake up in a pool of my own blood because I've slit my wrists and not remembered doing it? Would I not be able to get on a plane to see Mum?

He continues, "You said yourself that your flat stinks and your bedroom now gives you the creeps. I don't think you'll have a pleasant time."

"And we're concerned about you," Margie adds. "I think a change of scenery and a bit of R&R will do your mental health some good. You've had such a rough time of it recently. If you recharge your batteries for a couple of days, you'll come back stronger and more focused to sort everything out. We want to look after you. We've grown very fond of you."

"And don't feel you need to entertain us all weekend or anything like that," Mark says. "We're very relaxed. You can stay in your room for the entire time or sleep on the sofa all day and all night if that's what you fancy. We wouldn't mind in the slightest."

Margie fixes me with an intense look. "And besides, what if Brandon, or Tyler, or Kelvin try something? Or show up at your flat? If I can be completely frank, I don't think you're in the right state of mind to have to deal with any of them."

And I'm definitely not in the right state of mind to deal with my father, my sisters, or all three of them together if they rock up again. But I don't say that out loud. I've never mentioned them to the Maddens. I don't tend to talk about them to anyone.

My stomach twists at the thought of Brandon earlier. What had he planned to do? Push me back into my flat and then what? I'm sure he was going to kill me. Would he try again? Shove me in front of a bus for real? Or strangle me? The memory of his strong hands around my neck at the bus stop makes me shiver.

I need to get away from everything, to chill. I'll come back stronger; I know I will.

"You're right. I'd rather be where nobody knows where I am for a few days. I can sort everything else out next week. Yes. I'd love to come."

Margie claps delightedly. "Wonderful!"

"I'll cook a few times. And tidy up after."

"You don't need to do that," Mark says.

"It would be my pleasure."

"Well, that would be wonderful." Mark stands. He gestures to the dirty dishes on the table. "Leave all this, I'll sort it out later. I'm just going to call the housekeeper at Crimble to let her know we're coming and to stock up the pantry. We'll leave after breakfast tomorrow."

He picks up his mobile phone and strides out the room towards their bedroom.

Margie ushers me up, and we take our places back on the sofa. She picks up the remote. There's a knock on the front door. Margie looks in that direction, but doesn't move, perhaps waiting for Mark to go. But he must still be on the phone because the thump comes again.

"Strange," Margie says, frowning. "We're not expecting anybody." She glances at the large clock that looks like a Jackson Pollock painting. "Who could that be at this time?"

She puts the remote back on the coffee table, stands and goes to the front door, pulling closed the door between the lounge and hallway so I can't see or hear.

After a while, when she doesn't come back, I get fidgety. Who was at the door? Why hasn't Margie come back or invited them in? Is there a problem? My racing brain leaps to the worst conclusion.

When I can't bear the wait anymore, I stand to go and check the hallway. But the door swings open. Margie comes in, an odd look on her face. She pauses in the doorway.

"Everything okay?" I ask, alarm creeping up my body.

She flicks her long hair off one shoulder. "Yes. All fine. Just a neighbour bringing this back for Mark." She holds up a book. "I didn't realise Mark had lent it to him. I don't usually talk to him. He really chews your ear off, and I find him incredibly draining."

We both sit back down on the sofa. I reach for the book and look at the cover. *Meditations* by Marcus Aurelius.

Margie continues, "It's philosophy. Mark loves it. I read it a long time ago and have no plans to pick it up again. But Mark has read it dozens of times. You're very welcome to give it a try this weekend if you'd like."

"I might do," I say. And think of all the romances lined up on my Kindle to read. I could get through a few of those this weekend and completely switch off. I haven't read anything for a while. But my Kindle is at my flat. "If it's not too much trouble, could we swing by my flat tomorrow morning before we head off so I can pack some more clothes and grab my Kindle?"

"Oh no, not to worry. You can borrow any of my stuff, and there's loads of my daughter's old clothes and shoes there that I'm sure would fit. There's an entire library of books. And not all of Mark's kind, either. There are thrillers, mysteries, fantasy, and plenty of non-fiction too. Books that visitors have left over the years or swapped out. I'm certain you'll find something."

"Romance?" I ask hopefully.

"Goodness, yes. Danielle Steel, Nora Roberts, Colleen Hoover, you name it!"

"Perfect! Can't wait."

Margie squeezes my hand. "We're going to have such a fabulous time."

CHAPTER 24

I rest my head against the window and watch the city whizzing by. I woke up at Margie and Mark's feeling refreshed and excited for the long weekend away at their country estate.

At breakfast, Mark made us bacon sandwiches, but Margie wasn't hungry. I, however, had woken up ravenous and demolished mine and then ate Margie's too.

I take them in now. Mark drives and Margie sits in the passenger seat, with me in the back behind her. They're both dressed in country attire with matching khaki-green wax jackets and a lot of earthy colours. Mark has a tweed flat cap on, corduroy trousers and a zip-up fleece. And Margie wears shiny black riding boots, olive-green jodhpurs, a beige check shirt and a brown pullover. For once, she doesn't have a scrap of makeup on, and her hair, usually loose, is in a neat, low bun. When I first saw them this morning, they looked completely out of place in their modern apartment. Gone were Margie's high-fashion, brightly-coloured clothes and Mark's understated style. They look like completely different people.

It's making me curious about Crimble. Am sure they'll fit right in there. Do they have different looks for each of their six different homes?

I stifle a yawn. I feel exhausted all of a sudden, and the motion of the car is rocking me to sleep.

My phone dings with a message. It's from Kalisha:

> Hey, I'm not meant to be in contact with you but I know you were friends with Pete, and I thought you should know. This morning, Pete was in a freak accident and has severe injuries. He's in hospital, and it doesn't look like he'll make it. I don't know anything more than that.

My drowsiness is replaced by shock. I sit upright and reply immediately:

> OMG. That's awful news. I hope he's going to be okay. I've got everything crossed for him. Can you keep me updated, if possible, on his condition?

Kalisha replies:

> Yes, no problem. I shouldn't be saying this, but thank you. Kelvin was fired not long after you left. He didn't take it well. He smashed up his office and then smashed up your desk! You didn't hear that from me, okay? Gotta go. I'll let you know if I hear anything more about Pete xx

"Shit," I say out loud.

"Everything okay?" Margie says and twists in her seat so she can see me.

"Pete's in hospital. He had some kind of accident this morning. They don't know if he'll make it."

"But he's still alive?"

"Yes, thank goodness."

"Thank goodness," Margie says. She glances at Mark, who is concentrating on driving in the pouring rain, then back to me. "From the brief time we spent together, Pete seemed to me as if he's a fighter. I'm sure he'll pull through. I wonder what happened."

Mark indicates and overtakes a van. Once in the outside lane, he says, "Poor man." He points to Margie's bag by her feet in the footwell. "Could I have a drink of water, my love?"

Margie turns away from me to rummage in her bag and

hands a bottle to Mark.

A 'freak accident' – what could that mean?

The drowsiness settles back over me, and I slouch in the seat. But all the hairs on the back of my neck stand on end. A feeling of snakes slithering all over my body makes me squirm. I swivel and look out the back window. We're on a busy motorway during morning rush hour. Vehicles everywhere. I can't shake the feeling that someone in one of those vehicles is watching this car, watching *me* in this car and is following us.

It's so strong that I have to say something. I lean forward between the two front seats.

"Do you think we're being followed?" I ask the Maddens in the front.

Mark clears his throat.

Margie glances back at me. "I don't think so, Rach. Mark, what do you think? You're the one looking in the mirrors and paying attention."

"I really don't think so. But I'll keep my eye out for any vehicles that stay behind us for any length of time, okay?"

"Yes, thanks." I sit back.

"What made you ask that?" Margie says, still facing me. She looks slightly worried. "Did you see something?"

"No." I wriggle in my seat, attempting to put the feeling into words. It's the same feeling I had when I was walking alone in Bute Park. "I've just got a funny sensation in my gut."

The worry turns to humour. "That's probably Mark's driving making you car sick. He can be a bit jerky when changing lanes. Isn't that right, my love?" She playfully bashes his arm.

"The cheek," he replies and smacks her leg in return. "My driving is perfectly smooth, I'll have you know."

Margie chuckles and faces forward again.

I don't press the matter. The snakes still slither, but I know I sound ridiculous. Why would anyone be following me? Yes, both Tyler's and Kelvin's behaviour was worrying. Brandon's too. He was definitely watching my flat yesterday. Is he following me now? Did he sprint away to get his car to follow us back to Cardiff Bay and is behind us again right now? Was he following me in the park? I resist the urge to look out the back window again. It's all a figment of my imagination, it must be. I'm not quite right in the head at the moment. Out of sorts. I just need to relax and stop being so paranoid.

As the motorway blurs by, and I listen to Margie and Mark talk about what cheese they hope the Crimble housekeeper has managed to pick up, my eyelids droop.

I come awake with a start. My hands are tied. Someone is shaking my knee. It's Margie.

"Rach, darling, we're here. You slept for the entire three-hour journey," she says from the front passenger seat.

I'm still in the back of the car, my hands aren't tied, they're just tangled in my scarf. I pull them free. I must've been wringing my hands in my sleep.

Mark unloads the boot of the car and runs to the house through the heavy rain laden with bags.

"We'll wait for Mark to open the front door and then make a run for it," Margie says. "The rain's not letting up."

"I can't believe we're here already! I had the weirdest dream," I say.

"Oh?"

"I was a puppet and was being undressed with my arms manipulated by string. It was freaky."

"Very! Right, Mark's in. Let's go." Margie grabs her things, jumps out the car and legs it to the house.

I put my coat on, which I don't remember taking off, and grab my handbag. I open the car door and run to the house. The rain splatters on my face.

The front door is wide open, and Margie heads inside. Mark stands in the covered porch area and looks at the car, the boot still open.

"Few more bits to get. Just gearing myself up to go back out there," he says with a gesture at the lashing rain.

Before stepping over the threshold, I turn around to take in the place. Rolling hills, fields upon fields, and patches of dense forest.

"It's incredible," I enthuse.

"I promise it's not as bleak when the rain stops. The weather forecast for this weekend is snow. Which will be frightfully cold, but absolutely stunning with a white layer over everything. A proper winter wonderland."

"Can't wait. I don't know Wales all that well and have absolutely no idea where we are. What's the address?"

"It's just the name of the place, Powys, and the postcode – that doesn't tell you much, I know. But to be honest, you're here. And that's all you need to know." He smiles at me, and a look of contentment comes over him.

I scan the rural surroundings. "Do you have any neighbours? I can't see any other buildings."

"The nearest neighbours are miles away. As far as you can see in every direction belongs to us. We rent out the fields to nearby farmers and there are a few farm buildings over that hill that are occupied by various businesses, but pretty much it's just us here." He gestures to the wooded area to the right of the house. "And that's our largest forest area. We don't touch it, we're rewilding it. It's a designated nature sanctuary so no one goes in there apart from us occasionally. There are no paths or anything like that."

He points to the end of the gravel driveway. There are large iron gates, which are closed, and high hedges on either side, but I can just about glimpse the lane. "That's pretty much a road to nowhere. Hardly any traffic. The odd farm vehicle or tractor. It's very quiet here. That's why we love it. It's definitely our fuck-off world place."

He rubs his hands together. "Right, I'd better get the last of the bags." Hunkering down in his coat against the rain, he sprints towards the car.

The remoteness of the place feels slightly claustrophobic, as if the great open space is closing in on me. It's a while since I've been out of the city, out of the bustle, out of having people everywhere. I take a deep breath. It's fresh, clean, reviving. I turn to look at the house. It's a grand farmhouse building, perhaps a little smaller than I was expecting, but a striking, substantial property nonetheless. Positioned on a slight hill, and isolated from any other buildings, it looks out across the land in a rather haughty manner.

I step inside. Margie waits in the hallway.

"Welcome to Crimble," she says with her arms wide.

She's turned on a few lamps and already taken off her coat and hung it up on a row of hooks by the front door. She gestures to me to give her my damp coat. Mark comes in with the last of the suitcases and bags as I take off my coat and hand it to Margie to hang on a hook. I immediately shiver.

Mark closes the front door and begins to peel off his sodden coat.

I rub my bare lower arms. I'm only in my t-shirt. "Brrr, I think I must've left my pink jumper in the car."

I don't remember taking it off, but it must've been when I took off my coat. I probably overheated while half asleep.

Mark pulls his coat back on. "I'll go and check." He opens the front door again and dashes back out into the rain.

"There's plenty of spare jumpers upstairs," Margie says.

I nod. My mouth is dry and tastes strange. It's because I've not drunk anything for three hours, I'm sure. I can't wait for a drink.

The interior of the house is perfect. It has a country cottage feel with lots of dark-wood furniture and antiques. A complete contrast to their apartment. It's cosy and welcoming.

"It's a wonderful house."

Margie beams. "Thank you. Yes, we love it here. And I think you're going to love it too. I'll show you around in a minute."

Mark runs back inside, empty-handed. "No jumper in the car."

I frown.

"Are you sure you brought it?" Margie asks me.

"Yes, I was wearing it this morning. It's definitely not in the car?"

Mark shakes his head. He closes the front door. I notice he doesn't lock it, just like he didn't lock his car. That's not the done thing in the countryside, is it? Everyone leaves things unlocked. There's simply not the same risk of someone breaking in or a dodgy character showing up as there is in the city. He takes off his coat and boots.

Where's my jumper if not in the car? Was I wearing it? My brain whirs. I'm certain I had it on. Mark must've missed it. I'll look again when the rain stops.

Margie claps excitedly. "We'll find it later. It's got to be somewhere. Right, let's sort our phones."

"Our phones?" I ask.

Margie pulls hers out of her handbag, turns it off, and places it on a shelf in a wooden cabinet on the wall in the hallway.

"Yes, while we're here we put our phones in this cabinet. They're glued to our hands all the time normally so we like to use our time here to go tech-free for a few days. To live in the moment, to be more mindful. We don't have wi-fi here for that reason. And besides, there's never any signal anyway. So it avoids the frustration of stomping around the house trying to find some. Reducing our screen time and having a break from technology really helps us to de-stress. It might help you too."

"But what about your TikTok? All your followers?"

"A few days not posting will be good for me and will probably be good for my followers. They'll be desperate for my content when they realise they're not seeing it. Absence makes the heart grow fonder and all that."

I pull my phone out of my bag. I have one bar of signal that keeps dropping in and out.

Mark takes his phone from his trouser pocket and puts it on top of Margie's. "We've given the staff the weekend off so it'll just be us. We have everything we need here. Our fabulous housekeeper said she's stocked up the pantry with all our favourite things."

"I'm just going to text my mum," I say and tap out a quick message to Mum to let her know I'm having a quiet weekend away and will message when I get back. I tell her I love her.

I don't message anyone else. There's no one else in my life who cares where I am. And that thought makes me sad. I can feel Margie and Mark watching me, waiting for me to put my phone in the cabinet. I don't want them to get impatient.

But I hesitate. "What about Pete?"

Margie rests her hand on my arm. "Pete is in hospital. He's in the best place. There's nothing you can do for him. Clinging onto your phone in case you get a message about him is not time well spent. You need to focus on you. This is Rachel time. We'll pray for him. That's really all we can do."

"You're right." I gaze upwards, picture Pete's face in my mind and whisper, "Pete, I'm thinking about you. I really hope you pull through." I turn off my phone and place it on top of theirs.

Mark locks the cupboard and pockets the key.

"Locked?" I ask.

"Yes. Mark is much more disciplined than me when it comes to this. I get tempted to sneak down in the middle of the night to check my phone. Which is ridiculously unhealthy and behaviour I want to break. So Mark locks it and hides the key."

Mark taps his pocket. "Right, let's show you around,

Rach."

My stomach twinges, and I have the sudden urge to use the bathroom. "Actually, if you don't mind, please could you show me to my room? Or the nearest bathroom? I'm not feeling too great. I'm so sorry."

Mark pats my shoulder. "Goodness, don't be sorry. Like we said yesterday, you do whatever you like in this house. Right, I'm going to check out the cheese situation."

He strides off in what I assume is the direction of the kitchen.

Margie grabs my suitcase and points up the stairs. "Your room is this way."

After a nasty episode on the toilet, I slept all day. Missed lunch and dinner. Went downstairs at around nine in the evening to reheat a plate of food that they'd put aside for me. Mark had made Gorgonzola cheese, walnut and pear quiche with new potatoes and broccoli. I'm not a big fan of blue cheese, and the idea of pear and egg together didn't particularly appeal, but I already felt incredibly rude for sleeping all day and didn't want to reject the dinner they'd made for me too. So I ate it, briefly played a card game with them called Chinese Rummy, which I found confusing, and kept nodding off at the card table.

I apologised profusely for being a rotten houseguest, but Margie and Mark were very understanding and told me to just sleep it off.

Margie had said, "It's the stress. I always sleep more when I'm stressed. Mark goes the other way and can't sleep for toffee. I'd rather sleep than have insomnia, to be honest. Go back to bed, I think you need it."

So, here I am. Back in bed at 10.30 p.m.

It's a large room with an ensuite bathroom. It's decorated in the same country cottage style but has a huge, very imposing four-poster bed. I don't like it. It's obviously ancient, with a thick dark-wood frame and heavy red material draped all over the top and hanging as curtains all around. It feels like I'm sleeping in a box or – shudder – an antique coffin. When I first lay on it, it felt like there was too much stuff above me, that if it collapsed, I'd be crushed immediately. Thankfully though, the mattress – far from being old and lumpy to match the frame – is very comfortable. And the bedding is sumptuous and soft.

I almost immediately sink back to sleep.

A creaking floorboard wakes me. Was that above me? Is there someone walking around in the attic? The creaking comes again, followed by banging. Then a groan. It sounds like the Maddens are having sex. But the groaning comes again. It's not a pleasurable groan. It's a groan someone makes when they're in pain. Then sobbing. Very obvious sobbing.

Goosebumps dot my skin. The room is freezing. The bedcovers are all tangled up around my feet as if I've thrashed them off. My skin is clammy, and I'm out of breath. It's as if I've just run a marathon in a heatwave then come inside to an ice-cold air-conditioned room. I sit up.

It's almost pitch-black in the room, there's no light from street lamps to creep in around the edges of the curtains, only the moon. I get a whiff of disgusting aftershave. Too spicy, too strong.

The creaking comes again, louder. My eyes adjust and latch onto something. A shape...

At the end of my bed, a dark figure looms.

The Gorgonzola quiche lurches back up my gullet.

How long have they been there? Is it the person who has been following me? They've let themselves in the unlocked front door and have come to kill me! *Oh fuck, it's Brandon! It has to be!*

My body freezes, but my lungs are still working – I scream. And scream and scream.

The light switches on. I scrunch up my eyes.

"Rachel, are you okay?" It's Margie.

She runs towards me, jumps on the bed and puts her arms around me. Her long hair spills out of a silk scarf tied around her head. Mark is hot on her heels, doing up his dressing gown as he runs in.

My heart thunders. "I thought someone was in the room... the person following me... they were standing over my bed, right there."

I point a trembling finger and whimper into Margie's shoulder, sinking into her embrace.

Margie strokes my hair and shushes me while Mark strides around the room checking behind the window curtains, then the bed's drapes. He opens the wardrobe and looks inside. He crouches and checks under the bed.

I feel slightly stupid while he does this, like a child watching her father chase away the imaginary monsters. But I also feel relieved.

Satisfied he's checked everywhere, he says gently, "I can't see anyone."

Part of me wants to shout: *check on top of the bed! Someone could be crouched on top of this box hidden by the drapes!* But I don't. I feel a bit ridiculous.

"It was just a bad dream," Margie says. She kisses my forehead tenderly. "You're safe here. Safe with us. Nothing bad is going to happen to you here." She rocks me gently.

"I've never had a dream like that before. I've never screamed out loud like that. Well, maybe when I was a child, but not as an adult... It was so real..."

Margie shifts her position on the bed.

"Oh," she exclaims and looks down.

I look down too and see she's put her knee in a wet patch on the under sheet.

Realisation dawns on me: dampness in my knickers, in the crotch area of my pyjamas. Did I wet the bed? OMG. I pissed myself.

"I'm so sorry," I say, edging to one side as Margie shifts to the other.

"Dearest, please go and get some fresh bedsheets from the airing cupboard," she says to Mark and quickly strips the bedsheets off the bed.

"Right you are," Mark says with no fuss, as if his adult houseguest hasn't just urinated all over the bed in his spare bedroom.

Mortified, I stand to one side staring at the damp patch on my pyjamas.

Margie comes around to my side of the bed and takes my shoulders. In a kind, non-judgemental, motherly voice, which makes me immediately think of Mum, she says, "There are some spare nightclothes in the bottom drawer of that chest of drawers. Go and grab something and get changed in the bathroom. Pop those ones in the bath, and we'll wash them tomorrow."

She continues to strip the bed, and I do as instructed. But the only thing I can find is an ankle-length lacy white nightie with long sleeves and a frilly high neck – like something you'd see on a vintage Victorian doll. It'll have to do. In the bathroom, I get changed out of my pee-soaked pyjamas and knickers, dry myself off with loo roll and pull on the nightie.

When I come back out, Margie is dabbing at the mattress with a dry part of the balled-up bedsheet. Mark holds a pile of fresh sheets.

"There we go." Margie gathers up all the dirty sheets. "You two make the bed, and I'll just put these in the laundry basket."

She heads out the room while Mark and I make the bed. Margie comes back in and helps us.

"Right, let's go back to sleep, shall we?" She gets into the bed and pulls the duvet back for me. "I'm going to stay here tonight."

I get back into bed next to her.

"Right-ho," Mark says. "Night ladies."

"Will you switch the light off on the way out?" Margie asks.

"Certainly."

Mark leaves the room, switches off the light and closes the door so there's still a slight gap – no doubt so he can hear if anyone screams again.

Margie and I settle into the bed. It's plenty big enough for both of us. I turn towards her. I can only just make out her outline in the darkness.

"I can't apologise enough. I'm so embarrassed. That has never happened to me before."

"Shush," she replies gently and takes my hands in hers. "You had a fright, that's all. A nightmare. Our minds can play terrible tricks on us sometimes. Tomorrow is a new day. You'll have forgotten all about it in the morning, just you wait."

CHAPTER 25

Margie's gone when I wake up. It's deathly quiet in the house. I have no idea what the time is because I don't wear a watch, I don't have my phone and there is no clock in the bedroom. But the bright light outside tells me it must be mid-morning.

The hideous Victorian doll nightie reminds me of what happened last night, and I'm mortified all over again. Am I losing control of my body now too?

After showering, I get dressed in some of Margie's daughter's old clothes that are hanging in the wardrobe. They look completely new and all happen to be in my size, which is… weird. But then, I am average size so must be a coincidence. And that's possibly why the clothes were left – the daughter bought them, wore them once and didn't like them enough to take back to South Africa. I head downstairs.

"Margie?" I call out. "Mark?"

But there's no reply. I check in all the rooms downstairs. The house is empty. It's eerie being here on my own. I haven't been here long enough for it to feel familiar. My body cries out for coffee so I head into the kitchen. It's a big room with a double Aga oven, huge cream-coloured fridge-freezer, freestanding wooden units, and lots of red-and-cream gingham. There's a large dining table in the centre of the room, used as a counter to prepare food, as well as somewhere to eat.

I find a handwritten note on the table. It reads:

We've gone for a walk. Didn't want to wake you. Help yourself to anything you want, go anywhere, do anything – make yourself at home! See you later on. M&M xx

I put the kettle on and have a nosey in the fridge. I don't feel particularly hungry but eat some granola with yoghurt and banana. The rain has stopped, and it's a glorious morning. I decide to go for a walk too. I need to clear the cobwebs. My heart hasn't stopped fluttering since I woke up, and I'm on high alert. Every sound, every slight movement – from a bird twittering outside or a tree branch moving in the wind – catches my attention. Burning off some of this skittery energy will be a good thing, even though my legs feel exhausted, as if I've just hiked a mountain and not spent almost the entire day yesterday asleep.

Heading towards the front door, I pass the locked cabinet with our phones inside. I'm desperate to check my phone to see if Mum's replied. I can't wait to see her, to hug her, to talk to her face to face. This time next week I'll be in the air to New Zealand. That thought both soothes me as well as alarms me as I wrap up in coat, hat, Margie's scarf and gloves, and put on some welly boots by the front door that are my size.

The front door is unlocked, and I walk out into the sunshine and fresh air. I wander to the iron gates at the bottom of the driveway and look through at the lane and the hedgerow on the other side and the rolling hills and fields beyond.

I'm struck with the urge to see if the gates are open. I'm not certain why, I don't want to go out or leave the estate. But I have this twinge in my chest that I'm trapped. Ironic really when I'm surrounded by so much space. I rattle them. Locked. There's a keypad on the gate post that I hadn't noticed before. I don't know the code, of course.

Why do they keep the house front door and car unlocked and then lock the gates? But maybe that's exactly why, because the gates are locked. There must be another way into the estate if a burglar really wanted to get in. But I'm overthinking it.

It's then I notice the camera on top of the gate post. It's pointed right at me, and would pick up anyone entering or exiting through these gates. There are more cameras dotted around the outside of the house and outbuildings. Perhaps the Maddens are more security conscious than I realised. The countryside isn't such a safe place after all.

I look up at the camera on the gate post. Am I being watched right now? The hairs on the back of my neck prickle, and I look out across the lane to the hedgerow on the other side. There are a few gaps in it. Is someone hiding in the field and watching my every move?

A shiver hits me from head to toe. Of course there's no one out there. *Get a grip, Rachel. Stop being so paranoid. Nobody knows you're here. You're safe.*

I turn away from the gates and walk towards the outbuildings at the side of the house. The dense, gnarly forest on the other side does not look inviting, even on a sunny day like today. As I walk past Mark's car, I open the back passenger door and have a thorough look for my pink jumper in case Mark missed it. No joy. Perhaps I didn't put it on yesterday morning? Perhaps it's still sitting on the chair in the spare room at the Maddens' Cardiff Bay apartment? I'm certain I was wearing it, but my certainty doesn't mean much these days.

The outbuildings consist of a large, mostly empty barn, an empty stable with room for five horses and a smaller barn with a large cage along one side and a few cabinets along the other.

I venture inside, curious about the cage.

Behind the bars, something moves.

Fear punches through my chest. But a woof and a

waggy tail bring me back to earth. I didn't realise the Maddens had any pets. But they must be working dogs, and clearly not inside, sit-on-your-lap-for-a-cuddle dogs.

As I get closer, I see there are two in the pen. They look like beagles, but bigger.

"Hi there," I say.

The dogs eye me warily. They don't appear especially friendly. They look a bit too skinny. I can see ribs poking out under their skin. But I don't know anything about dogs or this breed or whether that's exactly how they're meant to look.

A flash of colour draws my eye. At the back of the cage, against the wall, are two raggedy dog beds. Under one is what looks like the very corner of perhaps a dog blanket. What's odd, is that it's the exact same pink as my jumper.

I lean closer to the bars to see better.

The dogs jump at me. Barking. Snarling. Growling. One snaps its jaws around the bars trying to get at me.

Startled, I stumble backwards out of the reach of teeth and claws and lose my footing. I blunder into one of the cabinets along the opposite wall. My shoulder connects with the corner as my bum hits the hard, cold concrete floor with a thud.

"Shit," I mutter.

The cabinet door flings open and spills its guts on top of me.

"Ow!" I shout as I'm hit by heavy, cold metal…

Guns.

Shotguns and rifles, more specifically.

I bundle them back into the cabinet and close the door. My breath comes hard and heavy. Guns are very usual on farms and in the countryside. I'm sure the Maddens, or the people who work for them, have the relevant licences. I'm sure it's all above board.

The dogs are still snarling at me as I pick myself up and head back towards the house. I don't feel like exploring the estate anymore. I bolt across the driveway and fly through the front door.

"Hey, Rach! We're in the lounge," Mark calls.

As I remove my boots and outerwear, I steady my breathing. What is wrong with me? Absolutely everything is giving me a fright. I need to chill out.

I head into the lounge.

Mark kneels in front of the fire, adding logs and blowing on it to get it going, while Margie sets up a bowl of fruit and some pencil-sketching gear on the table by the window.

"Nice walk?" Margie asks.

"Yes, thanks. Didn't go far. You?"

"Yes, we did three miles," Margie replies, settling herself to sketch and picking up a pencil.

"You have dogs," I say.

"That's Ronnie and Reggie," Mark says. He takes in my blank face and adds, "The Kray twins? Notorious London gangsters in the fifties and sixties."

"Oh, right. They, um, looked pretty hungry," I say, attempting to be delicate. I don't want to criticise another's dog-owning abilities when I don't own a dog myself.

"I fed them this morning. They'd eat all day if they could, the greedy buggers," Mark says. "Come in, take a seat." He gestures to the extremely comfy-looking sofa in front of the fire.

I nod but don't move. I hover in the doorway. I'm fidgety, anxious. I don't want to sit right now.

"They're not inside dogs, then? They're working dogs kept outside?"

"They're hunting dogs," Mark replies, stoking the fire so it roars. He leans back to avoid the heat flare.

"Hunting? Is that why you have guns too?" My voice rises a pitch. I'm not sure why I'm making this a thing.

Margie notices my tone and looks up from her drawing. "We don't hunt animals, my dear. Goodness no. The dogs help us to deal with illegal deer poachers and illegal badger baiting on the estate. The dogs are trained to track people. And the guns are used by our grounds staff for pest control, to manage lame or injured animals and what not. We also do clay target shooting in the summer."

Mark stands. "I'm going to bring in some bread, pickles and cheeses for lunch. Does that sound good with you both?"

"Absolutely," Margie replies.

"Yes, thanks." Before Mark leaves the room, I say, "I was wondering if we could go into town this afternoon for a mooch around? And have a look in the shops?"

They look at each other and laugh.

Margie stands and comes over to me. "There's absolutely nothing around here for miles. There's a tiny village but it doesn't have any shops and to mooch around it will take you five minutes, at the most."

"Honestly, it's best to stay right here," Mark adds.

He squeezes past me to head to the kitchen to gather lunch items.

Margie puts her arm around me. "Why don't we have a look in the library and find you a saucy romance." She guides me to the room next to the lounge.

The trapped twinge from earlier nips in my chest. Perhaps it's the complete change of tempo from a busy urban life or the fact that I'm used to being able to walk out my front door and go anywhere and do anything in the city, but I can't seem to relax. I chew at my fingernails and shift from foot to foot as Margie searches the bookshelves for novels I might like.

I need to settle, to enjoy this peace and quiet and this doing nothing on a Friday when I'd usually be hard at work. The Maddens are being so kind to me. I need to be a good houseguest and not so obviously weird and uptight.

I select a book from Margie's pile, and we go back into the lounge. She takes up her sketching once again, and I sit on the sofa, tell my body not to be so rigid, to relax. My eye is drawn by the crackling fire, and I watch it for a while before taking a deep breath and opening the book.

Hours later, Mark stands. "Right, time for dinner."

The day has passed in amiable, relaxed activity. Margie sketched, switching on lamps and lighting candles when the natural light dimmed. I half-read, half-daydreamed, put my pee-soaked bedsheets and jammies in the washing machine, and forced myself to sit still in the lounge. And Mark played the piano on and off, kept the fire going, as well as read the philosophy book that their neighbour brought back on Wednesday evening, on occasion reading out loud to us.

I stand too. "I'll help."

We head into the kitchen. Mark dons an apron and gets things out.

I sit at the dining table. "What's on the menu tonight, chef?"

"I was thinking beef stew with herby dumplings, root veg and potatoes and a side of green beans. Sound good?"

"Delicious. Can I help peel and chop the veg?" The manic energy is still pitter-pattering around my body. It needs an outlet.

"Certainly."

He grabs a chopping board and puts it in front of me on the table. He finds a turnip, potatoes, onions, carrots and parsnips and dumps them in front of me. He grabs the peeler from a drawer and slides it along the table and selects a large, shiny knife from the magnetic knife holder on the wall. He places it carefully in front of me.

"Take care with that. It's very sharp."

Margie comes in the room just as he says this. "Mark is very precious about his knives," she says to me. She kisses him on the cheek. "You have quite the collection, don't you, dearest."

Mark pulls open a drawer full of neatly lined up knives and selects a large cleaver. He places it carefully on the table next to another chopping board and then pulls a large slab of beef out of the fridge.

Margie gets out three wine glasses. "Shall we have the Château Le Pin with the beef?"

"Absolutely," Mark replies. "Punchy and peppery to complement the earthy, strong flavours."

He chops at the meat with the cleaver. His arm swings from above his head to land in the meat with a thud. He cuts it into small chunks with a skill that I find impressive but also slightly disturbing.

He notices me watching. "Did a butchery course a while back."

Margie pours us all red wine. "We've got twelve bottles of this stuff," she says to me with a wink.

"There's another case in the pantry, so actually we've got twenty-four," Mark says, grinning.

After a delicious dinner and goodness-knows-how-many glasses of excellent red wine, I'm feeling much more relaxed. And really quite drunk. On the vinyl player in the lounge, we've been playing old records from a large crate that Mark brought down from a bedroom. And dancing. Well, more like swaying, in my case.

I come back into the room after taking a toilet break for the umpteenth time and see my glass has been topped up again. I gladly take a swig then put it back on the coffee table that we've shifted to one side so we can dance.

"Ooooh, here's a good one!" Margie declares and pulls a record from the crate. "Not belly dancing music, I'm afraid, but something you'll definitely know."

She delicately lifts the arm from the player, and a bluesy tune, which was new to me but which Mark knew all the words to, stops abruptly. She switches the records, carefully slotting the blues record into its cover and placing it in the crate. She gently lowers the needle back down.

Nina Simone's 'Feeling Good' blasts out.

"Yes," I slur and punch the air. "I love this song!" I sing along.

Mark grabs my hand and lifts it up to twirl me around like he has been doing all evening to both Margie and me. And sometimes to us both at the same time. I twirl under his arm, but, this time, he pulls me into him so I'm leaning back against him and he has his arm around me.

He starts to sway but presses his body into mine.

Alarm bells ring through my booze-addled brain. This does not feel right.

He turns me and shifts his body at the same time so we're facing each other. His hand slides down my back and gropes my bum, and then he moves in for a kiss.

My reactions, all evening dulled by alcohol, immediately come alive. "What the hell, Mark!" I push him away. "Get off me!"

Mark's forehead scrunches up, baffled. Margie stares at us.

"What just happened?" Mark asks me.

"You just fondled my bum and tried to kiss me! That's what just happened," I shout at him.

Mark shakes his head.

I turn to Margie. "Margie, you must've seen that!"

She glances at Mark then looks straight at me. "No, I didn't see Mark do that. You must be imagining it, Rach."

"What?" I screech. "No, I am not *imagining* it!"

Mark holds up his hands and takes a step towards me. "You're very drunk. I wouldn't ever do something like that—"

"Get away from me!" I take a step back, stumble and knock into the coffee table. My glass tips over and spills red wine all over the beige carpet. "Crap..." I mumble, caught between being the polite houseguest wanting to immediately rectify the spillage and being infuriated that I've just been sexually assaulted.

Mark moves away from me and stands behind Margie. They share a very obvious *look*.

Margie comes towards me. "We've all had quite a bit to drink. And I think it's time for bed. I'll take you up."

Her lips are pursed and eyebrows knitted. She's angry with me. I allow her to guide me out the room and glare at Mark as I pass.

In the hallway, I stop dead. Margie tugs on my arm but I won't budge.

"I'm telling you the truth. Your husband just came onto me!"

Margie glances in the direction of the lounge. "He didn't. He wouldn't do anything like that. I know that's what you think happened, but that's not the truth."

Arguments, protestations, insisting she believe me – it all gets stuck behind my teeth. No words come out. I gape. Blink a few times at her, just to make sure it's Margie who is in front of me. Her outline is fuzzy, and there are three of her. But that's just the booze. Nausea does a merry jig in my belly. I really am ridiculously pissed. More so than the Maddens appear to be.

Did I just imagine that? Is my version of reality warped? My head hangs. It's so heavy, and I don't have the energy to lift it up.

I just want to vomit and go to bed. I can't trust my brain anymore. That stark realisation makes me crave the oblivion of sleep.

Margie tugs on my arm again, and I follow her through the hallway, up the stairs and into my bedroom. I trip over my own feet and cling on to her to stay upright.

In the middle of my room, I mumble, "I don't know what's going on in my head at the moment."

I look at my feet, shuffle closer to the bed. I just want to sleep.

Margie violently shakes me. She grabs my face so I'm looking at her. She looks over her shoulder towards the door and nudges it shut with her foot. My eyelids droop, and she squeezes my cheeks harder so I open them. I try very hard to focus on her.

Urgently, she whispers, "Mark did touch you and try to kiss you. I saw it. I need to tell you something about him… about our relationship…"

CHAPTER 26

My body tells me to *get up!* My eyes open. I'm lying halfway up the bed, fully clothed, my bum still on the edge and my feet still touching the floor. The bedroom light is on. The signal from gut to brain fires again, and I jump up and sprint to the bathroom, vomiting in the toilet.

It's the middle of the night. I'm drunk. But a hazy conversation with Margie, while we were sitting on the end of the bed, comes back to me in a jumbled mess. I concentrate on it. Everything in my being tells me it's important, that I have to remember. I can't have another blackout like on my birthday night.

But this time, the pieces slowly slot into place.

"I'm terrified of him," Margie had said to me. "He manipulates me, controls me, and I can't escape from him. I've tried. He holds this power over me."

"It's okay," I'd replied with a slurred voice. "Tell me everything."

"You're the first I've told. Mark makes me do it. I don't want to do it anymore," Margie sobbed.

I'd put my arm around her shoulders. It had taken some time, my coordination shot to pieces with the red wine sloshing through my veins.

Margie continued, "I'm so sorry I dragged you into this…"

"I'll help you. I swear. We'll sort this out."

And then, nothing… I must've passed out.

THE NEW GIRL

The shock jolts me as I sit on the bathroom floor. I'm still inebriated, clumsy, foggy. But I register the surprise that the Maddens aren't such a perfect couple. They appear so in love, so in tune. I envied their connection. I guess nothing is what it seems.

But what the hell does Mark want with me? Has he made Margie lure me here for some depraved sex thing? There's *no way* I'm going to let that happen.

I flush the toilet and stumble back into the bedroom. I sit on the bed, gulp down water from the glass by the side of my bed. I don't recall bringing up a glass of water, but perhaps Margie got it for me. It tastes disgusting. Like vomit, I realise. I should've brushed my teeth after I was sick, but too late now. I need to make a plan to get me and Margie out of here safely and quickly.

A creak comes from above. Footsteps. I stare up at the ceiling. There's a groan, a sob. It's the same noises as I heard last night. Is there someone up there? Has Mark locked Margie in the attic?

The creaking comes a second time, but then stops. The entire house is pin-drop silent. I need to find this attic. I need to check. I couldn't live with myself if I didn't. But I have to be quiet. I can't wake Mark. If only I had my phone, I could use the torch function. I don't want to switch on lights in the hallway or in other rooms in case that wakes him, and he comes for me.

I scan the room for a potential light source. And a potential weapon.

An old brass candleholder is up on a shelf. I take it down and see there's a small nub of candle still left. I scrabble through drawers and find a box of matches with only one left. Bingo.

In my suitcase, I search for my aerosol deodorant. Spraying it into the flame of the candle will make some kind of flame thrower. It's all I can think of. There are knives in the kitchen but going downstairs will make too much noise.

I pluck out the spray can with a tad too much enthusiasm, fumble it, and it rolls under the huge four-poster bed. I get down on my belly to grab it, but it's right at the back.

Wriggling in under the bed, I reach for the can. There's writing etched into the wooden frame of the bed that's against the wall. I crawl a little closer to read it.

HELP ME
I WON'T SURVIVE THEM
SAM EVANS

Who's Sam Evans? I run my finger over the scratched letters. They could've been made in the past week or in the past century. The bed is certainly old enough.

More creaking and a sob from upstairs brings me back to my purpose. Margie's up there. I wriggle out from under the bed and stand up. A massive head rush almost floors me, and I cling onto one of the posts of the four-poster bed to stay upright.

I have to find the attic. I grab the candleholder and pocket the deodorant and box of matches. As quietly as I can manage, I open the bedroom door and step into the hallway. It's deathly quiet. No more creaking or sobbing.

The Maddens are in the huge main bedroom through the door to my left. It would be better to keep my door wide open so the light shines into the hallway, but I don't want it glowing under the Maddens' bedroom door and waking Mark, so I light the burnt-down candle with the only match and pull my bedroom door to.

I lift the candle up to the hallway ceiling, but there's no hatch opening into the attic. Which is odd. Most of the time access to the attic is in the hallway, isn't it? Although it's not something I've really paid much attention to over the years. It must be in one of the bedrooms. It's not in my bedroom, I would've noticed. It might be in the Maddens' room, but I have to hope it's not. There are four other bedrooms and a bathroom that it could be in.

Even though all the other rooms are empty, all the doors onto the hallway are closed. I creep forward.

Footsteps from inside the Maddens' room make me freeze.

I put my hand on the aerosol can.

A door sweeps open on plush carpet. I brace myself for Mark to leap out at me.

But the door to the hallway remains closed. I don't move. A few moments later, a toilet flushes. The door sweeps again, footsteps.

Margie says something, and Mark replies. I can't hear what, only mumbles. Then, silence.

I've not been rumbled. He doesn't know I'm out of my bedroom. Vomit reaches the back of my throat, but I swallow it down. I need to keep it together.

If Margie's in the bedroom that means there's someone else up there. Pete's voice comes back to me.

"They pick up waifs and strays," he'd told me.

Is it Carrie up there? The woman who was never seen again in Cardiff after hanging out with the Maddens? Margie told me that I was the *first* she'd told and that she didn't want to do it *anymore* – implying that I'm not the first and won't be the last.

I creep forward again, keeping the old candleholder in front of me. There's dark-wood wall panelling all around the hallway, and I stifle a snicker. Thank goodness I'm not in that Victorian nightie otherwise I'd feel like I'm in some gothic horror movie.

Focus, Rachel. Put the drunken thoughts aside for a moment.

I put my hand on the doorknob of the first empty bedroom. I didn't pay much attention when Margie showed me round the upstairs, and she didn't linger on the other bedrooms, just showing me where I was sleeping and where she and Mark were sleeping. I don't know what's behind this door.

I take a deep breath, open it and immediately put my

hand on the deodorant in my pocket.

It's just an empty bedroom. With no access to the attic in the ceiling. The next two bedrooms and the large bathroom are the same. I get to the last spare bedroom. This room is the smallest and the farthest away from the Maddens' room. I don't risk turning the light on though.

The candle flickers. The wick is burnt down to almost nothing. I need to be quick before I run out of light.

I open the door slowly and step inside. There's a musty, old smell in this room, and it's very cold. It has bunk beds in one corner and, in the other, a tall glass-fronted cabinet. I scan the ceiling, but no attic access. It must be in the Maddens' bedroom. Dammit.

The cabinet is odd. Out of place. It's like something you'd display trophies in. I step closer and hold up the candle. It's almost out, getting dimmer by the second.

There are seven glass shelves, the lowest is empty. On each is just one object, placed in the centre. From highest to lowest is: a battered navy-blue baseball cap; a small lilac handbag; a cheap plastic ring in the shape of a flower; a chunky gold watch; a lock of brown hair tied together with a purple ribbon. And on the sixth shelf there is a small turquoise tin.

Curiosity gets the better of me. I pull open the glass door and pick up the tin. The lid is jammed on tight, but I manage to open it with a drunken, inelegant wrench. The contents fly out and hit me in the face and neck like little pellets. There's still one left in the tin.

It's a tooth. With old dried blood caked around the top.

I heave, my legs give way, and I drop to the floor.

What are all these items? Why are they on display like this? Are they trophies from all the women that Mark has used Margie to lure here? Why the hell are there teeth in a tin?

Does one of these items belong to Carrie? Does another belong to Sam Evans?

I pick up one of the teeth from the carpet. It's tiny. A

baby tooth, it must be. And it dawns on me: this is probably all stuff that used to belong to Mark and Margie's kids. And they keep it on display for nostalgic reasons. There's probably a lovely memory attached to each item.

I gather up the rest of the fallen teeth, drop them back in the tin and put the tin back on the sixth shelf. Shifting my body to stand back up, I notice that the seventh shelf, the one right on the ground, isn't empty.

There's an item on it, but pushed slightly back so it can't be seen when standing.

I recognise the colour – the distinctive burgundy of the older ones. I slide it out. Stare at it.

A British passport.

I open it up to the identification page. The candle flickers and splutters.

But I see it. My face. My name.

My heart soars – it's not lost! But then it sinks – what is it doing here?

The wick burns out with a little hiss. Smoke fills my nostrils. It's pitch-black in the room. I allow my eyes to adjust as much as possible, stand, pocket my passport and flounder around with my hand to find the glass door of the cabinet. I close it and tiptoe in the direction of the door, one hand holding the candleholder, the other arm outstretched.

I feel my way out of the room and into the hallway. My bedroom light shines just enough under the door to light the hallway for me to creep back. I shut the door and sit on the bed.

Clutching my passport, I fight the urge to lie back and fall asleep. I have to make a plan. I have to get out of here, get Margie out, save Carrie in the attic... Or maybe that's Sam up there. Or maybe it's me. Or maybe all four of us are merrily playing card games...

Stay awake, Rachel!

But it's no good, I go under, dragged deep, deep down into sleep.

CHAPTER 27

A gong clangs between my ears and throbs throughout my head. My hand clutches at my passport but grasps at empty space.

I sit up, groan, and stare at my empty hands. Although my pounding head screams at me to *lie back down!*, I jump up, hunt around in the covers, check under the bed, and search the room.

My passport is gone. Did I ever have it? Was that a crazy dream?

No.

I rub my forehead. This is more than a red wine hangover from hell. Mark drugged me. I'm sure of it. He must've come into my room and taken the passport back while I was out of it.

I shower, making sure to lock the bathroom door, get changed and stick my head out of my bedroom door. The Maddens are laughing together downstairs. A whiff of bacon comes from the kitchen.

I dash down the hallway to the smallest bedroom and go straight for the trophy cabinet. The cabinet is still there. But the contents are different to last night. It's full of antique trinkets, glassware, vases, candlesticks, small sculptures, and pottery. Nothing that was there last night. And no passport.

Confusion riddles my already aching brain.

Mark is screwing with me. This must all be part of his

sick game. He definitely tried it on with me last night. Margie definitely told me about their relationship. What does he plan to do to me? To Margie? To whoever was in the attic last night? I heard them, I know I did.

Back in my bedroom, I grab my set of keys and slot them through my fingers as a discreet weapon in case Mark tries anything. I head down to the kitchen.

Margie has her back to me, washing up. Mark has his arm around her waist and is nuzzling her neck. They're both chuckling, enjoying the intimate moment. Their behaviour is exactly how it's always been since I first met them: loving and deeply connected.

But I know it's all an act.

Mark spots me lurking in the doorway. "Ah! Here she is. How are you feeling this morning, sleepy head? As fuzzy as us? That was a lot of red wine we got through."

Margie glances briefly at me over her shoulder. "Morning, Rach!"

Mark goes back to the oven. "I'm just making some bacon and eggs. Can you believe it's almost lunchtime! Do you want some?"

He's been sneaking drugs into my food and drink. Although my stomach tells me it would very much like some bacon, I say, "No." Then instinctively add, "Thank you," as my politeness kicks in.

They're acting as if nothing happened. But I know what Mark is up to, and I'm not going to let him get away with it.

I edge into the room and stand behind the other side of the large dining table to where Mark is serving up the food. I fold my arms, making sure my keys are still in my fist.

"Mark, we need to talk—"

Margie swings around, washing up foam flying from her hands, and cuts me off. "I was just saying how I couldn't remember *anything* from last night! A complete blur. What about you?"

It's then that I notice it. Margie has done a good job at trying to conceal it with makeup, but it's obvious. She has a black eye.

"What on earth happened?" I say and point at her nasty bruise.

"Oh, this!" She chuckles. "I walked into the wardrobe last night while I was blotto coming back from the loo. What an idiot!"

She gives me a big smile. But I know that's a lie. Mark hit her. They have a toxic, physically abusive relationship. He's forcing her to play a part in whatever game it is he's playing with me.

I understand her message loud and clear: *He's violent. Do not confront him. Pretend you're not onto him.*

"Ouch," I reply. "That's the kind of clumsy thing I would do." I fake-laugh. "I don't remember a thing from last night either. We were dancing… and then I woke up this morning. I don't even recall how I got up to bed."

Margie beams at me. Mark comes to the table with two plates of bacon and eggs with buttered toast.

"Are you sure you don't want some?" he asks me.

I shake my head.

They sit, but I hover. When it gets awkward, I pick an apple from the fruit bowl and wash the skin thoroughly under the tap, not turning my back to Mark.

He eats a few mouthfuls and catches my eye. "What did you want to talk to me about?"

Margie stops eating and blinks at me a few times.

I lean against the cabinet eating my apple. I don't want to sit at the table near him. I take a bite and chew slowly to give me some time.

"Umm… I was just going to say that your food last night was sublime, and we need to talk about what we're eating for dinner later, because I'm not sure you're going to be able to top that."

He laughs. And launches into a monologue about what food we've got in and what he could cook and what do we fancy to eat and how it would be his pleasure to cook anything for us. While they finish their food, we talk about what's on the menu today and our favourite meals of all time. Mark clears the things away.

"Shall we head into the lounge for some cosy-fire-and-board-games action?" Mark asks. "I would've suggested a walk but it's snowing."

I hadn't noticed, too fixated on watching Mark's every move, and look out the window. White fluff drifts down.

He continues, "Don't think it'll settle. But bloody cold out there."

He heads out the room; Margie goes to follow.

I step in front of her. "Margie, can I have a quick word?"

Mark pauses in the doorway.

I continue loudly, "My period has come on. Don't suppose you have any tampons, do you? I forgot to bring any."

Mark keeps moving towards the lounge.

Margie replies, "I think there's a box in your bathroom cabinet that Simone left…"

I beckon Margie closer towards me. She frowns but moves in.

"We need to get out of here," I whisper.

"What?"

"Mark came onto me. You told me about him, about him forcing you to lure me here. Your black eye. He did that to you, didn't he?"

She shakes her head, her expression baffled. She glances in the direction of the lounge. "I don't know what you're talking about. Mark wouldn't hurt a fly. I injured myself."

I do an exaggerated wink. She's playing his game. She's terrified he's eavesdropping. If she tells me the truth, he'll be even more violent with her.

"Listen…" My voice is barely audible. Margie has to put her ear to my lips. "…I found my passport last night."

Margie leans back and claps her hands. At a normal volume, she says, "I'm so pleased about your passport! Was it in your suitcase all along?"

"It was in Mark's trophy cabinet," I whisper. "Which he's moved all around now." I point up. "There's someone in the attic, isn't there? I heard them. I thought it was you up there, but it's Carrie, isn't it?"

She looks at me blankly, although I think I see concern, and moves towards the door.

"There is an attic, yes. But there's no one up there. It's only us three here this weekend. You probably heard the wind howling. It was blowing a gale last night."

She turns away from me. "He'll kill me," she whispers so quietly that I'm not sure if I've heard her correctly.

I grab her arm. "What did you say?"

Margie frowns and smoothly extracts her arm from my grip. "I said, time for games!"

She leaves me and enters the lounge.

He'll kill her.

Every cell in my being snaps to attention. I need to work out how to play this. How to extract us safely from his talons – and fast. Mark needs to think that I haven't discovered he's up to something. Margie's terrified to go against her husband and is playing her part. I have to do this right. Her life is on the line if I don't.

The magnetic knife holder on the wall is now bare so I head straight to the drawer holding Mark's knife collection. It's locked. Has it always been locked? Or has he just done this? As quietly as I can manage, I tug and shake the drawer, but it won't open. What can I force it with? I spin around to scan the kitchen for some kind of tool, but Mark is stood in the doorway.

"Forgot my drink," he says and points at a glass of water on the table. "Can I help you with anything?"

Oh crap, did he just see me battling to open his knife drawer?

"Um, no, just coming," I say sweetly, as if I'm talking to one of the wrong side of my family. "After you." I gesture for him to lead the way out of the kitchen. There's no way I'm walking with him behind me.

He leans across the table, picks up his glass and heads back towards the lounge. I take a deep breath before I follow. The Maddens are on the sofa, a board game set up on the coffee table in front of them. The fire crackles.

Mark beckons me forward and points to a space on the armchair next to the sofa. "Come join us. We're about to play Camel Up. It's hilarious. You bet on racing camels."

"No, thank you. I was wondering if I could get my phone?"

"Are you having withdrawals?" he asks.

"Something like that."

"No, you know the rules!" he says with a smile.

"I'd really like it," I insist.

He shakes his head. "Honestly, it's like a craving that you just have to fight. Smartphones are addictive. This is better for you. It'll feel bad for a while, then you'll get over it and realise you didn't need to check it, not really."

"You just need to find something to distract yourself," Margie chips in, rubbing Mark's back affectionately.

"Maybe we could go for a drive somewhere? I know the nearest village hasn't got anything in it, but perhaps further afield?" I say.

And then we could make a run for it when you're not looking or get someone to call the police.

Mark shakes his head again. "Not in this snow. It'll be dangerous on the lanes, very icy in places. Best to stay here."

"Why don't you explore the house if you're restless? There are plenty of nooks and crannies to discover," Margie says with a big smile.

I smile back. "Yes, good idea. I need to burn off some energy." I exit the lounge and make sure to pull the door closed.

That was a massive hint, if ever I heard one. There's something Margie wants me to find. Or someone.

My mission from last night resurfaces. I need to prioritise. Find the attic. Rescue whoever is in the attic. Get Margie. Overcome Mark somehow. Get out of here. Three of us against Mark should work. Margie will know the code to the front gate, I'm sure. Perhaps she might even know where the keys to the phone cabinet are. Or maybe the car keys.

Right, first things first. I fly up the stairs and straight into the Maddens' large ensuite bedroom. It looks much like the rest of the house and has their suitcases and things dotted about. I scan the ceiling but there's no hatch into the attic. Where the hell is the access to the roof space?

I go through the drawers in the bedside cabinets looking for keys, but don't find any. I search the rest of the room and bathroom, but no keys.

Back in the bedroom, there's a very large, wooden wardrobe in one corner. It has huge double doors, as if it opens onto a patio rather than hanging clothes. I pull open the doors.

Either side hangs clothes, but the back of the wardrobe, right in the centre, has been cut away, and in the wall is a small hole with narrow wooden steps leading up.

A stairway.

Why is the access to the attic concealed like this?

I have to go up.

I step into the wardrobe, duck, and go through the hole. The stairwell opens up, and I stand upright. It's dark. My hands feel my way up. Every step creaks.

My chest constricts, and it hurts to breathe. Carrie has to be up there. But what state will she be in? What else is up there? A prison full of torture items? Or weird sex contraptions? Both? I need to save her. First priority.

At the top of the stairs is a door. Light escapes from the small crack all around it, casting the stairwell in a gloom just enough to see by. The door has a lock on the outside but no key in it. I try the handle.

It's unlocked.

I hold onto my flat keys. I should've perhaps found something else to use as a weapon, but too late now.

The door opens outward into the stairwell. I slowly pull it towards me.

"Carrie? I'm not here to hurt you."

But the sight of the attic space snatches the air from my lungs.

I take a few steps into the centre of the room. It's empty. Completely, utterly, empty. There is a small skylight window that is too far away for any human to reach, but looks like it doesn't open anyway.

The attic has wooden floorboards and wooden panels all around the outside. The ceiling slopes following the shape of the roof with the beams exposed.

There's a distinct smell of bleach. And blood.

The intuition in my gut yells at me. Bad things happened here; I can tell. It might be empty now, but this room holds dark, dark secrets.

Someone was locked in here last night and the night before. I heard them. So where are they now? Have they been moved somewhere else?

The stairs creak. Mark has snuck up behind me. That was his plan all along. For me to find this room. For him to lock me in here.

I will not be his prisoner.

I spin around and launch myself at the door.

CHAPTER 28

I fly through the doorway, slip at the top of the stairway as if someone's slicked oil there, and tumble down the stairs, landing in a heap at the bottom.

All the air is knocked from my lungs, and I black out momentarily.

When the fuzziness clears, I see there's no one in the bedroom. The door to the wardrobe is still wide open. If anyone had been on the stairs, I would've taken them out with my fall.

Lying very still in the position I came to a stop in, I scan my body for any major injuries, any part that hurts more than the rest. I ache everywhere. I'm going to be one big bruise. The back of my head throbs where I hit it on the way down. I touch my lip with my fingertip and wince. It comes away red. The taste of blood registers in my mouth. I must've bitten my lip.

Slowly, I push myself up to sitting. My head pounds. I listen carefully. The faint sound of music drifts up from the lounge.

An image pops into my mind. A set of keys. Hanging on a hook. I focus my swimming brain on it. The image sharpens. Above the gun cabinet opposite the dog kennels was a set of keys. Could one of those be the key to the cabinet where my phone is?

The guns!

A weapon.

I have no idea how to use a gun, have never even touched one before, but hopefully they're loaded. And, if not, then hopefully the ammunition is nearby and it'll be self-explanatory how to load it. I'll work it out. I have to.

I heave myself up, wobble out of the bedroom and down the stairs, and barrel through the front door before I can bump into Mark.

A blast of freezing air smacks me in the face as I stumble, shoeless, through the snow and towards the outbuilding that houses the dog kennels. With every step, my body hurts all over and my head throbs, but I can't let a fall down some stairs stop me. I have to push on.

The dogs snarl, snap, bark, shove their bodies against the bars of their cage to get to me. Drool flies and hangs from their jaws. They salivate like they want to eat me. I've never been afraid of dogs. Every dog I've ever met has wanted to be my best friend, but not these two. These two are teeth-baring, dangerous beasts. I keep as far from the cage as possible and head straight for the gun cabinet.

I yank the door open. It's empty. Not one gun. Mark's hidden them. Should I search for them? No, it'll be a waste of time. I doubt I'll find them. Mark knows this place, I don't. It could take all day, and I don't have that time.

A set of keys hangs from a hook above the gun cabinet. I snatch them up. There are three keys. My heart sinks. None of them look as if they'd open an antique wooden cabinet. But they are all labelled: Front Door. Back Door. Basement.

The last label gives me pause. On my tour of the house when we first arrived, I was never shown the basement. I replay our arrival in my head. Mark had gone straight to the kitchen after we all put our phones in that cabinet. There are two doors in the kitchen. One Mark and Margie go into all the time. The pantry. The other... the other I've never seen opened. I hurry back to the house.

I bound through the front door, which I left wide open, and Mark's voice comes from the lounge.

"What are you up to out there?" he asks.

"Oh, you know," I say as lightly as I can muster, "just had a sudden urge to run through the snow in my socks." I force a laugh.

"Fair enough," Margie replies. "You do you!"

"Are you going to come and play Camel Up with us?" Mark asks.

"Maybe in a bit. Just going to get some water and catch my breath."

"Right-ho," he says.

I dash into the kitchen, unlock the second door, and go down into the basement.

There's a pull cord at the bottom of the stairs that I can make out in the light coming from the kitchen. I pull it, and a single lightbulb flicks on in the centre of the space. It's large, with concrete floors and brick walls. It's as cold as outside, and my breath forms clouds in front of my face.

The room is bare, apart from seven large white chest freezers. The kind that in movies a dead body has always been stored in. They are positioned so each can be easily accessed. An electrical hum fills the space. At least one, if not all, of these freezers are on right now. I take a step closer to the freezer nearest the bottom of the stairs.

Mark's voice comes from the kitchen. "Rachel, will you come back up please. We need to talk."

I shout back. "What's with all these freezers?"

"The previous owners of this place used it as a hunting lodge. They stored the carcasses of deer and pheasant down there. The freezers were left, and we haven't got round to taking them out yet."

He's lying. My hand reaches out and finds the handle of the lid. "I found the attic."

"Ha, yes. What a fabulously bizarre thing that is! The previous, previous, previous owners had that added. We like to joke that they must've had loads of kids and put it in secretly so they could get away from them every once in a while." He laughs.

But I'm not laughing.

I lift up the lid of the freezer.

"Rachel," Mark calls my name again. This time more urgently. "We're worried about you. We locked the knife drawer and hid the guns, just in case you attempted to hurt yourself… or did something to hurt us. Margie told me what you said earlier. We think you might be having a mental health breakdown, perhaps some kind of delusional episode…"

But I only half hear him. The room spins.

Inside the freezer is only one thing. A woman. A dead woman. A layer of ice covers her clothed body. She has blonde hair. Her frozen eyes shock me the most. And her open mouth, as if she died screaming.

Carrie. It has to be. Did Mark kill her last night when I was drugged and passed out? I was too late to help her.

The contents of my stomach erupt out of my mouth, and I vomit on the floor. The room does more than spin, it turns upside down and inside out. I go dizzy.

"Rachel? I'm coming down."

Mark's voice snaps me back. I can't faint now. I can't be stuck down here with a murderer. I need to grab Margie and get out of here.

"No," I reply sweetly. "I'm coming back up."

There's nothing I can use as a weapon in the basement. I have two sets of keys, that's it.

As fast as I can manage, I ascend the stairs and burst into the kitchen, hoping for some element of surprise. Mark stands to the side of the door.

His eyes are wild. One hand holds a huge kitchen knife. Blood drips from its tip.

On the floor by his feet lies Margie. She's covered in blood from a wound to her gut, it pools around her on the tiles. Her face is angled towards me.

Her glazed expression is as dead as Carrie's frozen face.

I was too slow. He's murdered Margie, and I'm next.

How many dead bodies are in those freezers? How many women has Mark murdered? How many more does he plan to murder? I have to get out of here. I have to survive this serial killer and tell the police...

Mark grabs my arm and raises the knife.

I chuck the keys in his face.

It's enough to distract him, and his grip loosens. I yank my arm free, turn on my heel, and run around the large kitchen table for the door into the hallway, tipping over a dining chair in his path.

"Rachel!" he bellows as he chases after me.

The front door is closed again. I grab the handle; pray he hasn't locked it. Am I trapped in this house to be murdered and frozen too?

But the door flies open. I sprint out of the house towards the forest.

I shiver uncontrollably. Light snow flutters around me. I can only just about see it. It's almost pitch-black in this bleak, deserted forest in middle-of-nowhere Wales. I'm desperate to blow on my numb fingers, to rub my cold skin – skin so icy it feels prickly – but I don't. I don't move, I still my breathing. I have to stay silent, hidden.

I'm crouched low to the ground. My socks are soaked and muddy. Water rises up the bottom of my jeans, and the hems are caked in dirt. One sleeve of my jumper is torn from the scramble through a thorny bush. I'm thankful I'm not completely barefoot. I ran too quickly to put on shoes or a coat.

I need to focus. I'm going to have to move at some point or I'll freeze to death. But I don't know where I am or how to get out of this forest. I'll deal with that when I come to it. For now, I need to stay very, very still.

A twig cracks behind me.

Shit.

I've been found.

This can't be the end. It can't be. I will fight until I've

got nothing left. I want to live. I'm not going to go easily.

The footsteps get closer. My head spins. *How the hell did I get here? How the hell did it all lead to this?*

I curse myself. I should've seen it coming. But I didn't. I was blind to it all, and now it's too late.

"Rachel!" Mark shouts again.

Barks echo through the woods.

He's set the dogs on me.

I need to move.

CHAPTER 29

My entire body aches from the fall down the stairs. I can barely feel my feet, but I run deeper into the forest. I know I can't outrun the dogs. But I have to try.

The forest does everything to hinder my progress. I lose my footing on uneven ground and trip in hidden holes. Undergrowth tugs at my clothes, hits me in the face, scratches long gashes into any exposed skin.

There's no obvious path. I have no idea which way I'm going. I could be running around in circles for all I know. It all looks the same. And I know screaming for help is pointless; there's nobody around for miles.

The barks get louder. They're closing in.

Nobody knows I'm here. Nobody will miss me for a few days. They're not expecting me at work on Monday, and I told Mum I'd be quiet for a few days. Probably this time next week she'd start to worry about not hearing from me. Mark could easily bury my body in this forest, and I'd never be found.

I stumble into a small clearing. The forest canopy breaks, and I look up to see the sky, but it's full of snow clouds and gloomy.

Excruciating pain shoots through my ankle. A dog latches on and bites down hard. I fall flat on my face, turn, attempt to kick off the dog. But its teeth sink deeper. A piercing scream explodes from within me. The second dog jumps on my torso, it's front paws on my collarbone. It snarls in my face, drool drips on my cheek. Jaws open wide and go for my neck.

"Hold!" Mark shouts.

The second dog's maw hovers millimetres from my ear. It's hot, stinky breath blows across my face. The pain from the first dog's mouth clamped around my ankle makes my vision reel.

The dogs have me pinned down. I don't dare move but flick my eyes towards where Mark's voice came from.

He stomps through the forest into the clearing. He's bundled up in warm outerwear and wellies. A camping lamp hangs from his belt. He's aiming a shotgun at me.

When he's about a metre away, he lowers the gun, unhooks the lamp and places it down.

I wriggle, attempt to sit up, but the first dog's teeth sink in deeper and the second dog snaps its jaws in my face, its bulk heavy on my chest.

A second figure stomps through the woods behind Mark. The realisation shakes me to the core – Mark has an accomplice. They're also dressed up against the snow and hold a lamp, but no gun. I focus intensely on this figure, my pain-addled vision blurry.

I blink. My vision sharpens. And I see.

"No... it can't be..." I mumble. But the light from the lamp confirms it. "Margie?"

My heart soars that my friend is still alive. But then it falters with confusion. "I thought you were dead... that Mark stabbed you... there was blood everywhere..."

Margie puts down her lamp too. She and Mark share a long, desperate look. Mark shakes his head sadly. Margie wipes away a tear that I can't see.

What is happening? My brain fires on all cylinders attempting to make sense of what it's seeing.

What did Mark say earlier? That they were worried I was having a delusion. Did I imagine seeing Margie's dead body? And the woman in the freezer? Is none of this real? They set the dogs on me so I wouldn't get lost and freeze to death. To find me, not to hunt me.

A sob escapes my lips, and I stop struggling against the dogs.

"I need help…" I whimper. "Things are happening in my head that aren't real."

Margie's anguished face breaks. A grin spreads. She laughs and doubles over clutching her belly. Mark laughs too.

Margie stands, collects herself and unzips her coat. Underneath, her outfit is smeared with red.

"Fake blood," she explains through laughter. "From the fancy dress shop." She licks a finger and smears it across her black eye. It leaves a line of normal skin and a smudge of purple down her cheek. "And makeup."

I gawp at her.

She grins at me again. It's not the smile of my friend. It's demonic.

She continues, "Thank you for not attempting to put up a fight in the house and for running." She turns to Mark. "We love it when they run, don't we, dearest?"

Mark nods, beaming. "We love the thrill of the hunt."

I find my voice. "What is all this?"

"It's our game," Margie says happily.

She sweeps her hand to indicate the forest, their estate. "And this is our playground. You, my dear, are our plaything. We love toying with young women, luring you here, keeping you up in the attic. And when we get bored, well, then there's the freezer."

"This is a sick game?"

"It's the perfect couple's hobby for us. We first bonded as children over our shared love of torturing small animals." Margie blows Mark a kiss.

"You're murderers! Why would you do this?"

Mark mimes catching Margie's kiss and blowing one back to her. He turns to me. "Because we have all the money in the world. We can do anything we want. And we've done it all. Life got rather tedious. Until we devised this little game. It keeps us excited with life, with each other. We'll do it until the day we die."

My insides crack with the thought of all the other women they might lure here to murder.

"Why me?"

Margie takes a few steps towards Mark, reaches out and holds his hand. "We knew from the moment we met you on New Year's Eve that you were the one. You were our new girl. Vulnerable from a relationship break-up, new in town, no friends. Slightly… broken. And yet, intelligent with so much going for you. We don't want an easy target. We want a challenge. It makes it so much more fun to tinker with and slowly destroy the mind of a vibrant woman."

Mark lifts up Margie's hand and holds it against his cheek.

He says, "We drugged you on your birthday and paid that broke actor to wake up with you, staged that near miss in your work vehicle and tipped off your work, brought in all those coffees. Your landlord was more than happy to give Ivan the spare keys to your flat for a tidy sum. It always takes a lot of planning, but we love it. And all your personal dramas! They all added to your demise. You were always so keen to tell us all about it. Thank you for that."

"You were the ones following me? I thought it was Brandon, but it was you."

Mark snorts in derision. "No. That was your floundering little brain being paranoid. Totally played to our advantage though. You cracking up has been a pure delight to witness and help along."

"You hurt Pete, didn't you?"

Mark's face screws up with disgust. "That meddling friend of yours nearly ruined everything. Ivan should've taken care of that little problem by now. Pete shouldn't have survived the first accident. But Ivan will smother him with a pillow in the hospital and finish the job."

Poor, poor Pete. He'd only been trying to protect me,

and I'd ignored him, thought he was making things up, spreading gossip.

"That blonde woman in the freezer in the basement is Carrie, isn't it?"

Margie nods. "Yes, she's been there about a year now. This is our winter sport." She cups Mark's face. "You brought the syringe? Best to do that now, don't you think? We don't want her getting hypothermia."

Mark rests his gun against one of the lamps and fishes in his jacket pocket. Margie's smug face offends me in every way.

"Are all seven of those freezers full of women you've murdered?" I can't keep the disgust from my voice.

"Just six." She points at me. "The seventh one is empty, waiting for you."

Mark pulls out a large syringe filled with clear liquid.

I wriggle again, but the dogs won't let me get up.

"Don't worry," Margie soothes. "This is the same stuff you had on your birthday. You won't remember anything for hours while we fix up your ankle and move you into your new room."

Mark takes a step towards me. "We've got the attic all ready for you. I can't wait to hear you begging us to spare you." He pauses to look at Margie. "I do think that's my favourite bit."

"What the fuck do you plan to do with me in the attic?" I screech, attempting again to move.

The first dog's jaw tightens around my ankle. I can feel the blood oozing out of my body.

Margie clicks her fingers at the dog. "Easy, Ronnie. Don't worry, Rach. It'll all be psychological torture. That's our thing. Nothing sexual or anything like that. Not like what that actor may or may not have done to you in your own bed on your birthday. We paid him and told him no marks or noticeable damage." She shrugs with a little laugh. "So, who knows what he, or his friends, did to your body while you were out of it."

"You're insane! How long do you plan to keep me in the attic?"

"For as long as you amuse us. A few days, weeks, months. Maybe even years," she replies.

Mark hovers over me with the syringe angled towards my neck. "I've just had an idea," he says to Margie.

"Go on," she replies eagerly.

"I'd really like to practice my butchery skills. So how about we thaw out Carrie and feed her to the new girl?"

Margie's face screws up. "That's revolting, Mark. But I love it."

Mark grins, looks down at me again. "How about that, Rach? Are you hungry for some Carrie stew? You will be after we've starved you for a few days."

He pushes the second dog's head to one side and presses the syringe into my neck. It pierces my skin.

"No!" I yell and jerk my body.

Screw it if the dogs rip me to shreds, I can't be a plaything for this sick couple... I just can't...

The dogs react viciously to my movement. Mark kneels on my chest and holds me steady. I'm too weak from blood loss and pain to shove him off.

His thumb presses down on the plunger.

But a swinging garden spade comes out of nowhere and smashes Mark around the head.

CHAPTER 30

Mark flies backward and slumps in a heap on the ground. Margie screams.

What looks like a small stick sails past my face, the waft of Peperami trailing in its wake. The dogs immediately jump off me to chase the smell. The sound of a packet of crisps opening registers. The packet is chucked in the direction of the dogs, scattering crisps everywhere.

A hand grabs my jumper and pulls me up to sitting.

It's Caroline.

She nods at me and launches herself on top of Margie and Catherine, who are tussling next to us. Margie's arms flail as she shouts for Mark.

Caroline throws a punch in Margie's face. "Nobody fucks with our sister apart from us, bitch!"

The punch doesn't connect. Margie is wild, uncontrollably screaming for her husband and trying to reach him.

My ankle shrieks at me as I attempt to stand to help my sisters.

A hand grabs my hair, yanks me down.

Mark.

Blood pours from the wound in the side of his head. His pupils are pinpricks. He still has the syringe in his hand. He stabs it at me. I dodge it, roll away. He headbutts me.

Blazing pain blasts from my nose across my face. My

fingers scrabble on the ground and come upon a rock.

I pick it up and bash him in the head with it, in the same spot as the spade hit him. He screams, falters, his eyes roll back momentarily.

I grab the syringe in his hand.

He blinks, shakes his head, focuses once again on me. I bite his hand, prise the syringe from his weakened grip.

With all my strength, I shove it in his neck and press down the plunger.

His eyes immediately glaze over. His body sags.

Panting, I push him off me and scramble up.

The twins wrestle Margie. She elbows Catherine in the face, and the younger twin topples backward. The older twin goes for Margie's eyes, but Margie is too strong, too determined. Margie headbutts her. Caroline falls away, dazed.

I pick up the spade, limp forwards, heave it up with the little energy I have left. And swing.

The spade arcs through the air catching Margie full in the face. She collapses to the ground.

Caroline jumps on Margie, turns her over so she's face down and kneels on her back. Catherine picks up the shotgun.

All three of us pant. Margie shifts, grunts, tries to shake off Caroline, but Caroline is too heavy.

"Do either of you have your phone?" I manage. "Police…"

Caroline slips her mobile out of her pocket but instead of handing it to me, she glances up at Catherine.

The younger twin has the shotgun pointed at me, her finger on the trigger.

Fuck.

I sink to my knees; hang my head.

They've had enough of screwing with me. Of harming me. They want me dead. This is their chance.

A perfect opportunity to get away with it. I doubt that anyone knows they're here. The Maddens have no idea who they are to identify them. Well, that's if they leave the Maddens alive. Our bodies would never be found in this forest.

They've saved me from the Maddens just to bump me off themselves.

Caroline coughs.

Catherine sniffs.

They've just said something non-verbally to one another. Probably: *Good riddance to our despised little sister, to the new girl in our family who we've hated from the moment she was born.*

I squeeze my eyes tight.

The end.

A dog barks. The shotgun fires.

Right behind me, the dogs squeal and whine and run off into the forest.

I pat myself down searching for the holes in my body. There are none. I look up.

The gun smokes in Catherine's hand. She lowers it.

"We've been following you since New Year's Day," Catherine says. It's the most she's spoken to me since we were children. "We've been watching our perfect little sister and her perfect little life. But you know what, your life is just as fucked up as ours."

She nods at her twin. Caroline dials 999.

EPILOGUE

One year later

A dog barks and brings me back to the present with a jolt.

"She's a therapy dog," the owner explains. "We're on our way to the children's ward, but she likes to say hello to everyone on the way."

I pet the waggy-tailed, three-legged, one-eared dog in front of me for a moment before she moves on to greet the other people in the hospital waiting room with the same enthusiasm.

Mum has gone with a nurse to see the specialist and hear the results of some tests. I'm sitting with her for her chemotherapy treatment after. She's been gone for a while. I'm trying to stay positive about the results.

It's summer here in Auckland. We've just had a lovely family Christmas, and I spent New Year's Eve with my fiancé, Nikau.

So much has happened in a year. And yet, at times, I find myself back there. Back in that forest.

The Maddens are facing jail for the rest of their lives. It's still ongoing, but my part in it is done. It caused a huge scandal – a bored, wealthy, retired couple with glowing career histories, commendable charity work and shiny reputations holding captive, psychologically torturing, and then murdering six women.

And attempting it with a seventh.

They found and identified all six bodies in the freezers

at Crimble. All were missing persons cases that had gone cold spanning back a decade, including Carrie Donohue and Samantha Evans. The women will receive justice and their families now have closure.

They'd planned everything to the most minute detail to make me believe they were my friends and to get me to trust them. The house was full of hidden speakers, cameras, and heaters. Police even found a gadget concealed in the wall at the top of the attic stairway that sprayed oil, explaining why I slipped so easily and fell. And another in the mattress that squirted liquid making it appear as if I'd wet the bed. They'd used an AI photoshop tool to create those photos from my birthday night out that looked as if I was having a great time with them and that random stranger who ended up in my bed. The police found him. They also charged my landlord.

The Crimble housekeeper and staff had absolutely no idea what was happening at the house. The basement had always been locked, and the staff were always given time off when the Maddens were in residence, so were never there when they had a victim in the attic. The Maddens' children had no clue either.

Another woman came forward after seeing the case on the news to say that the Maddens – via Ivan – had paid her to play a recording of my laughter in a sushi café at the shopping centre. She'd thought they were playing a practical joke on me and had no idea that they were screwing with my head. They'd also paid a man to pull out in front of me when I was driving the work pick-up. He thought I'd maybe cut them up once before and they wanted to get me back. It's amazing what people will do for a wedge of cash.

Ivan was tracked down eventually. He was on the run in Albania. He'd been their 'muscle', their 'fixer', their henchman. However, he didn't know the specifics of what his employers were up to, he just carried out orders. I met him at their New Year's party. He'd opened the door to me dressed in sequins and star glasses. Ivan had beaten up a few people over the years for the Maddens, but Pete had been his first attempted murder.

It was touch and go, but Pete survived, although with life-changing facial disfigurement. He received a big payout. And is currently taking part in a documentary about the Maddens for a huge sum. He's also written a book and has become somewhat of a celebrity in Cardiff, now hosting a true crime podcast and having a regular guest slot on a local radio show. He's just been offered a national TV presenting gig, which I'm sure he'll accept. We speak regularly.

Kalisha messages me every now and then. She's still at the same place and steadily working her way up, receiving a promotion recently. Kelvin was charged with sexual misconduct, among other things. He'd been sexually suggestive to Kalisha on multiple occasions, although hadn't at that point been physical with her. She had been certain it was going to get physical on the day she asked me to go home due to period pain. Kelvin also admitted that he'd tried to coerce Pete and Kalisha into spying on me for him, on telling him everything that I'd messed up on. They'd both refused. I'd overheard one of the occasions when he'd attempted to convince Pete.

I take a sip of the hospital coffee. They didn't have my favourite peppermint syrup mocha with an extra shot of coffee, of course. The two options were 'with milk' or 'without milk'. The best place for coffee still remains the coffee shop near my old work. But I'll never go back in there. I didn't hear from Tyler again. Or from Brandon, thank goodness. Both are long forgotten.

I met Nikau on the plane from London to Auckland. He was sitting next to me, returning from a business trip. I was already panicking on take-off and doing breathing exercises, and at the moment the plane lifted off, I yelped and grabbed his hand. He was the sweetest to me and really helped calm me down. And when I looked at his face, really looked, I was instantly attracted. It turns out that outrageously flirting with a handsome man takes your mind off a fear of flying.

We live three doors down from my mum and stepfather in a gorgeous little house. Nikau has been slowly converting the spare room into a nursery. I organised a visa to live and work out here and now have a fabulous job that gives me flexible working hours so I can be with Mum during her chemo sessions. I'll never go back to the UK.

I pat my pregnant belly and look at my phone.

Heather has replied to me with congratulations. I shared my ultrasound scan with her. She was the one who gave the twins my new Cardiff address. She felt awful about it, but I know how persuasive they can be. Apparently, they showed up late one evening and wouldn't leave until Heather gave it to them. She thought I knew that was what had happened and I was in a mood with her. And I thought she was mad at me for missing Ella's birthday. We made up. She's still my best mate, even though we're now thousands of miles apart. She's planning on coming over for my wedding next year, and I can't wait to see her.

There are a couple of Happy New Year messages in the WhatsApp group I started with my sisters and Dad. I rub the gap where my left little finger should be as I read them.

I've finally got to a place with them that I'm comfortable with. I message them briefly on special occasions but will never see them in person again. They're on the other side of the world, and that's exactly how I like it.

But my sisters saved me, and I'll always be grateful for that. If it wasn't for them, I'd either be dead or still in the attic at Crimble.

They'd been following me since New Year's Day and living secretly in my neighbour Ralph's third bedroom. He never went in there and had no idea. He's deaf so didn't hear them, and they made sure to cover their tracks.

We didn't tell the police – or Ralph – that, of course. We told them that the twins had been staying with me because they were worried about me after the breakup. As close, loving siblings, they'd been concerned when I said I was going away with friends who I barely knew. So, they decided to follow and watch to make sure I was okay. They put on their sweet, cute, innocent identical twin act – and the police lapped it up.

Caroline and Catherine hadn't gone back into my flat. The Maddens had been letting themselves in with the landlord's keys to move my things and cause the flood in my kitchen.

The twins and Dad had come to my flat the day after my birthday. They'd planned to wait for me to get home from work, not knowing that I was already back after getting fired.

Dad had seen the car was still parked outside with an accumulation of parking tickets on the windscreen. He'd been furious and had given the twins the second set of keys and told them it was their gift now.

In the SUV, the twins had followed Mark and me back to the Maddens' Cardiff Bay apartment and then the three of us to Crimble, parking down the lane out of sight.

They'd watched as the Maddens had taken my pink jumper off me while I was still asleep in the car, released the dogs, allowing them to sniff the jumper and take it back to their kennels, and then woken me up. The next day they'd watched me attempting to open the locked front gates. And, the day after that, had seen me run into the forest barefoot in the snow and with a bloody lip.

"It had all looked so fucked up," Caroline had told me afterwards. "So we found a way into the estate."

Dad hasn't forgiven me for trying to shake him off by moving to Cardiff without telling him. He's happy to only message occasionally. He's pretty much disowned me. Which I'm totally fine with.

There's a message from my contact at the charity I

work with now. It helps victims of violent crime. The charity supported me, and now I'm giving back by taking part in online group sessions and writing blog posts.

I spend a lot of time in therapy. It's hugely helped. My therapist likes to remind me that most people are good, there are just a few rotten eggs out there. I have some lingering trust issues and find it hard to make friends now, but I'm working through it.

My relationship with my stepfather and two younger siblings is stronger than ever, and I have my mum and Nikau, who has proved to be an absolute saint and most definitely a good egg.

Mum comes out from a room down the hallway and heads towards the waiting area. I stand as she approaches. She's smiling.

She reaches me and says, "It's good news, Rach."

And my heart sings.

AUTHOR'S NOTE

Dear reader, I hope you enjoyed *The New Girl*!

Please could you leave a review on Amazon. Your review will help other readers to discover the novel and I hugely appreciate your help in spreading the word.

Subscribe to my email newsletter to be notified when my next psychological thriller is released, and for giveaways, price promotions, book recommendations as well as exclusive extra content. You can sign up here: www.noravalters.com/subscribe

Thank you for taking the time to read *The New Girl* – I'm very grateful for your support.

Nora Valters
February 2024

BOOKS BY NORA VALTERS

Her Biggest Fan
Now You Know
Here For You
The Party
The New Girl

ABOUT THE AUTHOR

Nora Valters grew up in the New Forest in the south of England and has lived in London, Manchester, Bournemouth, Oxford and Dubai. She currently resides in Weston-super-Mare.

She studied English Literature and Language at Oxford Brookes University before embarking on a career in marketing and copywriting.

Her debut psychological thriller *Her Biggest Fan* was published in October 2020. *Now You Know* came out in June 2021, *Here For You* in January 2022, and *The Party* in November 2022. *The New Girl* was released in February 2024 and she's currently writing her sixth novel, which will be out soon.

Nora loves to travel and has journeyed around the world. She enjoys exploring new places, knitting/crochet, painting, hiking, and is an avid reader. She's also a bit obsessed with dogs.

Subscribe to be notified by email when Nora's next novel is released, for giveaways, price promotions, book recommendations as well as exclusive extra content at www.noravalters.com/subscribe

Keep in touch:
Website www.noravalters.com
Facebook www.facebook.com/noravalters
X www.twitter.com/nora_valters
Instagram www.instagram.com/nora_valters
Goodreads www.goodreads.com/noravalters
BookBub www.bookbub.com/authors/nora-valters

For more information and to contact Nora, please visit www.noravalters.com

Printed in Great Britain
by Amazon